THOMAS FORD MEMORIAL LIBRARY

3 1908 00039

W9-BRB-070

THOMAS FORD MEMORIAL LIBRARY
800 Chestnut
Western Springs, IL 60558

Bound by Blood and Sand

Bound
by
Blood
and
Sand

BECKY ALLEN

Delacorte Press

THOMAS FORD MEMORIAL LIBRARY
800 Chestnut
Western Springs, IL 60558

This is a work of fiction. Names, characters, places, and incidents
either are the product of the author's imagination or are used fictitiously.
Any resemblance to actual persons, living or dead, events, or locales
is entirely coincidental.

Text copyright © 2016 by Becky Allen
Jacket title typography © 2016 by Pomme Chan
Jacket photo of girl © 2016 by Lee Frost/Millennium Images

All rights reserved. Published in the United States by Delacorte Press,
an imprint of Random House Children's Books, a division
of Penguin Random House LLC, New York.

Delacorte Press is a registered trademark and the colophon
is a trademark of Penguin Random House LLC.

Visit us on the Web! randomhouseteens.com

Educators and librarians, for a variety of teaching tools,
visit us at RHTeachersLibrarians.com

Library of Congress Cataloging-in-Publication Data
Names: Allen, Becky, author.
Title: Bound by blood and sand / Becky Allen.
Description: First edition. | New York : Delacorte Press, 2016. | Summary: "A slave living
in a dying desert world must decide if she wants to help the kingdom's prince save their
world"— Provided by publisher.
Identifiers: LCCN 2015044877 (print) | LCCN 2016021670 (ebook) |
ISBN 978-1-101-93214-8 (hardback) | ISBN 978-1-101-93215-5 (glb) |
ISBN 978-1-101-93216-2 (ebk)
Subjects: | CYAC: Fantasy. | Slavery—Fiction. | Blessing and cursing—Fiction. | BISAC:
JUVENILE FICTION / Fantasy & Magic. | JUVENILE FICTION / Social Issues /
Prejudice & Racism. | JUVENILE FICTION / Action & Adventure / General.
Classification: LCC PZ7.1.A438 Bo 2016 (print) | LCC PZ7.1.A438 (ebook) | DDC
[Fic]—dc23

The text of this book is set in 12-point Electra.
Interior design by Ken Crossland

Printed in the United States of America
10 9 8 7 6 5 4 3 2 1
First Edition

Random House Children's Books supports the
First Amendment and celebrates the right to read.

For Rachel.

When I FIND my sister,
I won't BE alone.

Chapter 1

SOMETIMES, WHEN THE SUN MADE HER DIZZY AND HER SKIN BURNED and peeled and there was no water to spare, Jae thought about revenge. She was in charge of the estate's grounds, and here in the garden, a cactus loomed over her work. Decades old, it overshadowed everything but the fountain. Back when it still rained, the cactus had grown enormous red flowers. Now there was no rain, there were no flowers, but the spines still grew, some of them as long as Jae's hand and as thick as her finger.

She tossed weeds into a sack so she could drag them out back, but she eyed the cactus for a long moment before turning away. She'd never be able to get her hands on a real weapon, but if she ever had a few minutes of freedom from the Curse, she could do damage with one of those spines.

"Jae? *Jae!* There you are! Don't move!"

Jae's body went stone still at the unexpected order, which locked her in place where she knelt. She could only shift her gaze to look up. Lady Shirrad was already moving away from the window she'd yelled from, leaving the faded gold curtains swaying in her wake. So Jae waited, using the moment to catch her breath. As orders went, just waiting wasn't so bad. Not yet, anyway. Though if Lady Shirrad was looking for her, it was to give Jae yet another task.

The Lady strode into the courtyard a minute later, the scent of noxious perfume accompanying her. That meant bad news. Lady Shirrad only covered herself in perfume when there wasn't enough water to bathe. That meant there would be even less water for Jae to use in the garden this evening—and less for Jae and the other Closest to drink.

The sneer on Lady Shirrad's face made her look older than seventeen. She and Jae had been born within a day of each other, but that was all they had in common. Lady Shirrad's features were softer, her skin a lighter brown, and she wore an embroidered red robe with sandals, where Jae had only a stained, shapeless tan dress and bare feet.

Hand on her hip, Lady Shirrad declared, "This garden looks horrible—like it's dead."

Jae just waited, still kneeling. The Curse didn't allow her to speak in front of anyone Avowed unless it was to answer a direct question. Lady Shirrad was right, though. The courtyard garden wasn't much to look at anymore—an open, square space in the middle of the building, with red and orange rocks ringing the cactus and a few scraggly bushes. The bushes' leaves were brown now, dying, just like the few tufts of grass that had fought their way up through the stones and sand.

Jae could just remember the way grass had covered the whole courtyard when she'd been a child, and that there had been real flowers. Those had died off years ago. Years before *that*, according to her mother, the fountain set back in one corner of the courtyard had actually worked, with fresh water flowing down into its trough, free for anyone to drink—even the Closest. Now the fountain was just an oddly shaped sculpture of four columns overlapping one another and linked together in the middle, representing the four elements that mages had once called upon for magic.

"I have guests coming, and it can't look like this when they arrive. What can you do about it?" Lady Shirrad continued.

Jae braced herself as she answered. The Curse forced all of the Closest to tell the truth as well as they knew it, but the truth didn't always make Lady Shirrad happy. This certainly wouldn't: "Without more water, I can't do anything at all, Lady."

Lady Shirrad narrowed her eyes, an expression that was usually accompanied by a sharp slap. But thankfully, she only said, "Then use what you need to, but don't you dare waste a single drop."

The weight of the order gripped Jae like stone sandals, so heavy that she'd barely be able to trudge forward until the order was completed or lifted.

"I can't have Aredann looking like this when they arrive. I don't even want to *think* about it. Do you understand?" Lady Shirrad demanded.

"Yes, Lady," Jae said, understanding what mattered: the order she'd been given, and that Lady Shirrad would be even more frantic and impossible than usual until her guests had come and gone again. Lady Shirrad had been Aredann's Avowed guardian—its absolute ruler—since her father had passed away when she was thirteen, and she hadn't had many visitors since. No one seemed to want to travel as far as Aredann, especially during the drought.

"Good. Now get to it." Lady Shirrad started back to the arched entryway, but then paused, her hand on her hip and her sandal tapping against the floor. "Do you know where your brother is?"

A bone weariness, worse than any day under the sun, wrapped itself around Jae's shoulders at the thought of Tal and Lady Shirrad. At least this truth came easily. "No, Lady."

Lady Shirrad gave her one last scowl at the negative response, then swept out, her swirling robe kicking up dust. Jae finally straightened up, her body protesting the change in position. She took a moment to stretch as she decided how she'd go about her work. The Curse would give her that much freedom, at least. As long as she was working, obeying Lady Shirrad's orders, she could do what she wished.

She stooped to pick up the last few weeds that had escaped her, annoyed at how those could grow even ages after the last proper plants had died. She'd want them all gone before she claimed one of the clay water jugs from the basement to use on the bushes and grass. There was no point in watering weeds.

At least Lady Shirrad had allowed her the water she needed. After a year of giving Jae only smaller jugs or water skins, barely enough to keep the garden alive, Jae could now use whatever she required. But rather than being a relief, that tiny bit of freedom left Jae dry, brittle. More water for the garden meant less for the livestock and the fields, less for cooking, less for bathing and cleaning. Less to drink. There simply wasn't enough to go around, and Lady Shirrad's order meant she cared more about impressing her guests than she did about keeping the Closest slaves from getting sunsick as they worked.

The garden's life was more important than Jae's own. Jae glanced at the overgrown cactus again as she hauled the sack of weeds out, stooping under the weight of her orders, and under the weight of the Curse of obedience that compelled all Closest.

The sinking sun stained the garden bright orange, and Jae shielded her eyes. Even her dark skin practically glowed under the intense light as she set about watering the garden, trying to save the dying grass.

In a landscape of unbroken browns and tans, under a sky that was endless blue all day and star-speckled black at night, green was the color of wealth. Green meant thriving plants, which meant thriving people.

The grass was brown. Jae frowned at it, dizzy for a moment, and sagged against the fountain until the spinning sensation passed. She heaved a deep breath, willing herself to move, to just get back to work. She had to return the rest of the water, the little bit that sloshed at the bottom of the massive jug. But the water was so tempting. . . .

A shadow flickered at the arched entryway into the courtyard. She reached for the jug, willing whoever it was to go about their business and not bother her. But the person stepped into the garden silently—barefoot, not causing the pebbles to grind. Jae's gaze flicked sideways, and she was relieved to see it was only Tal, her brother.

He caught her glancing, and smiled, then waved with an open hand, which signaled that no Avowed were near enough to see or hear him. It would be safe for them to talk. Even so, he walked toward her silently, and then stopped next to her on the path, brushing his hand against her elbow in a silent greeting.

They were twins, but he moved through the world with an ease she'd never mastered. It was in the way he glided from the doorway to join her; it was how he sat near her, light and relaxed, as if the Curse didn't weigh him down at all.

He nudged her elbow again, and when she glanced down at his hand, he opened his palm to reveal a date. He pressed it into her hand and murmured, "You look exhausted."

She had to lean in to hear him, and she chewed the fruit for a second before answering, "I've been outside all day. Be careful. Lady Shirrad was looking for you."

"I know, but she just keeps missing me." He gave Jae a sideways smirk. Lady Shirrad adored Tal, treated him with kindness she never bothered to show anyone else. He was the only one of the Closest who ever ate or drank his fill, a privilege he earned by smiling to Lady Shirrad's face and saving his scorn for when her back was turned. But he used her favor to get away with scrounging up the few scraps he could, and he shared these first with Jae and then with the other Closest. Sometimes Jae thought his position as the most favored of the

Closest was the only thing that had saved her from dying of exhaustion or sunsickness.

"Lucky you," she said. She didn't know how he managed it. The Curse would never allow them to lie with words, so Tal used his body instead, acting for all the world as if he adored Lady Shirrad. His smile was his only weapon, but he wielded it ruthlessly.

She didn't have Tal's advantages. They looked similar enough, but the sharp features that were handsome on him were awkward and boyish on her. Tal was gorgeous and knew it; Jae was a mess of scraped hands and gangly limbs. Where he wore his hair in long curls, bound at the nape of his neck, she kept hers cropped almost to her scalp. Considering that she was nearly as flat and curveless as he was, only the fact that she had a dirt-stained dress instead of loose pants made it clear from a distance that one of them was a girl.

She stood and took a step toward the jug, but the dizziness hit again. She paused, waiting for the sensation to pass, but Tal was at her side this time. He guided her back to the fountain carefully, his hand gentle on her arm. While she waited for the world to stop spinning, he grabbed the smaller water skin she'd been using for the plants and held it out to her. He pressed it into her hands, urging her to drink.

She tried to push it back, turned away, as if not seeing it would suppress the longing. "Not allowed," she said, mouthing the words because her throat was too dry to do much else.

He understood anyway, frowned, and didn't let her release her grip on the skin. "Tell me if the Lady actually said that."

She didn't have to obey an order from him, another

Closest, but if she didn't answer, he'd ask it as a question. The Curse *would* force her to answer that. No matter who asked, the Closest were compelled to answer all questions. So, to spare herself, she said: "She ordered me not to waste any. Tal, I have to work."

"I know, I know," he said. "Traitor's blood means a lifetime of toil. But you *can't* toil if you die of sunsickness. So you have to drink. She might as well have ordered you to."

Jae shook her head. If Tal explained that to Lady Shirrad, the Lady would laugh and let him drink what he wanted. If Jae tried to explain it, the best she could hope for was that Lady Shirrad would roll her eyes and tell her to get back to work. Jae knew full well what the lady had meant by her order.

But Tal was right. Lady Shirrad hadn't actually ordered her not to drink, and Jae couldn't work like this. If she got dizzy again, she'd probably spill all the water she had left, and that really would be a waste.

Hands shaking, she brought the skin up to her lips, telling herself that Tal was right. If drinking allowed her to obey, then drinking *was* obedience.

The Curse allowed her to drink. When it didn't immediately punish her, she swallowed greedily, nearly draining the whole thing before she stopped. It was like breathing for the first time all day.

When she was done, Tal pulled the skin closed and set it aside for her. She shot him a grateful look but said, "I still have work to do. The front path is a mess."

"I'll help."

"The Lady will see you out there," Jae said.

"She'll find me eventually anyway," he said, his head so

close, it nearly touched hers. "I might as well help you in the meantime."

Jae hesitated, torn. She wanted the help, anything to make the work go faster. Anything that would keep Lady Shirrad from deciding that Jae hadn't done a good enough job. But at the same time, she knew what Lady Shirrad wanted Tal for. The same looks and charm that won him relative freedom came at the price of him having to hold his smile when she brushed her fingers over his cheek.

Tal caught her gaze, gold-flecked eyes sincere. "Don't worry about me. I can handle the Lady," Tal said, then stood and offered Jae a hand up.

She ignored it and stood on her own, guilt warring with anxiety in her gut. Accepting Tal's help would practically offer him up to Lady Shirrad for the evening, but without his help she'd be working all night. All she wanted in the world was to rest. But Tal was her brother.

"Jae," Tal finally said, barely audible. He wasn't smiling at her, pretending things were fine. He was as tired as she was, but he was still waiting for her. "Ask me if I mind helping you."

She shook her head. She didn't have to ask; he wouldn't have offered to answer if he didn't mean it. And while he might find ways to twist the words of his answers when Lady Shirrad asked him questions, he wouldn't do that to Jae, so she nodded, trusting him.

Tal helped her for as long as he could, until Lady Shirrad came out to find him and lead him away. He brushed a hand against Jae's shoulder as he left, a silent goodbye. That left her on her own, working until the moon rose and the temperature dropped, and finally there was nothing else that had to be done immediately and the Curse would allow her to rest.

The Closest's quarters were dark and quiet. They were tucked away in a corner of the house, rooms with low ceilings and few windows, where the Closest ate, slept, and gathered in their few free moments. The rooms had housed paid Twill servants once, but as the drought had gotten worse, fewer Twill had been willing to stay at Aredann. Jae had occasionally overheard some of the Avowed complaining that it was disgusting to allow traitorous bloodlines to live under the same roof they did, yet somehow, she'd never heard them complain about having Closest slaves to replace their servants.

The Closest's main room had ancient, stained squares of carpet covering most of the floor, layered over one another so that no one would have to sit on the bare stones. There was a small fire pit where they could cook, and a stone cistern that sat empty. People gathered near enough to the fire to see each other, close enough to hold murmured conversations.

Tal was kneeling in front of an old woman named Asra, her hands in his—Jae had to walk close before she could see he was applying a salve to burned skin on her hands. Jae had no idea how he'd gotten it, when he couldn't even speak to ask Lady Shirrad for it, and she didn't dare ask him. She didn't know whether he was really stealing, and as long as she didn't find out for certain, that was the truth she'd be able to tell if she was ever asked.

Tal saw her and mouthed "Hello" then stood. "You might as well keep the rest of that, in case you need it," he said to

Asra, and then joined Jae. "I'm assuming you haven't eaten yet. Come sit with me and Gali while you do."

Jae helped herself to a small portion of the stew that had been left near the fire, then sat with Tal and Gali, another of their friends. Tal was cross-legged, but Gali knelt facing the wall, her fingers brushing across it, painting it with ash and charcoal. The walls in here were plain tan bricks and had been covered in designs for years and years now, drawn over each other, blending together to cover the bricks almost all the way up to the ceiling. It wasn't like the brightly colored Avowed art that adorned most of the halls and rooms in Aredann. Avowed art was always a celebration, eye-catching and beautiful, meant to be kept forever. Closest drawings were subtle, nothing but grays and black, nearly impossible to make out. It would be washed away if they ever had water, and drawn over again and again in the meantime.

Jae sat with her brother and Gali and reached out to lightly touch Gali's elbow. She looked over at Jae and nodded tiredly before getting back to her drawing. This close, Jae could see it was a person in profile—Tal, probably, judging from the hair.

"I was going to go looking for you soon," Tal said. He wasn't loud, but he didn't whisper, either, and a few people glanced over at them. "I was starting to worry you'd never be done."

"So was I." Now that Jae was sitting, her feet throbbed. The idea of standing up again, even just to walk to the smaller room where her sleeping mat waited, was unbearable.

Gali added a detail to the wall. When Jae studied it, she could make out the sharp lines of Tal's nose and jaw. "Today was long," Gali said.

Jae gave her a concerned look, not daring to hint that she'd like to know more. Gali had been selected to join the household because she was pretty, and when her days ran long, it was usually because she'd been called to someone's sleeping chamber, another order the Curse wouldn't let her disobey, another punishment for crimes that had been committed generations ago. It happened to all of the Closest who worked in the household.

When Lord Rannith had summoned Jae, it had been the only time she'd fought to disobey an order, struggled against the Curse's grip—not that struggling had done any good. If she ever had even a heartbeat free from the Curse, Rannith was the person she'd seek out with her cactus spine. But Gali caught her glance and shook her head.

"I'm fine," Gali said. "The Lady wanted everyone's sleeping mats cleaned, and all of their blankets. It's the first time in weeks. And there's no water."

"It's the same everywhere, even the garden, I think," Tal said.

Jae nodded. "I was told to use whatever I need. But I don't know where she thinks the water will come from."

"The Well will provide, as long as the Highest rule," Gali intoned, rolling her eyes as she mimicked the serious tones Lady Shirrad's advisors used when they said that. And they always said that. Even now, in the midst of a drought and with their reservoir dropping lower and lower.

The Highest still ruled, but the Well barely seemed to provide anything. Maybe that was what the Highest intended, at least for the Closest, but the rest of Aredann wasn't descended from traitors. Jae couldn't believe that an Avowed guardian like Lady Shirrad would be left to suffer.

"Listen."

The word all but echoed in the room. There was no compulsion behind it from the Curse, but the entire room went silent. Jae scowled as she turned to look at Firran, the Closest who'd spoken and who was now standing by the fire pit. Years ago, Lady Shirrad's father had appointed Firran their leader, so that the Lord would only have to speak directly to one Closest. Firran had snapped up that scrap of power like one of the dogs Lady Shirrad's family used to keep. When he spoke, it was always loud and demanding—orders like most Closest would never give one another.

Even aside from the order, he wasn't exactly polite. Closest always shared what they knew with one another; it made all of their lives easier. But they didn't go demanding and interrupting, or speaking in the loud tones of the Avowed.

Still, the rest of the Closest now gathered around Firran, knees touching, sweaty shoulders brushing, as closely as they could. Firran didn't mind raising his voice, but the rest of the Closest preferred the quiet.

Except Tal.

"What is it?" he asked, smirking a little, meeting Firran rudeness for rudeness. Closest didn't order each other around, and they *never* asked each other questions.

Firran glared at him as he was compelled to answer, "I know who Lady Shirrad's visitor is." He waited a moment, and when no one else interrupted him, he continued in that same booming, pompous tone. "He is the son of one of the

Highest, the grand warden of all reservoirs—Elan Danardae. His father sent him to tour Aredann to see our plight."

"They already know our plight," Gali muttered, not quite loud enough for Firran to hear—but Tal stifled a laugh. Jae stayed silent but had to agree. The Highest were the ones who'd cursed them, generations ago, when the Closest's ancestors had rebelled. If they were sending someone to visit Aredann, it definitely didn't have anything to do with the Closest's desperation.

"No wonder the Lady was in such a tizzy today," one of the others said. "But it's good news, if the Highest are finally coming to our aid."

"But they aren't," Firran said, some of the bluster dropping from his voice. "Lord Hannim told Lady Shirrad that there are other estates like Aredann, where the reservoirs are going dry. There's not enough water, not even in the whole Well, so some estates are being cut off."

"But there's *always* been enough," Asra said, voice creaky and unsure, as someone else said, "They can't just cut off whole estates," and someone else snapped, "I don't understand; talk sense!"

Firran held up his hands, waiting for the commotion to work itself out. "They say there are too many people in the world now, more than ever before, and that's why there's not enough water anymore. All of the wardens agree, the Well can't sustain everyone. So some estates . . . The Highest have decided to leave some estates entirely, take their Avowed and even the Twill and leave the rest of us here to die in the drought."

This time, no one seemed to know what to say. It made a

sickening, twisted kind of sense. If there were too many people in the world, then of course the Closest would be the ones left to die, to bring that number back down. Their ancestors had been spared all those years ago, allowed to live as slaves, so long as they were cursed so they could never rebel again— but the Highest would never hesitate to trade Closest lives for the rest of the world.

"That can't be," Tal said finally, standing, but even he sounded shaken. "Lady Shirrad would never leave Aredann to be abandoned."

"You mean Lady Shirrad would never leave *you*," Firran said. "They certainly won't take the rest of us Closest."

"She would never leave *Aredann*," Tal repeated. "And the Well will provide. It has to. The Highest will make it."

Firran shook his head. "Believe what you will, but I know what I heard. If the Highest order it, Lady Shirrad will have to obey. They'll send the water somewhere else, Aredann will turn to dust without it, and we'll all die here."

Tal shook his head, but he didn't argue. There was no point. Firran was telling the truth as well as he knew it. He spent more time with Lady Shirrad than any of the rest of them, even Tal, and he overheard all of the Avowed's business. Jae didn't like him, but she also didn't doubt him. And if what he'd heard was true, then soon—maybe only days from now—all of the Closest at Aredann would be left alone, without the protection of the Well, and with no water, in the middle of a drought.

"Come to bed," Gali murmured, wiping her sooty hand on her dress and leaving a smudged handprint, a new stain on a garment that hadn't been cleaned in months. She offered that same hand to Tal, who accepted it but looked at Jae. He nodded toward the chamber they shared with a few others.

Jae followed them slowly, stiff and sore in a hundred different places, still thirsty and too warm after her day in the sun. Tomorrow would be just as bad, or worse. And so would every day after—somehow, it always seemed as if things got worse. Every day was hotter, drier, and longer, and the Curse had no mercy.

She thought about that as she lay down on her sleeping mat, a few hand spans from where Tal and Gali were now intertwined, exchanging comforting words so low that Jae couldn't make out what they were saying.

Without the Well's protection, the Closest would die in days, of sunsickness if not thirst. But if the Avowed all left Aredann, then there would be no one to give the Closest any orders. For those few, precious days, it would be almost like they were free. And maybe a few days of freedom would be better than a lifetime spent as a slave.

Chapter 2

ELAN DANARDAE SLUMPED IN HIS SADDLE AND LOOKED AT THE desert through the mesh across his face. Brown and orange rolled on in front of him endlessly, broken only by rock outcroppings. He'd have thought they were lost and wandering, if not for the occasional trees that had been planted to point the way—if they could even be called trees. They were only trunks, leafless and twisted into odd shapes, stunted reminders of better times before the drought, back when there had been enough water for everyone. Now the trunks were all that marked the way to Aredann, the edge of the world.

"Highest! Look!"

Elan squinted, barely able to see through the sun's glare, despite the mesh that covered his face to keep out the worst of the sun and sand. At first, he couldn't make out anything, then just a speck that grew more distinct as they came closer: cultivated land, and the Aredann reservoir and estate house.

As they drew closer, his tutor—his watchdog—Desinn drew up next to him and said, "I suggest you prepare yourself. We're nearly there."

Elan rolled his eyes, knowing Desinn wouldn't be able to see it from under his hood, but nodded. Not that he could do much to prepare in the saddle, and he refused to stop just to change clothes, with Aredann finally so close. After four days of camping, sand caked his travel robe and the loose garments under it. It had worked its way inside his clothes, too, fine grit rubbing his skin raw. His demeanor, not his appearance, would have to impress Lady Shirrad Aredann.

"You should be aware. The messenger your father sent will surely have started rumors about the abandonment, and the Avowed at Aredann will turn to you to ask questions. Your role here—your *only* role—is to be your father's warden, and remind them they must obey." Desinn paused, smugness dripping from him like sweat. "Try to remember your vows."

"I will," Elan snapped, and turned his attention back to the dry, dismal landscape.

As they approached, Elan found that Aredann wasn't any more impressive up close than it had looked from a distance. He could see most of its layout—the mage-built house, tiny compared to buildings in the central cities, but larger than anything else out here. There was a smattering of a town around it, no more than a handful of dull tan buildings. The fields and orchards sat off to one side, closer to the minuscule reservoir. It was the reservoir that most drew his eye, glistening like a blue jewel, but infinitely more valuable.

The main street they rode down was also the only street, aside from some tiny sandy lanes. A few Twill gaped at him from the glassless windows of their houses, so he tried to look regal, like his father. Worn tracks led them to the estate's outer wall, with an enormous stone gate that was pulled open by guardsmen as they approached.

A small crowd waited inside, the girl at the front wearing a vibrant red robe with gold embroidery, much nicer than anything anyone else had on. It took Elan a moment to realize she was Lady Shirrad—he'd expected a grown woman, not someone close to his own age.

Growing up among the Highest families had taught him to school his expression, so he was careful not to let his surprise show as he pushed the hood and mesh from his face. No one so young should have been the Avowed guardian of an entire estate and reservoir. Something must have happened to her parents, but he couldn't remember Desinn mentioning it.

The riders finally halted, and as Elan dismounted, Lady Shirrad fell into an elegant curtsey. With that cue, everyone else who had gathered bowed, as protocol demanded.

Elan tucked his gloves into his belt and stepped forward. He stood in front of Lady Shirrad and held out his hands, sand falling from his draped sleeves. Someone handed Lady Shirrad an elegant cup, intricately carved, with damp spots dripping from the top. Lady Shirrad ducked her head as she handed it to him, an offering of loyalty to the Highest. Elan accepted it and drank. The ceremony only required him to take a few mouthfuls, but he was thirsty enough to empty the cup entirely.

He nodded when he was finished, handing the cup back. "My thanks, Lady Guardian."

"All I have is yours, Grand Warden," she answered, and gestured to the arched gate of the inner wall behind her. "And I'd be pleased to show you all that this estate offers."

"Highest is fine—or Lord Elan," he said, though he was inwardly pleased she'd used his full title. He was young to hold it, but carrying out his father's will and upholding order was an honor. And, despite what Desinn thought, it was a role he was perfectly capable of handling. "Before anything else, I'd like to change into something less travel-worn." He brushed sand from his robe, not that it did much good. "And I'm certain my traveling companions would like to do the same. Ah, Lady, I should introduce you. . . ." He glanced over at Desinn, now dismounted and following them as they walked toward the house itself. Desinn wasn't as good at keeping his feelings off his face, and right now it clouded with impatience. "This is my tutor, Lord Desinn Loerdan, one of my father's most trusted stewards for many years now."

"I'm very glad to meet you, my lord," she said, almost stumbling as she looked back at him while leading the way.

"Lady," Desinn answered, amused. Shirrad's cheeks reddened, but that could have been from insult as much as embarrassment at her misstep. As the guardian of an entire estate, she certainly outranked Desinn enough that he should have bowed. But then again, Desinn was close to Elan's father, which was a kind of power all its own.

"Highest, we haven't had our evening meal yet," she said after a moment. "I'm sure you must be exhausted from your trip. Why don't you rest before dinner, and we'll eat in private when it's ready?"

"Certainly," Elan agreed. "Perhaps I'll bathe while I wait."

Her smile went tight but didn't waver. "Of course, Highest. I'll have a servant draw a bath for you immediately. And of course, here, ah"—she turned down a hall—"the finest rooms in the estate." She opened a door and stood aside politely.

The room was nicer than he'd expected, with high ceilings and bright orange-and-yellow walls, an intricate tile design that proved that, poor though this place was, the house had been built by mages. No one since the War had constructed houses where the walls themselves were art.

The sleeping mat was on a raised platform and draped with lush, bright blankets and pillows, with a carved stone cistern in the corner, several more cushions for guests to sit on, and a padded bench in front of the window. The room's decorations weren't as intricate as the ones in his father's house, but the blankets and cushions all looked just as comfortable and equally embellished, and he was sure these were Lady Shirrad's quarters. Giving up her own rooms for him was beyond the politeness required from a host, but she scurried off before he could thank her for it.

Elan stretched, sore from the journey and too warm, even in here. He loosened the cord that fastened his robe at his neck and tossed the robe off. As he walked to the window, he absently tugged the neck of his shirt down, allowing his fingers to trace the well-healed brand below his collarbone, near his heart. A circle, divided into four sections—one for each of the Highest families; one for each of the elements. It was a mark of his rank, given to him when he'd taken his vows of loyalty to his father at thirteen. All Avowed wardens and guardians had one, including members the Highest families—the guardians of the Well itself. The brand was a reminder of the vows they'd all taken.

He pushed aside the curtain and gazed out at a dusty courtyard. It wasn't much of a view, but he supposed that was to be expected. There was nothing to look at in Aredann, because there was nothing *to* Aredann. As its water supply dwindled, so did Aredann, and soon it would be left to the desert, battered by wind and sand until it crumbled into dust.

Elan ran a hand over the decoration in the tiles, staring down at the empty, ugly courtyard. It was hard to believe that the last battle of the War of the Well had been won here.

Aredann may not have looked impressive, but its history was worth saving. It wasn't just the battle, or the fact that the great traitor had been born here. No one knew for sure why the Highest's ancestors had seen fit to build a reservoir so far removed that it didn't support a city or even farming lands, but legends said the estate had actually been a way-marker. Aredann was supposedly the last reservoir before the Well itself, out to the west somewhere. No one was sure that was true; no one had ever found any proof.

But here Aredann was, and here Elan was, too. They were both out of favor with his father, and Elthis rarely forgave. He certainly never forgot, and his respect, hard enough to earn in the first place, was all but impossible to win back after it was lost. So while Aredann turned to dust, Elan would spend years struggling to prove that he deserved the grand warden title he'd so nearly lost. Unless, somehow, he could prove he deserved it while he was here.

If Aredann was a signpost, the last reservoir before the Well, then maybe, hidden somewhere in this forgotten, desolate estate, there was a map or a clue or a key to finding the location of the Well itself. If there was, and if Elan could find it, that would be a service to his father large enough that all of his misdeeds would be forgiven. His father would accept him back with open arms, would trust him the way he trusted Elan's older sister and so few others.

Elan wasn't naïve enough to believe it would be easy, but if there *was* a secret hidden at Aredann, he was determined to be the one who uncovered it at last.

Much like Lady Shirrad's chamber, the room where they were dining had high ceilings and enormous windows, but that was where its grandeur ended. Low shelves had been built between the windows, stacked with books and a few decorative mugs and plates. There were some large, faded mosaics hung higher up, but the cushions around the table were plain and, frankly, didn't look particularly comfortable.

Not that it mattered. Elan still settled himself on one, cross-legged in front of the low stone table, as a servant brought in their meal. He didn't expect much, but was pleasantly surprised by the smell and then the sight of the meal: a well-baked bread with herbs, cheese, and even goat meat. He hadn't thought there was enough cultivated ground out here to keep animals, and this was much, much better than he'd expected from such a water-poor estate as Aredann.

Lady Shirrad watched him nervously as he ate, waiting for

some kind of reaction. He smiled, nodding to her. "Delicious, especially after days of eating while traveling."

"I'm so glad you like it," she said, smiling too hard.

Desinn was watching for her reaction, too, even as he ate. He didn't seem particularly appreciative of the meal, though it must have taken a great deal of time to prepare.

But that was why, Elan realized. As Desinn had warned him, Shirrad knew full well why Elan was visiting, and what that would mean for her future. When Aredann was abandoned, Shirrad would lose her standing as guardian. Her only hope was to be given a decent new title by Elan's father—and a good word from Elan would smooth that along.

No wonder Desinn didn't seem impressed. The play for their favor was obvious. But while Desinn sneered, Elan smiled. Desinn had nothing to lose if he was obvious about his disdain, but Elan wanted Shirrad's help, and he didn't want Desinn to know about it. So let Desinn be rude, and let Shirrad resent him for it. That would make it even easier for Elan to ply her.

He changed the subject from the meal. "Aredann has been beautifully kept—I could swear mages still walk the halls."

Shirrad tittered nervously. "Well, we do try, Highest. I know it's only a small estate, but I take my duties to it very seriously."

"And it shows. Don't you think, Lord Desinn?"

Desinn shot him a sharp look, but said, "Of course. It's as nice as one could expect, being so far away from civilization."

Lady Shirrad giggled again, as if it had been a joke and not an insult.

24

Elan took another few bites, then changed the subject again. "I hope you won't think this question is too rude, Lady, but until we arrived, I expected you to be . . . older. How did you come to be in charge here so young?"

Lady Shirrad's smile faltered for a heartbeat. When she began to talk, her voice was still light, but the bright tone rang false. "My mother died in childbirth. And my father, several years ago, he . . . I hope you won't take this the wrong way, Highest. My father was always very strange, and . . . I suppose my family has always been strange, but . . ."

Elan nodded. The current Aredann family had been installed here years ago—as a punishment. Shirrad's great-grandfather had angered Elan's grandmother but hadn't directly challenged the Highest's rule, so he couldn't be disavowed. Instead, Elan's grandmother had sent him to rule Aredann. True, being made a guardian was supposed to be an honor—but serving as guardian of an estate as removed as Aredann had meant the family had rarely been seen in the central cities again.

"When the drought started to become noticeable, several years ago, my father was convinced there was something wrong with the Well. I know that's impossible," she said, hands folded on the table, the meal forgotten. "I know your family would never allow that to happen. It's a drought, that's all; even the Highest can't control that."

"Of course," Elan said, glancing at Desinn, whose expression was unreadable. The four Highest families had crafted the Well and protected the magic that kept water flowing from the Well to the reservoirs. Without the Well, the world would be lost, but it wasn't only the drought that was a problem.

There were simply too many people in the world now, thousands and thousands more than the original Highest had intended the Well to provide for.

To protect the world as it was now, the Highest had decided to abandon outlying estates like Aredann. With people gone from them, the Well's water could be diverted back to larger reservoirs, areas that needed the water more. Changing the way the water flowed was a huge work of magic, which was why the Highest only did it in dire emergencies, but now it was necessary.

It was a brutal solution that left estates to be buried in the desert, and none of the Avowed who had stood as estate guardians and stewards had been happy about the relocation. Elan had sympathized with them—more than he should have. No one was allowed to question the Highest about the Well, not even their own families. Their decisions may have been cruel, but the Highest only ever acted to keep order and protect the Well. Kindness was a gesture they couldn't often afford.

"He thought he could find the Well himself," Shirrad continued. "He took a search party into the desert, but . . . there was a sandstorm. It was enormous enough that we felt it, even here. Half our crops were buried, unsalvageable. And my father, he . . . he was lost."

"I'm so sorry, Lady," Elan said. "How old were you?"

"Thirteen, Highest. I'd only just returned from taking my vows at Danardae."

Elan sagged on his cushion. Thirteen was far too young to rule over any town or city, even one as insignificant as Aredann. He gave her a sympathetic look and went back to his meal, but he was already thinking it over. Lady Shirrad's father had believed he could find the Well from Aredann. He must have had reason to. He must have found something—hopefully something still here, not lost with him in the desert.

Maybe Lady Shirrad knew what it was. She'd definitely never talk about it, with her situation as precarious as it was. She couldn't afford to look like she questioned the Highest. But once Elan had a chance to speak with her alone, he'd reassure her, and find out everything she knew. And Desinn would never know what was happening, until Elan was ready.

Chapter 3

L ADY S HIRRAD OFFERED TO SHOW E LAN AND D ESINN AROUND
Aredann after the meal, but Desinn declined, tired from all
their traveling. Elan was just as exhausted, but even so, he
said, "I'd love to see more of Aredann this evening, at least
enough to start to learn my way around."

Shirrad gave a shrill, nervous laugh but stood and gestured toward the hall. "I know Aredann is a small estate. It
certainly can't compare to Danardae. But it is beautiful here,
Highest."

"So I can see already," Elan agreed, eyeing the designs
in the halls. The large, swirling patterns built up to peaks,
their shapes echoing the arched hallway itself, dotted with the
occasional burst of yellow or red flowers. Legend said Lord

Aredann, the guardian the estate had originally been named for, had been an almost obsessive gardener and that under his rule, the estate had been blanketed by blossoms year round.

"It is remarkable what the mages were able to do, isn't it?" Shirrad asked, reaching out to drag a hand along the wall.

"It's a shame so much magic was lost after the War," Elan said. And then, carefully, he continued, "One of the final battles was fought here at Aredann, wasn't it? If I remember my history right . . ."

"Yes!" Shirrad chirped.

"I'm fascinated by your estate's history. Are there any artifacts left from the battle?" Elan asked.

"Not many, I'm afraid," Shirrad said. "It's hard to tell what was used in a magical battle—I suppose we're lucky the house was even left standing!"

"Yes, we are," Elan agreed.

They turned down another long hall, one with enormous, empty windows. "But we do have the mosaic in the main hall that was created only a few years after the War, to celebrate Lord Aredann's victory. And oh!" She stopped short. "Of course he loved his garden. It's nothing to look at now, but . . ."

She gestured to a large, open arch, which led out into a courtyard. Elan squinted in the dark and started forward as his eyes adjusted, peering across the yard at the strange shapes of the bushes—

And he walked directly into something. It gave, and cool liquid hit his sandals. He jumped back, and Lady Shirrad crashed into him from behind. It took him a second to spot what he'd hit—a large water skin had been propped open on the path. He managed to steady himself and Lady Shirrad, while someone else scurried in the darkness—a barefoot servant girl.

No—servants would never go around barefoot. That was a sign of the Closest. He frowned in confusion as the girl hurried to save the rest of the water, but it was too late. A little still sloshed inside the skin, but the rest puddled and spread across the garden path. The Closest froze, still clutching the skin, then dropped into an awkward bow, shoulders hunched and gaze cast downward.

"Jae!" Shirrad shrieked, and pushed past Elan. "All that water! Blood and bones, how could you be so careless?"

Elan's vision had finally adjusted enough for him to see the Closest more clearly. He'd never seen one so closely before. Her hair was cut short, close to her scalp, and her clothes were filthy. "It was an accident, Lady. I was watering the garden. . . ." She trailed off, looking down at her muddy footprints.

"You never should have left that open!" Shirrad yelled. "And now it's all wasted." She turned to Elan, eyes wide and glistening as she said, "I'm so sorry, Grand Warden. We are *never* this careless with water. Please believe that."

The Closest girl had sharp features and dark skin. Elan couldn't make out the color of her eyes, but her mouth hung half-open and her hands trembled. Shirrad raised her arm, and the Closest tensed, eyes screwed shut. The sound of the slap echoed through the courtyard, a sharp noise like a thunderclap. The Closest didn't react except to quiver in place, but Elan's gut twisted with horror. Back home, they'd never dream of striking one of their servants—but then again, they'd also never have a Closest inside the house or on its grounds. Their servants were all well paid. Some of them were even Avowed, working not for money but for a chance to impress the Highest families.

Lady Shirrad raised her hand again, and Elan reacted without thinking, grabbing her arm to stop her. She whirled around to face him, her lips twisted in an angry sneer that turned to shock when she remembered herself. She dropped her hand quickly and asked, "Highest?"

"What is she even doing inside like this?" he asked.

Shirrad shifted awkwardly, and finally explained, "With the drought being what it is . . . the servants have mostly left. I know it's . . . it's unusual to allow the Closest into the household, but . . ."

"I see," Elan said.

"But I promise, I will see her punished for that waste," Shirrad finished, her voice growing a little stronger as she spoke.

The Closest girl's eyes shut for a moment, and she looked away, defeated, silent. Something in Elan's gut twisted unpleasantly, and he said, "No, that's not necessary."

"But we never waste water like that," Shirrad insisted. "You *must* understand that. We—"

"I do understand," he said. He was a water warden, after all; he knew the difference between waste and an accident. But Shirrad still looked nervous, so he sighed and said, "I'll take care of this."

Shirrad glanced at the girl, then nodded. "Very well. Jae, go wait in His Highest's room until he's ready to deal with you."

The Closest girl fled.

Jae felt as if she'd eaten a bowl of sand: her throat was dry, her stomach hurt, and she wanted to throw up. She sat on the windowsill and hunched over, her arms wrapped around her stomach. She'd spilled water in front of a grand warden, a member of one of the Highest families. The Highest had no mercy, and there was only one reason he would choose to discipline her in his quarters.

She sank into the bench at the windowsill, waiting, trying to calm down. It wasn't as if it mattered anyway. In a matter of weeks, maybe days, the Avowed would abandon Aredann and leave the Closest for dead. No punishment would compare to that, but she still couldn't stop shaking.

Long minutes later, his Highest walked in. Jae swallowed, tasted acid, and stood so she could bow as protocol demanded. Or maybe she should have knelt. The Curse didn't demand it, since it was only tradition, but she probably should've erred on the side of caution, shown extra deference.

Lord Elan threw her an unreadable glance, but if she'd broken with the protocol he expected, he didn't say anything about it. He shut the door behind him and undid the cord at the neck of his robe. He tossed the robe off thoughtlessly, leaving him in only a long, vivid green shirt and loose pants.

"Cursed heat, I don't know how anyone stands it out here," he said as he sat on one of the cushions—or lounged, really, completely at home among the freshly cleaned pillows.

He gestured her back to where she'd been sitting, then tilted his head and looked her over intently. Jae crossed her arms over her chest, her heart beating too fast, wishing she could sink into the floor and disappear. But all she could do was wait.

Finally, he finished his examination. "What's your name?"

"Jae, Highest," she murmured, not sure he'd be able to hear her from so far away. She glanced up to make sure he had, then went back to staring at the floor near his feet, then looked farther away. She didn't dare look any closer. She was already in trouble; she didn't want to make it worse.

"Jae," he repeated. "It's so bizarre to see a Closest inside like this. It isn't done back home."

She kept her gaze steady on the floor. He didn't sound particularly angry, but he could cause her just as much trouble in a good mood.

He gestured at the stone cistern at the edge of the room. "I'll have a drink."

The Curse nudged her, and the base of her skull suddenly ached as if something had hit it, the Curse pain starting more quickly than it ever did with Lady Shirrad's orders. Especially tiny, flippant ones like that. Jae rushed to fill a mug and brought it to him, kept it clenched tightly until he took it, willing herself not to shake. She was here to be punished, but she wouldn't give him the satisfaction of seeing how much she dreaded it.

He nodded at her and drank, then settled back down on the cushion, holding the mug lightly in his hand. She tried not to stare at it. Her throat was dry, and she'd barely had a drink all day.

She looked down at the floor again, thinking of Tal instead of Lord Elan. Tal would know what to do here—he'd silently smile, relax, somehow put Lord Elan at ease, make him think they were friends. Jae just had no idea *how*. She could never do that, not when all she wanted was to run for her life.

Lord Elan held the mug out to her, and she took it to pour the rest of the water back into the cistern. But she'd barely taken a step toward the tank when he said, "You may have the rest, if you want it."

She turned to stare at him sharply. It didn't sound like he was joking, and he wasn't smirking at her. He just looked a little bored, as if he really didn't care whether she drank it or not. As if *any* Closest would turn down even a few mouthfuls of water after a day of work. But why would he offer her a drink if he intended to punish her? Lady Shirrad would never waste water that way, and he was a water warden.

She didn't give him a chance to change his mind. She drank, and the water soothed her throat, if not her nerves. She set the mug down by the cistern and waited. Now when she watched him, it was with curiosity. He tossed his head, shaking black curls out of his eyes, and sighed. "If I miss my servants for anything, it's chatter. I've heard people say 'as quiet as the Closest' before, but I never realized how cursed silent you really are."

She waited for him to ask her a question, something she could answer, and he frowned at her.

Then: "Oh!" and laughter. "If I give you permission to speak, then can you?"

"Yes, Highest," she said.

He nodded. "Then fine, speak if you want to. I hate the quiet."

She nodded but had nothing to say. She shrugged helplessly at his expectant look, and finally managed to whisper, "Thank you for the drink, Highest."

"What was that?" he asked, squinting at her as if that would let him hear better.

She cleared her throat and repeated herself, surprised at how loud she sounded. She wasn't yelling—she'd never yelled in her life—but she'd almost never spoken above a whisper. And she'd certainly never spoken *with* any of the Avowed. Answered their questions, yes, but she'd never been granted this kind of permission before.

"Of course," he said, and gestured toward the cistern again. "Help yourself, if you're still thirsty."

Jae all but dove for the mug, filled it, and took a few enormous gulps before he could tell her to stop or rescind his permission. When he didn't say anything about it, she drank another half mug before setting it down.

"Are you really *that* thirsty?" he asked, eyebrows raised.

"I—well—yes, Highest," she said. "Always."

"Oh." The surprise faded to a frown. "The Lady rations drinking water?"

"Yes, Highest," Jae said. "There's so little left at the end of the day. . . ."

"And the reservoir is low," he said, shaking his head. "So wasting water is a crime."

Jae tensed again, the water now churning in her stomach. She'd let the drink lull her into calm, but if Lord Elan wasn't used to rationing water, he probably wasn't used to withholding it from anyone, either. So offering her a drink hadn't been a sign of mercy—even though *he* was the one who'd tripped and spilled the water. If he'd bothered to watch where he was going, nothing would have spilled at all. Not that anyone of his station would ever think of it that way.

Jae set her jaw but didn't look away from him. He laughed and asked, "What's *that* look for?"

The Curse tore an answer from her before she could brace herself, try to stop the words and shape some half-truth instead: "I was ordered to care for the garden. I do the best I can. And now I'm to be punished for *your* misstep, Highest."

He stared at her silently, and she flinched. She was already here to be punished, and what she'd said had only made things worse for herself. But she couldn't help it. The Curse compelled the truth, no matter the consequences.

But it didn't matter, she reminded herself. She had only weeks to live anyway. Nothing that happened tonight mattered at all.

Lord Elan finally leaned back on his cushion and gestured dismissively. "There's no need to be so angry about it."

Jae didn't dare respond to that, even though she still had permission to speak. She *was* angry, but disrespecting him would only make the punishment worse.

But all he said was "This place is miserable enough, and that water—that was an accident. Not treason, even if you do carry traitors' blood. I don't see any need to punish you for it. You're dismissed."

She started toward the door immediately, obeying the implied order to leave, so quickly that the Curse didn't even have a chance to nudge her—and he didn't have a chance to change his mind, because after her outburst, she was certain he would punish her if he paused to think about it. But if she got out of his sight quickly enough, he might forget or decide she wasn't worth caring about at all, even for that slight.

But before she could make it out, he called, "Wait!"

She stopped sharply, one foot still partially raised. When he didn't give her another immediate order, she set her foot down carefully, trying to make it clear—to herself, to him, to the Curse—that she wasn't going anywhere. She was just waiting.

"As thirsty as you were, did you work outside like that all day?" he finally asked.

"Yes, Highest," she said, turning around. "I'm the grounds-keeper."

"The groundskeeper is a Closest, of course," he said, shaking his head a little. "Well, I can do something about that, at least. Tell whoever you answer to that I want you to serve inside while the sun's at its peak. Does that suit you?"

Jae was braced better now, after their conversation, and was able to set her jaw and force back the immediate answer—*no*. No, she didn't like being inside, where Lady Shirrad and the Avowed could see her. Where *Rannith* might see her. There was no telling what Lord Elan might do if she said that, but the Curse would never allow her to lie, and with every moment, the thrumming in her head grew louder, the compulsion to speak getting stronger.

At least this time, she hadn't been caught totally off guard. She cast around for anything she could think of, anything that was true enough to speak, related enough to his question to be an answer, and finally gave in. Very, very carefully she said, "It would be a relief to escape the sun."

Which *was* true. She forced herself to exhale quietly,

calmly, as if she hadn't just battled the Curse for that. Drawing his attention to her pause would do no good—she didn't want him to ask anything else.

"This place is miserable," he repeated, which meant if he had noticed anything, he didn't care enough to ask about it. "I've seen what sunsickness can do. Even back home, it's not uncommon. And with the drought as bad as it is . . ." He shrugged. "I was the one who tripped, after all. You may go."

She fled. Maybe she should have thanked him, but she didn't want his eyes on her any longer than necessary. And besides, what did she owe him her thanks for? She didn't want to work inside, and her life was nothing to him.

Leaving without speaking had been the smart thing to do, even if she had had permission to talk. After all, she could still only tell the truth. Better to keep quiet like the Closest always did, and not to let slip what she thought of him.

Chapter 4

RUNNING ATTRACTED ATTENTION, SO CLOSEST DIDN'T RUN. BUT Jae moved as fast as she could while keeping silent and unnoticed, and didn't slow until she'd left the house and was safely out behind it. There was a large open space between the inner and outer walls, which had once held more yards and gardens and even trees. Most of the trees had died the same year her mother had, and had been dug out ages ago. The yard was now covered in sand, with neglected pebble paths. Only the outer stone wall kept the yard separate from the desert.

Jae felt like she could breathe again once she stepped outside, into the night. Unlike the front of the house, where people came and went, or the courtyard, which was overlooked by several rooms in the house, no one ever bothered to come back here. That was the reason it had been allowed to fall into this state, gloomy and abandoned, the way all of Aredann would be soon.

Still, Jae walked toward the few remaining trees. Their bare branches scraped at the sky, and the wind made eerie noises as it caught them. But Jae liked the trees anyway. She didn't have the water to help keep them alive, but they remained here, somehow, stubbornly surviving. Jae let a hand rest against one's rough bark and sighed.

Before the drought, Aredann had been a true oasis in the desert—or so her mother had told her. The courtyard garden had rivaled the splendor of gardens in the central cities, and this empty yard had been an orchard. Jae couldn't even imagine that, and almost didn't want to. In some ways, she preferred the yard as it was now: dismal and desperate, but still clinging to life. Like the Closest. Like all of Aredann. For now, at least.

She passed through the trees to the back wall. It came up to her hip, made of rough stones that she knew by heart. She rubbed her hand against one, almost surprised that she hadn't rubbed it smooth through the years. Here, blocked from the view of anyone in the house, was the one place where she could be alone, and where she felt safe enough to finally stop moving, to sag in place and catch her breath.

The moon was a bright sliver hanging over the open desert. Jae picked a dead branch off the ground and tossed it over the wall, leaned out and looked at the endless expanse of sand and stones. When she squinted, she could make out a few stunted bushes. She'd spent hours staring at them as a child, wanting to look more closely, to explore everything out there, to see what the other estates were like and if there were really cities with reservoirs ten times the size of Aredann's.

Those estates were as much a legend to her as the War of the Well, the rebellion her ancestors had started, that had left their descendants shackled by the Curse so that they could never rise up again. The Curse would never let her leave Aredann—not that she wanted to, necessarily. Aredann was her home. It was all she knew, and every blade of grass that survived was thanks to her care. It would turn to dust without her.

But if Aredann was abandoned, it would turn to dust anyway. So would she.

She heard pebbles crunch behind her, and went still, her heart racing. She hadn't been given further orders for the night, but if one of the Avowed saw her like this, simply standing in the night without doing any work—

"Jae."

Tal's voice, a whisper in the wind. Jae relaxed and turned to face him. He must have kicked those stones intentionally, warning her that he was coming instead of creeping up next to her silently, greeting her with a hand on her elbow. She didn't like to be startled.

"I heard that you were in trouble," Tal said, coming to stand at the wall with her. "But no one knew where you were. I thought you might have come here to be alone."

"And yet, here you are," she said, smiling a tiny bit so he'd know she didn't mean it. She liked being alone, but having Tal at her side was better.

They stayed like that for a few minutes as the chilly wind

raised bumps on her arms. The night felt enormous, but it wasn't silent. There was the wind in the trees, and even, when she listened carefully, the sound of insects singing. A tiny lizard skittered across the top of the wall and down the far side. She watched it go, sure no one else at Aredann stood still like this long enough to notice tiny details of the night.

"If you don't mind, I'd like to hear what happened," Tal finally said.

Jae scraped a fingernail along the wall. "I'm fine."

"I heard you were punished by Lady Shirrad and Lord Elan." He watched her plaintively, pleading for information without asking any questions. She could see his worry in the way he stood, the crinkled skin on his forehead.

"I wasn't. I was . . . His Highest said he was going to. He called me to his room. But all he did was give me a drink and send me on my way with orders for tomorrow." She stared out at the desert, still not sure what to make of all that.

"A drink," Tal repeated, incredulous.

She nodded. "And he allowed me to speak, which was . . . I don't understand."

"It sounds as if he was kind."

Jae snorted. Maybe it sounded that way, but none of the Avowed were kind, and the Highest were the cruelest of all. "Not exactly. It's more as if he just didn't care."

"Hmm." Tal let that go, but she could see he was thinking hard, reconsidering everything he knew about Lord Elan.

"I should go talk to Firran," Jae finally said.

Tal made a face like he'd eaten something sour, and she laughed. Firran was one of the only Closest who didn't like Tal—because one day soon, Lady Shirrad would probably give Tal his job, and there would go his precious scraps of power. So Tal had decided not to like Firran right back.

Jae felt a little steadier now, as if the conversation with Lord Elan hadn't been quite real. She knew it was, she had orders to obey or the Curse would punish her, but the idea that she'd actually spoken *with* him, not just answered his questions, was too strange. Like his order to protect her from sunsickness and his decision not to punish her, she had no idea what to make of it, or of him.

Firran was in the main room within the Closest's quarters, sitting next to the fire and eating a thin slice of bread and lentils. He was speaking quietly with a few others, but stopped when Tal put a hand on his shoulder. Firran frowned and stood.

Jae had to force out the words, self-conscious with so many people waiting for her to speak. "I've just been with Lord Elan. He gave me orders."

"What?" Firran demanded.

Her body went tense with the compulsion to answer, and next to her, Tal glowered. But at least it was an easy enough question. "I'm not to work on the grounds during midday."

"And that's it?"

"Yes," she snapped.

"Why, are you in a hurry to get back to your meal? Did we interrupt you?" Tal asked, arms crossed over his chest. The questions were pointless, inane, and while everyone else's eyes went wide, Firran's were narrow with anger.

"Yes. And yes," he said.

"Does it annoy you when people ask you questions? Do you want me to stop?"

"Yes. And. Yes."

Tal started to say something else, but Jae brushed his elbow and he stopped, looked at her, and shrugged. He turned pointedly away from Firran and murmured to her, voice dropping back to its usual soft tone, "I haven't eaten yet."

Jae hadn't, either, so she sat with him and let him serve them both small meals. He caught her eye and winked at her, and then passed his hand over the bowls quickly, sprinkling them with something he'd produced from his pocket. Lady Shirrad had probably given him the dredges from one of her spice shakers. Or simply hadn't forbidden him to help himself.

Slowly the rest of the Closest returned to their quiet conversations, to their drawings on the walls, to braiding belts and jewelry from scraps of fabric too small to be used as clothes or rags.

Tal didn't say anything else about it as they ate. But Jae knew him, knew that the way he stared into the fire meant he was still thinking. If anyone could make sense of Lord Elan's strange behavior, it was Tal.

Jae was awake and off to work before dawn. She may have had other orders for the afternoon, but the grounds were still her responsibility, so she went to work at the front of the estate. It wasn't until the sun loomed higher overhead, sending sweat pouring down her back and heating the stones up enough that her hands and bare feet ached from touching them, that Firran stepped onto the path and beckoned her in. She hoisted her tools and followed, careful to scuff off the dirt that clung to her feet and dress before she went more than a few steps in.

Firran turned and examined her again. "Put those things away and clean yourself up properly. If Lord Elan wants you inside so badly, he can have you—you'll be serving the Avowed their lunch, and attending them this afternoon."

Jae swallowed, nodded, and walked away, trying not to let anything she felt show. When she glanced back at Firran, he was smiling grimly. He knew *exactly* what he'd done. Jae would rather risk sunsickness than spend a minute near any of the Avowed. She wasn't like Gali and Tal, who could smile and move gracefully, even under Lady Shirrad's exacting gaze. Being watched by any of the Avowed made Jae's skin crawl, especially since Rannith—

Rannith was going to be there. Firran *knew* that.

Jae staggered to the side of the hall, leaned against the wall for a moment, her heartbeat echoing so loudly in her ears that she couldn't hear anything else. She hunched forward, trying to breathe, dimly aware of every scrape and scab on her body, every smudge of dirt. The armor that turned her invisible, kept her beneath their notice and away where she was safe—armor that she now had to strip off.

The Curse started throbbing slowly at the base of her skull, a nudge because she had to move. It didn't matter that she'd rather work outside with no water, and it didn't matter if Lord Elan had intended to do something kind. This was the task she'd been assigned, even if it was just by Firran, and she had no choice at all.

She stowed her equipment and went to clean herself up. Her hair was too short to do much with, tight spiral curls clipped close to her scalp, but she wiped the sweat and sand from her skin and changed into one of Gali's plain tan dresses. It was unwashed, but nowhere near as filthy as Jae's clothing. It fell straight down from her shoulders, with long loose sleeves and a belt around her waist. It didn't quite fit, too short because she was taller than Gali, and the belt was just old scraps braided into a flat strip, hanging down too low because Jae's figure was so much flatter than Gali's.

There was no mirror in the Closest's quarters, which was just as well. Jae knew she looked ridiculous. But ridiculous was safer than pretty.

Lady Shirrad's kitchen was run by a cook, one of the few Twill who hadn't fled back to the central cities as the drought had grown worse. He had two assistants, but the rest of the kitchen workers were Closest, including Asra tending a pot on the fire. Asra glanced at her and gave a tiny almost-nod in greeting before turning back to her work.

Only the cook bothered to say anything to her. "You're not the usual server."

Jae shrugged silently. The cook wasn't Avowed, so the Curse would allow her to speak, but he probably wouldn't like it. It would be the same when he gave her orders in the kitchen. Magic wouldn't force her to obey, but she'd still end up in trouble if she tried to resist. All he'd have to do was tell Lady Shirrad or one of the other Avowed—if he even bothered. No one would say a word about it if he beat her himself.

"Well, we're not ready to serve yet—take the ladle and get to work." He shoved the scoop into her hand and nodded toward where one of his assistants was pulling the lid off a stone pot.

As Jae began doling stew out into bowls, the assistant

looked up at the cook and asked, "Did His Highest like breakfast?"

"He didn't say anything about it," the cook snapped. "And he's not all *that* high. Just the second child."

"High enough," the other assistant put in.

"Not even close," the cook said. "That tutor of his told some of the Avowed all about it last night. Lord Elan's not the heir, and he won't ever be now that Lady Erra has children of her own. He's not even in favor with his father."

"I don't believe it. How does the Highest's own son fall out of favor?"

Jae began arranging the bowls on a platter. The assistant garnished them with something green and slightly wilted.

"Well, what Lord Desinn says—not that we were meant to hear this, of course—but *he* says that Aredann isn't the only estate where the reservoir's run too low. Most towns are all right, and the central cities are all fine, but the farther out you get, the worse it is. It's bad enough that they've left some estates behind entirely—just packed up all the Avowed and moved. They're going to leave Aredann soon, too."

Just like Firran had said. Jae frowned down at the bowls.

"But of course, the guardians don't like that too much. No one's going to question it, not when it was ordered by the Highest themselves. No one would dare . . . except Lord Elan. That's what Lord Desinn said, that Lord Elan heard the grumbling and asked his father about it, and, well, Highest Lord Elthis wasn't very happy with him. *He* said it was traitorous talk, even if it was coming from his own son. So now Lord Elan's here, to see what it's like in the *real* drought, to learn his lesson, and he's cursed lucky he wasn't disavowed. He definitely won't be questioning his father again."

"But surely they won't really just leave Aredann behind," one of the assistants said. "There's still *some* water here."

"Not enough. And once the people are all gone, they'll work it so the Well sends its water to other reservoirs."

Jae stared resolutely down at her work. Once the people were gone—once the Closest were dead.

"Hey—hey you there, Closest. The platter's ready. Get it out there before His Highest complains."

Jae heaved the platter up, braced herself, and headed into the dining hall. The gossip had at least given her something to think about other than her terror of the gathered lords and ladies, but when she stepped out into the open, the fear flickered back to life. She moved as quickly as she could manage without risking tripping or spilling anything, making her way to the head of the table to serve Lord Elan first. He nodded his thanks when she set it down, though no one else at the table bothered to. Lady Shirrad sat next to him, along with her advisors, Aredann's few other Avowed.

Lord Rannith sat at the far end of the table. Jae's stomach clenched as she stepped near to him, hating how close she had to be to set the platter down. He was too large for her to reach around easily, with hugely muscled arms from his work as the captain of Shirrad's tiny guard squad. He reached for his fork and Jae darted away quickly, forcing back the memory of those hands on her body.

Thankfully, he didn't even look at her. He just leaned forward to eat and listen as Lord Elan talked about how everyone who went to search the desert for the Well left from Aredann.

Jae caught her breath as she walked back to the kitchen, her skin crawling. The work wasn't hard, but she was tense, worried that a misstep would have everyone's eyes on her.

Eventually the meal wound down. She cleared the dishes and delivered them to the kitchen to be cleaned, then had to wait in the corner of the dining room. She stood like stone, schooling her breaths to come as silently as possible while she watched and listened to see if anyone needed anything.

Lord Elan gestured lazily with his mug as he spoke. "With all the desert lore I've read, if I had to guess, I'd say the Well is just beyond Aredann. It's to the west; it must be."

"The Well was hidden for a reason," the Avowed steward who'd arrived with him, Lord Desinn, said. "There's no point in anyone trying to find it—or wasting time with guessing games."

"It's not a guessing game," Lord Elan snapped. "It's easy enough to see, when you look at a map. You there—Jae." He smiled for a split second when he recognized her. "There's a bundle of papers up in my rooms. One of them is a map. Go get it."

"Highest, this a waste of time," Lord Desinn said as Jae started to walk away.

"If you have something better to do, you're welcome to leave," Lord Elan said behind her, his voice fading as she hurried off.

The papers were easy enough to find, tied together with gold ribbons and left on top of one of his trunks. She untied the ribbon carefully, amazed at how soft and clean it was, and then leafed through the papers. Most of them were lines and loops of text, which meant nothing at all to her, with a few illustrations decorating the pages. They were drawings of plants: leaves, the kind the trees in the orchard had had during better seasons, and flowers she'd never seen before. Fruit—grapes, melons, and some she didn't know.

Other pages were less detailed, barely sketches—of the quartered circle that Lady Shirrad and the other Avowed had branded on themselves, and other strange, flowing lines and intersecting circles.

Finally Jae found what she hoped was the map. It was like one of the illustrations but more detailed, with drawings of what looked like houses grouped together. Everything was carefully labeled, but since she couldn't read, she couldn't be sure. Still, she pulled it free of the stack carefully and carried it down to Lord Elan.

He just nodded at her, accepted it, and set it aside. The conversation had moved on to something else. He was talking with the Avowed about what they all did at Aredann, laughing and joking about what they might do if the estate was abandoned. Rannith seemed eager to be sent to a new estate, where he'd get to work with a larger group of guards. His booming laugh as he described how pathetic Shirrad's guard was made Jae shudder.

Finally the conversation died down. Lord Elan reached out to grab her arm as she walked by, and she nearly jumped out of her skin, but all he said was "Put that away, would you? Carefully."

"Yes, Highest," she murmured, compelled to speak, even though he probably hadn't even meant his order to be a question. She took the map and hurried back up to his room, then flitted through the papers, trying to remember where it had been placed. As she slid it back between two pages, she felt an insect wing's worth of annoyance that they hadn't even looked at it—and then she stopped, staring at a sketch on the paper beneath the map. More careful lines and shapes, more text she couldn't read, though it looked somehow different from the writing on the other pages. But at the center of the page was a figure she was sure she'd seen before: four circles, overlapping one another, all coming together in the middle—but she hadn't seen it quite like that. It was the design in the fountain. She was used to looking at it from the ground, where it looked like columns rather than circles. But from up here . . .

She went to the window and peered out, just to check. There it was, down in the garden. From the top, the fountain was four interlocked circles. She couldn't imagine why the fountain would interest anyone enough for it to be drawn on any of Lord Elan's papers. It had been dry for years, nothing but a useless sculpture.

But when she looked back at the papers, there it was, drawn in dark ink as if it were the most important illustration on the page.

Chapter 5

THE AVOWED HAD MOSTLY LEFT THE DINING HALL BY THE TIME
Jae got back to it, including Lord Elan and Lady Shirrad.
They were off having a discussion in Lady Shirrad's library.
The meal was over, and though the sun was still high overhead, it was well past noon. Yes, it was still too warm out to
work comfortably, but Lord Elan had only ordered her inside
while the sun was at its peak. She was free to return to her
usual duties—well, as free as she ever was. At least out in the
courtyard, she knew what needed to be done, so no one bothered to give her orders, and she was away from the Avowed
and their demands.

She stole glances at the fountain as she worked. She knew
the four columns—circles, she now realized—represented

the four elements, and that mages had once called on those elements for their power. But that didn't mean the fountain was anything special; the four elements were part of almost every piece of artwork and decoration at Aredann.

As the sun set, Jae took a half jug of water out to the garden so she could try to coax the plants back to life. She set the jug in the fountain's trough so there was no way someone could kick it over this time, and took a moment to run her hand over the smooth stone of the fountain. Dirt and sand caked its surface, but when she rubbed the grit away, it was a white-silver that almost shone.

The fountain really was unlike everything else at Aredann, she realized as she worked. She'd never paid much attention to it, but where the rest of Aredann was tan and red, the fountain was silver; and the rest of the estate was covered in intricate patterns and designs, but the fountain was solid, plain, and gleaming.

She didn't have the water to really wash the fountain clean, but she could still scour off most of the dirt. She probably didn't need to; it wasn't like the plants, which would die without constant care, and she doubted anyone else would even notice. But she'd know, and besides, she wanted the excuse to examine the fountain in detail.

Jae grabbed the sack that she'd use to gather up weeds later and dropped to her knees at the fountain's base. She used the sack to rub the worst of the grit off, scrubbing with her whole weight where the dirt was the most caked on.

From this angle, there was no way to see the linked circles of the fountain's design. Looking up, Jae could see only smooth columns rising from inside the trough. The highest was at the back, the lowest in front, and the crevices where the front column interlocked with the two on the sides were covered in dirt. She scraped off as much of it as she could easily, then scooped it up, using her hand as a makeshift dustpan so she could dump the dirt onto the ground.

Jae dug at the trough with her finger, scraping more stubborn dirt off—only to feel her finger dip slightly, into a tiny depression in the stone. No wonder dirt built up there, where it had a little texture to cling to.

Though that was odd. The rest of the fountain was smooth and even. She finished cleaning the area and looked down at it. Nothing looked different at first, until she shuffled to the side and light from the sinking sun reflected off it. There was definitely something there in the base of the fountain, an area where the surface dipped just slightly.

She squinted. It was almost impossible to see, but she ducked back down and ran her hand across it, tilted her head to see how the sunlight's reflection shifted. And there it was, finally taking shape in front of her, just as subtle as Gali's soot-and-ash sketches on the walls inside—the impression of a hand, as if someone had pressed their palm into wet clay. In the middle of the print was another shape—a teardrop, etched even more lightly.

Jae traced her finger along the handprint, amazed at how subtle the whole marking was. She couldn't think of anything it could be except a signature of whoever had built the fountain originally—but no builder would want their signature to be too subtle to spot. And it *wasn't* like Gali's drawings, designed to be washed off or drawn over, again and again. Even as subtle as it was, it would take generations for the handprint to wear away. It had been left there to last.

Jae pressed her palm against the print. It was barely larger than her own hand, and her fingers tingled a little.

She jerked her hand away. The tingling felt almost like the Curse—but the Curse always started in her head, right at the back of her skull. It sometimes spread and got worse, but she never allowed that to happen anymore. The pain spreading meant the Curse would take over her whole body soon, wrenching control away from her and forcing her to obey orders, no matter how hard she resisted. The agony when that happened was incredible, so bad that she'd heard stories of Closest who'd passed out, and their bodies had carried on working anyway.

Jae shuddered and shook her hand out. The tingling stopped.

She went back to work, grabbing her sack and stooping to pull weeds. They were nasty, thorny, almost as bad as the cactus that loomed at the back wall. She plucked them carefully, one by one, and shoved them into the dirty sack. As she picked up the sack, she found another weed, still growing between the rocks. She yanked it, and one of the thorns sank into the tender skin of her palm.

Biting down a yelp, she dropped the weed and the sack both. Her palm was bleeding, damp spots blotting her brown skin, and her whole hand had started tingling again. She shook it, sending a few more droplets trickling out, then pressed her other thumb against the wound. It was only a small scrape, the bleeding would stop in a moment—

She whipped her head around and stared at the fountain. The mark was a hand, and a droplet, but maybe *not* a teardrop. Maybe it was something else. Water would make sense—it was a fountain, after all—but maybe . . .

The tingling in her hand felt like a hundred thorns piercing her, and her breath came in shallow gasps. She stared down at the empty fountain basin, at the handprint she'd never noticed before, and wondered how many times she'd cleaned the fountain and never seen the mark.

She hesitated for a moment, heartbeat echoing loudly in her ears, then pressed her bloody hand down against the etching.

Pain exploded inside her head, a sudden onslaught from the Curse instead of its usual warning pressure. She screamed, the noise sharp against the stillness of the courtyard, as the whole world went white, bright flashes and flickers like sparks—

"It's the small touches that count," Janna said. She laughed, staring at the gleaming stone. She had already given it shape and linked it to the streambed they'd built under the house. It was nearly finished, except for a final touch. Hovering in other-vision, she could see all four of the elements' energies and the whole house, as if she floated above it. Seen like this, the way a mage would see it, the fountain's design was much clearer—four circles, one to represent each element, all locking together in the center.

Janna drew on the elements' energies and concentrated on the fountain, building the image more clearly in her mind. Not just the shape this time, but the texture, the smoothness. She saw it gleaming, she focused, and then she poured the energy into the fountain until it glowed almost as brightly in real vision as in her other-vision. Finally she linked that to the water that was now beginning to gather at its base. The link was a simple binding that would give the magic permanence, tying the magical energy to the physical fountain itself. Now, as long as there was water to pull from, the fountain would shine.

Tandan shielded his eyes until the glow died down to something more subtle. "I think you have better things to do with your magic these days."

"I don't have many days left now, so why shouldn't I use them for something frivolous and beautiful? Anyway, this is what people will remember me for," she said.

Tandan scoffed. He'd always been impatient. "They'll remember you for creating the Well."

"The Well wouldn't exist without all of us," she corrected. "And when it is done, it will belong to all of us. But this fountain—this is mine alone. And I'm giving it to you, to remember me."

He scowled again, but she recognized the sadness he was trying to mask. "It doesn't have to be you, then, Mother. If the Well belongs to all of us, then someone else—"

"No," she said. "It isn't my Well, but it is my responsibility. It's an honor, and I would never ask this of anyone else. How could I?"

"If it's an honor, then someone else will volunteer. We can't lose you. I can't."

"Oh, Tandan." She opened her arms, and even though he was a grown man and embarrassed by his own emotions, he stepped into her embrace. She held him for a minute, knowing this was hard on him—harder than it was on her, by far. "This is how it has to be. If I do this, it will bind the Well until the Bloodlines die out, and you know they never will. Not with you and Mirrad going on like this."

"Mother!" He backed away, horrified, and she couldn't help but laugh. She would be leaving them all behind soon, but she was grateful that crafting the Well had taken long enough for her to see her grandchildren, another generation of the Bloodlines that would bind the Well's power. With so many families making up the Bloodlines, the Well would last forever.

"The only thing I regret is that I won't be able to see my grandchildren grow up," Janna said. "But this way, I know they'll be safe." She reached for him again, tugged him down until she could kiss his forehead the way she had when he was a little boy, even though now he towered over her. He'd grown up well, and she'd made the right choice in trusting him with the Well's power and its secrets. He and Mirrad would guide the others when the time came to make choices, and they'd raise their children, Taesann and Aredann, to do the same. The Bloodlines would continue, and so would the Well. And they would all be safe.

Jae's startled shout echoed back at her. She hit the ground, unable to even catch herself, her head only missing the base of the fountain by inches. Then everything went silent. The world faded to black this time, and the pain finally, finally faded with it.

Chapter 6

IN HER DREAM, THE GARDEN WAS FLUSH WITH LIFE. RED STONES still marked the path across it, ringed the fountain, divided the courtyard into careful sections. Grass grew up everywhere else, bright green and high enough to tickle her ankles.

The cactus bloomed with red flowers, and the stunted bushes had come back to life, with deeper green leaves hanging from each bough. The flowers around the base of the fountain were an amazing rainbow of rich reds and yellows and even purple. Their blossoms were full, delicate petals rimming their pollen insides, and they smelled sweeter than Lady Shirrad's perfumes. The fountain burbled behind them, the water fresh and cool, despite the sun—splashing, sometimes overflowing as the breeze picked up.

Jae stood in the middle of the garden, turning in a slow circle, staring at it all, *feeling* it all. Not just the damp breeze on her skin and the soft grass under her bare feet, but the life in all of it. More than anything else, she felt the fountain. It wasn't alive, but it hummed with some kind of energy she didn't recognize, brimming more with power than with water.

"Jae, Jae, please wake up, *please.*"

She could just make out Tal leaning over her, shaking her. She moaned, lances of pain shooting through her body, and managed to say, "I'm awake."

He stopped, thankfully, and pressed a hand to her forehead, his palm cool against her skin. "You're sick. You must be sick; you're *burning.* But you were inside today."

He stared at her imploringly, waiting for the answer to his unasked question. She tugged his arm away from her face and mumbled, "I don't know. I think I just . . . fell."

"Let me help you," he said, and stood, then leaned down to offer his hands. She clenched her jaw so no scream of pain escaped when he moved her, but she must have gasped anyway, because he murmured, "I'm sorry. I'm sorry, Jae. You'll be fine. I'll get you inside. . . ."

The pain was too much. She felt like she'd been in the sun all day without a drink, as if she'd been straining, hauling enormous water jugs by herself for hours until her body had given out. Everything *hurt.* The Curse throbbed in her head, and she didn't even know what it was punishing her for.

When Tal finally managed to get a grip around her and pull her up into his arms, it was too much. The world went black again.

"These drawings are . . . They're not as clear as I was expecting," Lady Shirrad said, leaning forward over the papers with a slight frown. Elan waited, schooling himself to be patient and relaxed. Now that he and Desinn had settled in at Aredann, it was hard to find time to talk to the Lady alone.

The whole day had been long, boring, and hot. He'd spent it sitting in this same chamber with Shirrad, Desinn, and all of her Avowed. They'd been discussing how much water they had left at Aredann. It was Shirrad's duty as the reservoir's guardian to see it was used wisely, and doled out to the Avowed who served her, but the Avowed had spent the day quibbling over how many jugs each of them had been allotted. As if that made any difference. Aredann was going to be abandoned soon. But that just seemed to make them greedier, as if whoever finally drank the reservoir dry before they left would win.

Desinn had watched them all with a superior smile. He and Elan both knew how little any of this would mean, once the Avowed were sent to the central cities. But Elan had been sent here to see just how desperate the drought could make people, to be reminded of why the Highest had to make careful, sometimes even cruel, decisions for everyone's safety.

It wasn't until after dinner that Elan had finally managed to walk with Shirrad out around the grounds and mention that he was interested in learning more about Aredann's history — and that he'd brought some old books and papers about it. The information in them was obscure, some of it seeming to be a completely different kind of writing, nothing he'd ever seen before. That was probably from before the War, maybe even before the Well had been crafted; he knew she wouldn't be able to read it any more than he could. But she might be able to do something with the rest of it. If she recognized something, it might lead him to the Well's location.

"Maybe that one isn't the best to begin with," Elan said. "There are some other drawings, here." He shuffled the pages around, looking for one of the more complete images. There had been shockingly little information about Aredann in any of his father's books, and Elan had barely had time to copy any of it properly before being sent away. What had been hard to decipher in the originals was all but impossible now, though he finally found one that was more clear: a quickly copied drawing of a garden.

Lady Shirrad studied it, then looked up, wide-eyed. "Highest, of course I know what this one is. Look."

She pointed above his head. He turned to look over his shoulder—and there it was, the same image, the largest of the mosaics hanging on the wall. He bounded to his feet to examine it more closely.

The mosaic was enormous, some of the tiles as small as his fingertips and others as large as his fist. The wall was opposite the room's windows, so the tiles themselves had lost some of their vividness, but they still gleamed in the torchlight. It must have been quite a sight when it had first been created, huge and bright, showing a man kneeling in a garden as he planted a flower.

"My father told me that it's an image of Lord Aredann himself," Shirrad explained.

Elan nodded a little, studying the picture. Aredann had

been one of the greatest heroes of the War, a mage whose own brother, Taesann the traitor, had joined the Closest when they'd tried to seize the Well. Taesann had been the Closest's final mage, and Aredann had eventually been forced to kill him. The estate where Aredann had grown up had been renamed in his honor. The mosaic itself was as tall as Elan, though it was hung above the shelves, with its bottom as high as his ribs. It was set within a green-gray frame with a rough texture.

"How long has this been here? Has it ever been moved?" Elan asked.

"Not in my lifetime, Highest," Shirrad said.

If it truly was an artifact from right after the War, the era when it had been decided to hide the Well, then it really *might* hold a clue. But if he had the mosaic removed from the wall so he could study it more closely, Desinn would definitely hear about it. Elan would have to explain himself, and at best, Desinn would scoff at his quest to find the Well. More likely, he'd spin it into a tale that would make Elan look worse to his father, attempting to solidify his *own* influence with the Highest. Elan couldn't afford to appear any worse in his father's eyes.

Finally he said, "Lady, we haven't discussed this much, but when Aredann is abandoned . . ." She winced but didn't say anything, so he pressed on. "When we leave, we won't want to leave anything *this* valuable behind. Can this be taken down from the wall? Cleaned and prepared to move?"

She didn't say anything for a long moment, her lip trembling; then she took a deep breath and said, "Of course, Highest."

"Thank you," he said. "Is there anything else you can tell me about it?"

"Only a little," Shirrad said. "The garden—well, it's not as large as it looks up there. The courtyard just isn't that big."

"The courtyard?" he asked. "This is *that* garden?"

"I know it's hard to believe," Lady Shirrad said. "But before the drought, the garden was a wonder to behold—or at least, that's what my father told me."

"You're *sure* it's the same garden?"

"Yes, Highest," Lady Shirrad snapped. Elan glanced at her again, surprised by the bitterness in her voice, but she recovered herself quickly and gave him a cheerful, obviously false, smile. "That's the fountain. It's still there. It seems to have been built by mages, just like the house."

"So it *can't* have been moved since the War," Elan realized. "Then—then I need to go look at it."

Lady Shirrad's pleasant, polite smile didn't waver this time. "Of course, Lord Elan. I don't think we'll be able to move *that* anywhere, though, when you leave Aredann."

She led him to the courtyard, and he tried to memorize the way as they walked. The house at Aredann wasn't nearly as large as the ones the mages had built around the enormous reservoirs where he'd grown up, but he still needed to learn which corridors connected to which wings. The sitting room they'd left was central enough that he'd gotten turned around and didn't know which way led toward the garden.

When he stepped into the courtyard, he realized that it was a little silly to examine the fountain now after all. It was dark out, and though the moon was bright enough, everything was shadowed. It would be easy to miss details.

The fountain itself was impossible to miss, though. It towered over everything, silver-white in the moonlight, bright enough that it was almost a light in and of itself—bright enough that his eye caught on something at its base.

"Lady—Lady, look!" He crossed to it, crouched down, and caught his breath.

Lady Shirrad joined him, her eyes widening in surprise. A single flower, bright purple and delicate, was growing at the fountain's base. There was no grass around it, nothing but sand and stones. Elan put his fingers to the ground, and they came back dry and dirty, not damp. But this flower was just like the one in the mosaic—and it was alive, which was impossible. It needed water to grow, and he hadn't noticed it the previous night, when he'd first glanced around the miserable little courtyard.

"The Closest," he said. "The one who tends the grounds—Jae. I need to speak to her immediately."

✤ ✤ ✤

Once again, Jae woke to Tal shaking her. The room was only lit by a torch, which threw strange shadows that distorted Tal's features, deepening his frown into something frightening.

"You're awake," he finally said, and let out a deep breath. "I was starting to worry."

"Everything still hurts," she said, answering his unspoken questions. She squinted at the dim light, then screwed her eyes shut. Even that was too much. Her head ached from the effort of looking at Tal. She tried to roll over, away from him, but her whole body seized, throbbing, and she fell back on the mat, eyes squeezed shut as tears formed. "I don't . . . don't understand," she mumbled, her heartbeat echoing in her ears. "I didn't disobey or . . . I don't know what I *did*."

"You must have done something," he said, and reached for her hands. "Because Lord Elan just summoned you. He sent Lady Shirrad herself, but she found me first. But it's definitely you he asked for."

Now her eyes flew open and she stared at him in horror. "He . . . But I didn't . . ."

"He's waiting for you in the garden, and he wanted you to hurry. I wanted to explain that you're ill, but . . ."

But Lady Shirrad wouldn't have asked, so Tal couldn't have said anything—and even if he *had* managed to speak, it wasn't as if anyone would care that Jae could barely move. Jae grimaced and nodded. That set her head spinning, and it got worse when Tal hauled her up to sit, as if someone were smashing her head with a stone, over and over—but at least that was familiar. She had an order to obey, and the Curse had no pity for traitors. It didn't matter that she'd had some kind of fainting spell, or whatever it was that had knocked her flat. She didn't even know what had happened, could only remember a flash of shining stone and the moon, and fleeting, muddled images of faces and flowers. Whatever she'd dreamed was fading as she woke.

At least the focused pain of the Curse in her head seemed to ease the pressure on the rest of her. As Tal guided her to her feet, she felt as if she were a grape left in the sun too long, withered and dry.

Her legs were unsteady under her, and she had to lean

on Tal as they walked. Some of the ache started to ease as she moved, as if she'd simply been in one position too long and her muscles needed to unclench. It also helped her head, since she was doing her best to obey the summons, and that calmed the Curse.

Lord Elan stood waiting in the garden. The moon was high overhead now, bright silver, and the stars were sprinkled across the sky like sand waiting to be swept away. He stood in front of the fountain, and Jae had to squint to see him at all. It was as if the moon had set the fountain on fire and it was throwing silver flames all over the courtyard. Everything looked strange, unfamiliar, as if she hadn't spent every day of the last year in this very spot.

She and Tal both tried to make the bow protocol demanded of them, but it was hard with them tangled together. Evidently Lord Elan didn't care. He just said "You can go" to Tal.

Tal hesitated, his grip on Jae's arm going tight for a moment. He couldn't argue—couldn't even speak, since he hadn't been asked a question—and he couldn't disobey. He helped Jae get balanced, then brushed her elbow with his hand as he glided out. Jae watched him go, wishing she could keep him with her somehow, hoping he'd stay nearby. She wasn't sure she'd be able to make it back to the Closest's quarters by herself, assuming Lord Elan let her go when he was done.

"Jae," he said. "Look at this."

He pointed down at the fountain's trough, but when Jae shifted her gaze, the world started to swirl in front of her again.

Everything turned sideways; she couldn't tell which way was up, could barely move her arms to try to catch herself—

Lord Elan sprang forward and grabbed her as she toppled, pulled her up until he had his arms wrapped firmly around her. She shuddered, wanted to pull away but couldn't. She didn't dare, and wouldn't be able to move even if she did.

"Are you all right?" he asked, quietly, concerned. "What happened?"

The Curse nudged her, and she was too exhausted and achy to even attempt to control her answer. "I'm *not* all right! I had some kind of fit before, and now—now I'm dizzy and exhausted and I don't want you to touch me!"

His eyes widened, the whites catching the moonlight, the brown so dark she couldn't tell iris from pupil. His mouth fell open, and he just gaped at her. She braced herself as best as she could. The Curse required honesty, but she wouldn't usually have shared that particular bit of truth.

"You can't stand on your own," he finally said, once he got over the shock and regained control of his jaw. "I'll set you down."

He wasn't as gentle as Tal but managed to maneuver her down onto the ground without dropping her. He left her kneeling, hunched over, her fingers digging into the dirt beneath the pebble path. She concentrated on breathing, on not shaking. He didn't move any closer, just waited.

Finally her trembling subsided. She could move again, though she didn't dare go far. All she did was force herself to relax, to sit back on her legs, kneeling upright instead of hunched over. The garden was still too bright, the fountain still glowing under the moon. Not even just the fountain—

everything seemed to be cast in an eerie light, as if a silver fire burned inside the cactus and the pathetic bushes. Even Lord Elan glowed, though he looked a little different. That light was dimmer, steady instead of twisting and pulsating like a flame.

He stepped forward a little and pointed at the base of the fountain again. Not at the trough but at the pebbled ground in front of it, where a single purple flower was growing.

Jae gasped.

"That's what I needed to speak to you about," he said. "I don't remember seeing this flower yesterday. Was it here?"

"No, Highest," she murmured, still staring. The flower, like the fountain, glowed brightly—but that was impossible. It was *all* impossible. Stone as smooth as the fountain could reflect light, but a flower or a cactus couldn't. She'd heard of some people who got headaches so severe that they saw strange things, but it had never happened to her before.

"Did you plant it today?"

"No, Highest," she repeated.

He frowned, but at the flower, not at her. "I don't understand it. The flower—it *can't* grow out here; the soil is too dry. Back home, we have to water gardens twice a day to get blossoms like this, and I know you don't do that. The water I spilled yesterday, do you think that might have done it? That it was enough for the flower to grow?"

"No, Highest. The flower's grown too quickly, and it wasn't all that much water. . . ." She trailed off, squinting at the flower. Something about it was familiar, floating just beyond her grasp, but the thought vanished like the last rays of daylight.

Lord Elan scowled, his mouth pulling to one side. "Well, it can't just have appeared here."

She swallowed, glad he hadn't asked her if she agreed with him. It was impossible, but it had just appeared, sometime in the hours since she'd tended the garden and had her fit. And she'd dreamed about the garden, about flowers just like this one. . . .

Maybe that was all it was; she'd seen the flower as she'd fainted and had turned it into a dream. But even as she thought that, she knew it was wrong. The flower *hadn't* been there that afternoon.

She waited for Lord Elan to ask her something else, but he didn't, instead saying, "It must be nothing, then. Stupid of me to hope otherwise. But I want you to care for this flower, at least. Give it the water it needs. There's only one, for now, so it won't be all that much."

She nodded that she understood as the Curse accepted the order. Then he strode out, not looking back at her.

She heaved a deep breath, relieved to have him gone. Tal didn't come back into the courtyard, though, which meant that either he really had left her alone or he'd been pulled off to a more important task—or any task at all. Maybe Lady Shirrad had found him again. It wasn't as if the Lady would care that Tal wanted to help Jae.

Instead of pushing herself up, Jae crawled forward until she could reach out and brush a finger against the flower's petals, awed. It was like something she'd seen in a dream, dancing at the edge of her memory, just out of her reach. Jostling the flower released the scent of pollen into the air, sharp and sweet, and *familiar*. But dreams didn't come with scents, and she'd never seen a flower like this before.

Maybe Lady Shirrad had perfume that smelled like the blossom. . . .

But once Jae touched it, she couldn't shake the strange feeling that she had seen the flower before, and not in a dream. Maybe she *did* remember it from some long-ago time, when she'd been a child and the drought hadn't started yet. But that felt wrong, too. She knew the flower, and it felt more intimate than that, as if it belonged to her alone.

It was impossible, but as Jae stared up at the fountain that was practically writhing under the moonlight, then down at the flower in front of her, she knew that she'd created it.

Chapter 7

"I'M NOT SURE YOU'RE WELL ENOUGH TO BE UP," TAL SAID AS THEY
walked down the corridor toward the courtyard together.

Jae let out a huff. She'd woken him just before dawn, but
they would have been up soon anyway, and the Curse would
have forced her to rise and work no matter how sick she was.

Even this early, Closest roamed the halls, preparing for
the day. Jae and Tal should have been doing the same thing,
but thanks to Lady Shirrad's favor, Tal didn't have specific
orders, and Jae's only orders were still to tend the grounds
and to serve inside during the worst of the sun. Since she
was dragging Tal out to the garden anyway, the Curse hadn't
stopped them.

Besides, no matter what Tal thought, she felt much better than she had the previous night. She was still stiff, but the throbbing through her body had finally eased, and she could walk on her own again. The bright colors and glows she'd seen had faded. She wasn't dizzy. Everything that had happened during her fit had subsided—except her certainty that she'd created the flower outside, and a strange feeling that there was something more to her dream, something she'd forgotten.

They managed to slip into the garden without being noticed, and she led Tal over to the fountain. Leaning close to him, she murmured, "Look at the flower, Tal. *Look*."

"It's beautiful," he conceded. "I've never seen one like it. But I don't understand—"

"I grew it."

He just lifted his eyebrows, waiting.

"I don't mean—I didn't *plant* it. I imagined it was there. I dreamed about bunches of them. I pictured them when I fainted, and this was here afterward." She dug her hand into his arm but kept her voice low. "Tal, I *made* this."

"Made it how? I don't mean to be rude, but you're not making any sense."

As loud as she dared, she retorted, "Because *this* doesn't make any sense!" She dropped his arm and grabbed the fountain's brim. Her hand tingled, but it was a pleasant, warm feeling. "I don't know how. But yesterday I saw some of Lord Elan's papers," she continued, and explained as quickly as she could what had happened.

Tal stared at her but didn't interrupt and didn't contradict or tell her she was crazy, even though she knew it *sounded* crazy.

"I can't explain it," she finally finished. "But I *know* I did this."

"That isn't possible," he said at last. "You must *think* you did, but . . ."

"Then explain it some other way." She crossed her arms.

He looked down at the fountain, stooped to examine it, reached for the flower. For a terrifying moment, Jae thought he was going to pick it, but he just ran his finger down the delicate stem and across one of the leaves. It was lush, deep green.

"Magic," he finally said, quiet and reverent. "I can't believe . . . It just seems so impossible."

He was right. Growing a flower with magic sounded entirely mad. No one had used magic since the end of the War, but it had been common once, before then. It had been generations, but . . .

"The flower can't grow without water, and I didn't plant it. There wasn't even a bud there before I fainted yesterday. And I felt something." Thinking she had magic may have been madness, but Jae knew deep in her core that it was also the truth. She was so doubt-free that the Curse didn't even stir.

"But then . . . that's amazing," he said, and then looked her in the eye. "And dangerous."

She nodded. True, all those generations ago, magic had been used to craft the Well, to save the world—but their ancestors had also used it for war. Taesann, the great traitor, had gathered an army of rogue mages for his rebellion, and had nearly toppled the Highest in his attempt to seize the Well. As long as there was magic in the world, another war could happen. That was why the Highest had turned away from it after casting the Curse, and why they'd hidden the Well's location, even from their own descendants. Now they used magic only when there was no choice, when protecting the Well required it.

Now, looking down at her flower, Jae could almost feel the echo of her ancestors' power. Magic could be life—or death.

"If it really is magic, we need to know how it works, what you can do," Tal finally said.

"I don't know much yet," she said, answering the implied question. "I was cleaning the fountain, and everything just happened."

He hesitated again, looked around, up at the windows, and finally said, "You should try it again—carefully. See what you can do. If you can really do anything at all."

"I *can*," she said, stubbornly sure of it. She reached for the fountain, pressed her hand into the bare trough. The tingles grew stronger, climbing up her arm, and the fountain started to glow. Not as brightly as the previous night, but also not reflecting the first rays of dawn. It came from within the fountain.

"Look at that," she breathed.

"I don't see anything except you."

"Then . . ." She stared down, *focused*, but there was no sudden spike of anything. No pain, no dizziness. No visions. "I don't know what to do."

Tal made a low *hmm* in his throat, and for a moment she thought he'd tell her she was crazy after all. Instead he said, "You dreamed of flowers."

"It was so real," she said, and inhaled. She could just

barely smell the single blossom, tickling inside her nose. In her dream—her vision—the scent had been a hundred times stronger—a thousand. There had been so many flowers.

She closed her eyes and imagined it. She didn't even picture the fountain or the garden, just a rainbow of flowers. Purple, like this one, and rich blues and reds. A blanket of colors over a bed of green leaves and stems, twisted and tangled together.

Jae felt like an army of ants was crawling over her skin, and the fountain went hot under her hand, pressing back against her where she leaned on it. She didn't open her eyes. Instead she thought about her beautiful, imaginary garden, and *pushed*—

The Curse hit her all at once. She swallowed a scream, only letting out a tiny noise as she toppled back, her body seared, her head pulsing with agony. Tal grabbed her, and he was glowing, too, the light flickering and twisting inside him. He helped her down to the ground, letting her sit, and perched next to her. His hand on her shoulder burned.

After a silent moment, he murmured, "Jae, look."

She pried her eyes open, squinting against the too-bright courtyard, the strange glows of Tal and the fountain both, and saw what he was pointing at. A bed of flowers—only a few, small but glowing more brightly than even the fountain itself. She stared at them, her heart beating too fast in her chest, echoing in her ears.

Finally she managed to breathe, "I did it."

"But it hurt you," Tal said.

"But I *did* it!" She wanted to laugh despite the pain, because she *had* done this. She'd created it, done something impossible—and even though the Curse had punished her, she'd never felt more powerful. She opened her eyes wider, let the bright lights flood in, and it was like laying her hands on the smooth fabric of one of Lady Shirrad's best dresses. She could *feel* it, pull it, rip it—it wasn't light. It was energy. The fountain burned with it, and so did the flowers. So did Tal, and, when she looked down at her own hands, so did *she*. The energy, whatever it was, wherever it had come from, was hers to command. She could do anything with it, anything she could imagine, anything she wanted—

Until someone found out about it.

"Quick," she gasped, scrambling forward even though it made her dizzy. "We have to get rid of them. If someone sees— It's bad enough Lord Elan found the first. If he finds out . . ."

Tal nodded, understanding immediately: if Lord Elan or any of the Highest found out, any advantage Jae's power gave her would belong to the Highest instead.

"We have to find a way to get rid of these," Jae repeated. "And hide all of this until Lord Elan is gone—until all the Avowed have left Aredann."

"But we can stop them! We have to tell— Jae, if they know you have magic, they won't leave us for dead."

"No," Jae said. "I want them to go. Let them leave, and assume we'll all die, because if I have magic . . . Tal, once they're gone, I might be able to save Aredann."

His eyes went wide as he realized, understanding dawning. He gaped a little and said, hushed, "Jae, if you have magic, if you can save Aredann . . . maybe you could even break the Curse."

She stared back at him, at the flickering, twisting glow within him. Maybe she didn't know where the magic had come from yet, but for the first time in her life, she had something of her own, something the Avowed didn't control. Again, she felt that echo of her ancestors through the ages, a reminder of their power.

Of their rebellion.

Jae could barely focus all day, even when serving the Avowed's lunch. Her mind kept escaping her, drawing her back to the small bouquet of flowers now hidden under her sleeping mat. They'd be crushed there and their petals would dry, and once the Avowed were gone, she'd be able to take them out, use the dry leaves to make the room smell better. And out in the garden, she'd be able to grow dozens more.

She worked until well after the sun set and she'd finally fulfilled all of her daily duties, so she could slip out back to the trees. She and Tal had agreed to meet, but he wasn't there yet. She frowned a little, nervous, but it was only a few minutes later that he appeared, a gentle hand on her elbow as he mouthed hello.

"I was worried you wouldn't be able to make it," she said.

He waved that concern away. "Lady Shirrad is so busy trying to impress His Highest, she didn't even notice me," Tal said. "Maybe I should be insulted, but it's actually a relief."

Jae had no idea how he could even joke about that, but he smiled and gestured to the dry, dirty ground. Jae sat facing him, her back against one of the trees, and he sat with his back to the wall.

"I've been thinking about it all day," he said. "What we really, truly need is water. And if the Highest mages were able to craft the Well, you *must* be able to use magic to find some."

"That makes sense," she agreed, nodding slowly. She had no idea how she'd do it, though—but then again, she hadn't known how to grow flowers, either. All she'd done was shut her eyes and imagine it, so she did that again now.

She could feel the energy around her, even with her eyes shut, and slowly the glowing started—even if it was just in her mind. She opened her eyes again, and sure enough, there the bright lights were, illuminating everything around her. It made it hard to tell one thing from another—the wall from the ground, Tal from the tree—and it was almost too much.

The Curse began rumbling in the back of her head. It was a soft pulse, not yet too painful. She ignored it and thought about water: cool, quenching, soothing. She remembered it damp on her toes when Lord Elan had spilled it, and the sloshing noise it made inside water skins. She could practically taste it, sweet against the heat of her breath—

Some of the lights swimming around her tugged at her, drawing her toward them. She twisted, and it was as if she could see through walls, drawn to the basement, where water jugs were kept locked up; to the kitchen, where they needed water for cooking and cleaning. Even the cistern in Lord Elan's room.

The Curse exploded in her head, and she gasped, clutching her skull.

"Jae!"

Tal's voice was painfully loud as she waved him back,

forced herself to focus on here and now, on her body's shape and feel and not the glow. As the lights subsided, so did the Curse—a little.

"It hurts," she said when she looked up and found Tal hovering scant inches from her, ready to catch her if she pitched over. "The Curse is . . ."

"But you weren't ordered not to do this," he said.

"No, but we're Closest." They'd been cursed because of the mage-led rebellion. Of course the Highest wouldn't want them to use magic. Of course the Curse wouldn't allow it.

"But has anyone ever, ever said to you—have they ever said, 'Jae, don't use magic'?"

She was forced to answer honestly: "No."

"Well, there you go." But his voice softened as he added, "I don't want this to hurt you. I just . . ."

"I know," she said. "I have to do it. I have to, or Aredann is lost, and we're all . . . dust. I'll try again. Just let me breathe for a minute."

He settled back on the ground again, and she caught her breath. The Curse was still thrumming lightly, but she thought about the truth she'd spoken. No one had ordered her not to do this. She wasn't disobeying anyone. She wasn't.

This time, the lights came to her more easily, and it was easier to tell one thing from another. The wall and the ground were both steady and bright, but Tal and the tree flickered and changed. And the water was brighter still.

Just finding the water already at Aredann wouldn't be enough. The Avowed would probably take it all with them when they went, fill jugs from the reservoir and carry off as much as they could. Aredann would need new water, coming from somewhere else.

She concentrated on the idea of that particularly bright glow, until she realized the glow was all around her, too—hard to see, hidden within other shimmering lights. Her head throbbed with Curse-pain again, but she ignored it and reached for the nearest glow she could—pressed her palm against the tree trunk and pulled and pulled.

Her palm was damp.

She gasped, the glows fading, as she pulled her hand back from the tree, twisted around to look closely. There it was: a tiny trickle, no more than a few steady drops. Tal moved closer, staring over her shoulder. He reached up to press a finger against it, and a moment later the trickle was gone, dry. There was water in the tree, but not much. Not enough.

But it was a start.

"You really did it," he said, amazed, and reached up to run a damp finger across her cheek. She ducked away from his hand, a quiet laugh forming in her chest. Feeling reckless and giddy, she let the laugh out, let the noise into the sharp night air.

"We'll need more than that," she said. "I'll need more practice. But . . ."

"But you did it," Tal repeated. "And you . . . you really are going to save Aredann."

Jae wondered if this was what it was like to be Tal. She technically obeyed all of her orders the next day, she did the work she needed to—but she practiced magic as she did it. Because she never neglected her duties, the Curse didn't do more than rumble slightly, and she quickly learned how to work while examining the glows. When she focused, she could use them to tell weeds from bushes, to sense where the rocky garden paths ended and the dead tufts of grass began. Or she could let herself go, her mind soaring over the estate. She could identify people that way—not just pick humans out from the walls of the estate, from the floor and ceiling, all jumbled together, but tell who was who.

As long as she worked while she did it, she was fine, and getting stronger. The trickles she called got larger. She could pull water from weeds and feed it to the bushes instead. It was never much, no more than a palmful at a time, but it was getting easier. Surely once the Avowed left and she didn't need to be so careful, she'd be able to do even more. She *had* to be able to, if she was going to save anyone.

The one time she didn't dare practice magic was when she served the Avowed their lunch. She banished even the glowing energy whenever she was close to one of them. The Avowed still made her nervous enough that she gave them her full concentration—and besides, an extra hour of practice wasn't worth the risk. If any of the Avowed caught on to what she could do, the whole gambit would be over. They would control her *and* her magic. Better to be careful in front of them; better to wait until she was alone again, working, beneath their notice.

Evenings were her favorite. Anytime she was alone in the garden or the yard, she could practice. She started by counting water jugs in the basement, learning not just to recognize the bright, beautiful glow of the water, but to separate out each individual jug by its clay. When she finally got to use the water itself, she would watch carefully in this, this other-vision, and see how it was absorbed, how the plants would glow more brightly. She practiced calling water from weeds, and, daring, finally brought the water in her palm up to her mouth to swallow.

It was sweet and cool, and she smiled in satisfaction. She'd find more. She'd call it, or she'd create it, somehow. But it would be like this, free for everyone.

A footfall on the path startled her. She dropped her hand guiltily and looked up to find Lord Elan taking in the garden. She stayed where she was, crouched by the bushes, hoping he'd somehow overlook her, or at least ignore her—but no, his gaze lingered on her, and he smiled.

"I wish I could see what this garden was like when Lord Aredann first planted it," he mused, looking around. "It's nothing like the mosaic."

She said nothing, trying to stay calm. He liked to talk, she already knew that much. Hopefully, if she just waited, he'd talk himself out, get bored, and go find someone who could actually answer him. She banished the glowing visions as she waited, worried he'd seen her do something.

"The fountain, though, that's the same," he continued, walking over to examine it. "Lady Shirrad tells me it was crafted by Lord Aredann himself."

Jae couldn't say anything, just waited, listening, but when she looked at the fountain, she knew that was wrong. She had that strange feeling again as if she wasn't quite able to remember something important, but she could swear she'd heard something different. Lord Aredann hadn't crafted the fountain; a woman had. Someone tied to the Well, back when it had been founded. Jae must have heard a legend about that once, but that didn't make any sense, either. If Lady Shirrad and the Avowed knew that Lord Aredann had crafted the fountain, then no Closest would dare say otherwise—none would even be *able* to say otherwise, legend or no.

Elan stooped to look at the blossom. "How has our mysterious flower fared?"

"Quite well, Highest," Jae said softly, swallowing her anxiety. He'd ordered her to care for the flower, so she had, painstakingly ensuring that it continue to grow and bloom. But the flower was a dangerous subject, because now she knew for certain where it had come from. She was safe, as long as he didn't ask, but if he did . . .

"Good, good." He laughed a little and straightened back up. He looked up at the moon and mused, "It's not a bad evening out, now that the sun's down. Back at Danardae, we spend the evenings in gardens, too, though they have more than just one flower."

She forced herself to smile. Let him scoff at her garden—let him scoff, and then leave her be. She'd smile at anything if it meant he'd go back inside. And he seemed like he was going to when he glanced to the arched entryway.

But then he looked back at her and added, "It's still cursed strange, it growing out of nowhere like that. I take it you haven't seen any other mysterious flowers?"

He sounded amused as he said it, but Jae couldn't help but think of the bouquet under her sleeping mat, of the feeling of growing flowers up out of nowhere, and the Curse erupted in her head as she panicked. She tried to swallow it, tried to think of any other truth she could say, but when she opened her mouth, her voice betrayed her and she said, "I have, Highest."

❖ ❖ ❖

Elan stared at the girl. She was cringing, all but cowering, her face twisted up in fear. He looked around the garden but didn't see any other splashes of color. "Where?" he demanded.

"They were here," she said. "I—I hid them."

"Blood and bones, *why*? Where did they come from?"

Her voice shook as she said, "I didn't want you to see them—to see any of it. Not ever. Because I grew them—*I* did it." She clamped her jaw shut, winced from something Elan couldn't see, and a moment later spat, "With magic."

Magic. That was so impossible that he actually gaped, his mouth open as he stared. No one had magic anymore, except what the Highest needed to guard the Well. And even if there were still magic, it wouldn't come from some filthy Closest girl. She must have been mistaken, somehow.

But Aredann had always held secrets. And there was no denying the flower by the fountain, or that Closest couldn't lie.

"Explain," he said.

Her voice grew stronger, the tremble vanishing, as she said, "I saw some of your papers. There was a drawing of this fountain."

"Why didn't you tell me?"

"I *couldn't*," she snapped. "No one asked me."

"But surely you could have said . . ." He frowned. The

Curse was strict, but it must have made allowances for this kind of thing. He just couldn't think of any. "But what happened? How did you . . ."

"The magic was locked in the fountain, and I unlocked it."

"*How?*" he demanded again, eyeing her carefully. Everything she said had to be true—the Curse wouldn't allow anything else—but she wasn't saying much of anything at all. He added, "Tell me everything you know."

She narrowed her eyes but did as he'd ordered, explaining that she'd bled into the fountain and it had caused her fit—but that it hadn't just been a fainting spell. And she told him about everything that had happened since, how she'd managed to will flowers into existence. That she could summon water out of weeds.

"Show me," he ordered.

She stared at him for a long moment, and he couldn't read her expression. Finally she grabbed a weed up off the ground, held it in her hands. She didn't seem to *do* anything, except her gaze went unfocused, her expression went soft. But then she held her hands out to him.

There were tiny pools of water in each.

"Impossible," he breathed again as she stooped and let the water fall onto the flower. He turned to examine the fountain, but it looked exactly like it always had: dusty and dry. He plucked the thorny weed from where she'd dropped it, and winced as he tore his hand the way Jae had described. He pressed his hand down onto the fountain trough and waited.

Nothing happened.

"Why didn't anything happen?" he asked, frowning down at the fountain.

"I don't know," she said.

He pressed his hand down again but didn't feel so much as a tremor, and certainly didn't see any of the strange things she'd described.

"That makes no sense," he said. Surely he should have seen *something*. If there was magic in the fountain, it must have been meant for him or another member of the Highest families. "Why would it work for a Closest and not for me?"

"I *don't know*," she repeated.

"Curse it," he said. "That's ridiculous. The magic, if this *is* magic, wasn't meant for you. It's too dangerous. But at least I found it now, before we leave. . . ."

Jae looked away from him, silent but scowling, her arms crossed.

"Don't worry, I won't leave *you*," he assured her. "The magic is too important; you'll have to come with me when we all leave Aredann."

She didn't look relieved. If anything, the opposite—her eyes narrowed and her mouth tightened into a thin line, and she was glaring at him as if she were Avowed and he were one of the Closest, as absurd as that thought was.

"What?" Elan asked.

"You'll save *my* life. But you'll leave my brother to die. My brother, my friends, everyone I've ever cared for—all dead. And you assume I'll be happy that you spared me." Her voice was venom, the words as sharp as the thorns on the vine.

"Well, I can't bring them all!" Maybe he could bring a few more, but no one would understand why. Jae had magic, but there was no *reason* to bring anyone else. Their deaths were what would save the rest of the world, bringing the population back down far enough that the Well could serve everyone. It was a grim thought, and he could understand Jae's anger, but there was no other choice.

Or there hadn't been. But maybe now there was. Elan had been sure there was something at Aredann that would help him find the Well, and that would be the key to saving lives. And now there was magic. In traitorous hands, yes, but still magic.

"The power you found . . . could you use it to find the Well?" Elan asked.

"I don't know," Jae said.

He glanced at the flower again. It was impossible, growing out of the dust, surrounded by bone-dry ground. Surely if Jae could bring it to life, create flowers out of nothing, she could do plenty of other things. He'd have to find out what, learn more about it, but all the stories about the War were of mages who did incredible, impossible things. Surely finding the Well would be easy enough.

And magic appearing like this, even if it was in the hands of a Closest girl, had to be a sign. It wasn't what his father and the other Highest had planned for Aredann—but they hadn't known the estate held magic. Elan would have to bring his father here, show him what Jae could do, convince him.

But he'd have to be very, very careful. Convincing his father of anything was next to impossible. A flower and a palmful of water wouldn't do it. Elan would need Jae to know precisely where the Well was first, and be able to prove it, somehow. Once Elan had that ready, he'd send for his father. Until then, he'd keep this secret. If Desinn or even Shirrad found out, they'd send for his father immediately—and

Desinn, at least, would try to take the credit for it. But this discovery was all Elan's, and if he handled it right, waited until he was certain he was ready, it would get him back into his father's favor.

"I believe the Well has been hidden for too long," Elan said finally, watching Jae carefully. "I think it's time to find it, and I hope that once we do, we might be able to increase its magic, make it serve more people—including the people here. With your magic, Aredann can be saved. No one has to die."

He smiled at her, a little relieved. He hadn't given much thought to what would happen to the Closest after Aredann was abandoned, and dwelling on their deaths didn't sit well with him. If it was necessary, then so be it—and the longer he spent at Aredann, the more he understood that it was. Just as his father had said, the drought made people desperate and scared, and Elan could see it all around him. There *had* to be enough water for everyone, and if there were too many people, there would have to be sacrifices. It was a nasty thought, but the Closest might have to die. But not if there was any other way, and now there was.

Jae still didn't smile back at him. Her angry expression didn't waver, didn't lighten.

"What?" he finally demanded when he couldn't stand her silent seething for another moment.

"I was going to save Aredann—from the drought, and from *you*. That's why I hid those flowers. I don't want to help you. I want you gone from here. Forever."

Elan shook his head. Closest could *never* be left alone alive, with no Avowed guardian to keep watch over them. An

89

enclave of uncontrolled Closest was dangerous. Surely Jae realized that much.

"Aredann will be saved either way. You'll just have to live with that."

She made a scoffing noise in the back of her throat.

"*What?*" Elan demanded again. Having to converse like this, to demand or ask a question instead of just talking, was maddening.

"I already know I have to live with it, *Highest*," she spat, her voice still quiet but no less nasty for it. "I have no choice in the matter. I never did."

Elan faltered again. No, she had no choice—but that didn't matter. He was right about the Closest, and he *would* save Aredann. She wasn't going to die, and neither was anyone else, as long as his plan worked. There was no reason for her to be so furious about it, and no point in arguing with her about it, either.

"I'm not ready to tell everyone what you can do, yet," he said instead. "I want to know as much about your power as I can before I tell anyone. Does anyone else know about this?"

"My brother," she said.

"Another Closest," he said. "That's good. You will not speak of this to anyone else—and make sure he doesn't, either. Do you understand that?"

"Yes." She glowered for a moment before adding, "Highest."

He ignored the disrespect as he continued, "And there's too much at risk here for me to let you wander about this estate alone. From now on, you'll serve as my personal attendant, so I can keep an eye on you. Your brother can tend the grounds, or someone else. It doesn't matter."

That finally seemed to break through Jae's wall of rage. Her gaze dropped, her shoulders hunched a little, and she nodded.

"And finally, you will *not* use magic unless I'm there to supervise you. Is that clear?"

"Yes, Highest," she said.

"Make sure you remember—and that your brother knows, too."

Again she nodded.

"Good." But as he spoke, the hair at the back of his neck pricked up as if it were caught in a breeze, and his skin went oddly chilly. He shuddered, glancing around, sure someone was watching him from a window or—or *something*. But Jae was the only one there.

Jae, who still stood rigidly, again lifted her head to glare at him. She would obey him, though he had no doubt that she hated every single order he'd given her. But that didn't matter. Nothing mattered but the magic.

He turned and swept back inside, knowing she'd follow.

Chapter 8

SERVING AS LORD ELAN'S PERSONAL ATTENDANT SHOULD HAVE been an easy job, but Jae couldn't stop seething. The work wasn't physically demanding—just running errands for him, serving meals, and pouring drinks as she had during lunch recently. The rest of the time, instead of working outside, she waited nearby, silently mending a basketful of old clothing. Sewing wasn't her strongest skill, but her mother had taught her along with Tal and Gali before she'd died. She'd explained that they had to be useful, prepared for any task at all, because they were so lucky. The rest of the Closest—dozens, maybe hundreds, from the way Gali described them—worked in the sun all day, tending the fields that kept Aredann alive. It was grueling, difficult labor, and the sun had even less mercy than the Avowed. Jae's mother had always reminded her, no matter how much she hated the jobs she was given, she was still lucky.

She didn't *feel* lucky. Not if all being lucky meant was suffering less than the others, with just as little choice in the matter. Not if being lucky meant sitting in a room with Avowed who didn't care that the Closest were all going to die, who saw her as nothing but a set of hands to put to work, or worse, a body to use. Not if being lucky meant being near Rannith.

Lord Elan barely even glanced at her, caught up in the Avowed who were fawning over him. They acted as if they were grateful that he was going to force them to leave Aredann—as if it were a kindness he was doing for them, pulling them away from the only home they'd ever known. But maybe they did see it that way, because *they* were going to survive.

It didn't help her any to think about what Lord Elan had said, that he'd use her power as a way to save Aredann and the Closest's lives. Saving Aredann his way would mean the Avowed would stay, and the Closest would be ruled over by Lady Shirrad and the others forever. Nothing would ever change, and even though Jae had only been learning how to use her magic, she'd felt as if she'd been so close.

Now, ordered not to use magic without his supervision, her power wasn't even her own. She'd only had it for a few days, and already it had been stolen from her.

She served the Avowed lunch and dinner. After dinner ended, Shirrad finally glanced at her, and stared for a moment. Even cleaned up, Jae knew she didn't look like much: a stick figure in a plain tan shift, bare feet showing under the frayed hem. Shirrad frowned at her and then looked at Lord

Elan. "I'm sorry I couldn't provide you with a proper attendant, Highest. But are you certain that girl is . . . I'm sure I
could find *someone* more suitable."

Jae went still, waiting by the kitchen door, but he gestured
for her to keep moving, clearing dishes. "She's fine, Lady."

As Jae walked into the kitchen, her grip on the dishes so
tight that her hand almost ached, she heard Shirrad mention
Tal. Lord Elan laughed in response. Lady Shirrad didn't say
anything more about Jae after that, and no one else seemed
to notice her at all.

The last of her duties was to help Lord Elan prepare for
the night. She followed him to his room silently and poured
him a mug of water while he stripped off his robe, shirt, and
pants, leaving him in just his underclothes. She was careful
not to look too closely at him as she handed him the mug,
nerves suddenly outweighing her simmering anger.

He watched her, though, as he drank his water and she
put his discarded clothing away. Her skin crawled when she
sensed his gaze, but all he said was "Drink, if you want to."

His tone somehow made it a peace offering, and she took
it even though she had no interest in making peace. For all
she'd been inside all day, it was still cursed hot and she'd only
had a few gulps of water with lunch and dinner.

As she drank, he added, "We'll make time to see what you
can do tomorrow. I'll tell Shirrad . . . I'll think of something.
They can't keep me busy constantly."

Jae glanced at him, nodding just slightly in acknowledg-
ment so he'd know she heard, while she put the mug away.

He gestured again. "And that—there's no point in you doing that, nodding instead of talking when there's no one else

around. I hate the silence, and you certainly had plenty to say yesterday. You may speak, when it's just the two of us."

At his expectant look, she said, "Very well, Highest."

"Good. You may go."

She nodded again out of habit but didn't have anything to say to him. He watched her for another long moment but didn't say anything to her, either, so she let herself out.

Tal wasn't in the Closest's quarters, though Gali was, trying to smooth her hair back into a braid. She was muddy and sweaty, and groaned, "I don't know how you do it, Jae. Every day outside like that."

"You're the one Firran assigned to the grounds," Jae realized. All Jae had told Firran was that Lord Elan had asked for her as his attendant—Lord Elan hadn't cared who handled the grounds.

Gali nodded miserably. "I'm no good at it. I wish Lord Elan had asked for *me* as his attendant."

Jae thought about the water Lord Elan had given her, and it only made her angrier. She should be using her magic to help Gali, not him. But she'd been forbidden to talk about any of it, so all she said was "I hate being inside, surrounded by all of *them*."

"I'd switch back with you, if I could," Gali said. "I'm used to them. And when Lady Shirrad sees what a mess I've made of the grounds . . ."

"I'll help you," Jae offered. "If I have the time."

"Thank you," Gali said, finally tying off the twine at the end of her braid. "I don't know what I'd do without you and Tal. He's been helping me, too, when he can. This is *awful*."

Jae nodded again, glancing over at the mat Gali and Tal shared. Tal still wasn't back by the time she fell asleep.

She dreamed of flowers in a ring again. Not around the fountain this time but around an oasis— No, it was too big for that, more water than even the largest reservoir. Perfectly calm, a bright blue reflection of the sky, with barely a ripple across the surface. A rainbow of flowers ran the whole way around it, a circle broken only by patches of trees and bushes, plants too large to grow anywhere without so much water.

Jae rose well before dawn to get ready for the day. She glanced out at the garden and took a quick walk around the grounds so she could give Gali a better idea of what needed to be done, ducked into the kitchen for a few mouthfuls of breakfast, then hurried upstairs to wake the rest of the household. The cook and kitchen attendants were already up, and the Closest never slept in, but most of the Avowed needed to be woken for the meal. It was one of the few times Closest had been granted permission to speak.

Most of the Avowed woke easily, with relatively little coaxing. Jae's heart thudded in her chest as she knocked on Lord Rannith's door, but he yelled that he was awake before she let herself in, thankfully, so she moved on without having to see him.

Lord Desinn, sleeping in the guest quarters, woke grudgingly as Jae repeated his name. Then he waved her away. She padded out of his room quickly, grateful he hadn't needed anything else. She was still anxious after being so near Lord Rannith, and she didn't know Lord Desinn or his habits at all. Some Avowed were always unhappy to get up in the morning.

Next was Lady Shirrad, also in a set of guest rooms, as she'd given up her quarters to Lord Elan. At least Jae knew what to expect when she opened the door, the Lady's name on the tip of her tongue.

Tal was lying on the mat next to her. Lady Shirrad was on her side, eyes still shut, but Tal was studying the ceiling, perfectly still except for his blinking eyes and the rise and fall of his chest. Jae swallowed hard, shuddering as she realized they were both undressed.

Tal pushed himself up to his elbows and waved silently. He wasn't allowed to speak, or to wake Lady Shirrad; that was Jae's duty this morning, and the Curse would allow only her to do it. Jae swallowed again, her stomach churning, and managed to say "Lady Shirrad. *Lady*, please, it's time to wake."

Shirrad stirred, rolling over on the mat, and then sat up. Tal echoed the gesture, silent and graceful, and Shirrad placed a possessive hand on his arm. "Yes, yes, I'm awake. Tal, bring me something to drink before you help me dress."

Tal nodded, standing up from the mat. Jae padded back out of the room and waited in the hallway for a few moments until Tal came out, still tying his braided belt. He touched his hand to her elbow, smiling, but she could tell it was forced, an expression he hoped would put her at ease. As if she didn't know him well enough to recognize what he was doing.

"I'm all right," he breathed, barely a murmur, and led the way toward the kitchen. Only Lord Elan's room had water kept in it for convenience.

"Tal—" Jae started.

He shook his head. "I really am, Jae. You know she treats me better than you or Gali."

"But—"

"It's *fine*," he interrupted. Then, his voice softening, "She's going to give me Firran's position soon. Everything will be easier then, for both of us."

Something dark and hard formed in Jae's chest as Tal walked into the kitchen and she continued down the hall toward Lord Elan's quarters. The Curse had let Tal say all of that, so maybe he'd convinced himself it was true, that what Lady Shirrad did was fine because he'd get something out of it. But just because he believed that didn't make it right. Gali had spent the night alone and miserable, and whether Shirrad treated Tal well or not, he still had no choice in the matter. It wasn't fair. What Shirrad did to Tal was no better than what Rannith had done to *her*—

The world around her went bright, even though there were no windows in the stone corridor. She fell backward against the wall, letting it hold her weight as she gasped in breaths. Her fingers scrabbled at the smooth stone, and she tried to focus on that, to let the sensation ground her. All she could think about was Tal, lying awake on Shirrad's mat, what had happened to him, to her, to Gali, to every other Closest in the household.

Energy sang around her, bright and pure, begging her to reach out for it. Her head pounded as the Curse reminded her: she wasn't allowed. Lord Elan had forbidden it, and even though all she wanted was to pull that energy into herself, to find a way to use it to take revenge, she couldn't.

She took a deep breath, then another, pressed her palms flat against the stone and leaned on it, the wall cool against the back of her neck. She shut her eyes and waited until the sense of power receded, the light dimming, the need to do something with her magic fading away.

She woke Lord Elan and helped him dress. He regarded himself critically in the mirror, rubbing his palm against the stubble on his chin, then ran his hand through his curls. "Help me pull this into some kind of order," he said. "I can go a few more days without shaving, but I'm starting to look like a mess."

Maybe she was allowed to speak, but holding her tongue seemed like the better idea, especially when she was so close to him. His hair was finer than hers, his curls falling in loose ringlets instead of tight spirals, and it was just long enough for her to pull back at the nape of his neck. She tied it with a piece of bright green cord, fingers brushing his neck accidentally. His skin was warm where she grazed it, and he smelled like sweat and perfume. Her chest tightened, and it was all she could do to keep her hands steady. Gali would have been much better at this; Gali, or Tal, or anyone else.

She took several long steps back the moment she finished, while Lord Elan looked in the mirror and frowned. Even Jae could see he wasn't as polished as when he'd arrived at Aredann, but he was still handsome, with sharp cheekbones and a strong jawline despite its current stubble, and warm, dark eyes. Jae turned away quickly, not wanting him to notice her looking and get the wrong idea. Or get any idea at all.

The day continued the same way the previous had. Jae worked and waited, fetched and carried and cleaned and sewed, and longed to be outside with her plants instead. The Avowed gathered in Lady Shirrad's study after lunch. With no choice but to serve as an attendant in case Lord Elan needed anything, Jae followed, and sat in a shadowed corner so she could continue with the estate's mending while they talked.

3 1308 00339 4806

"Now that Lord Elan and I have been here for several days, I can see just how dire the situation at Aredann is," Lord Desinn started. "I've sent word to His Highest, asking him to come oversee the abandonment personally, and immediately."

A few of the Avowed's mouths opened, to gasp or to talk, but Lady Shirrad cut them all off. "Are you truly certain that's necessary? Our reservoir isn't all *that* low. The Well still provides."

"Yes," Lord Desinn said. "It does, but that's the problem. There simply isn't enough water, and what the Well sends to Aredann could be better used in the central cities. Once Aredann is empty, that's where the Highest will send it."

"But that's not fair!" Lady Shirrad snapped, her voice breaking.

Jae looked up at her in surprise. She'd thought the Avowed were all happy to move closer to the central cities, where the drought wasn't as bad, but Lady Shirrad obviously wasn't. Then again, the rest of them would have it easier, but as a failed guardian, Lady Shirrad would probably never again be trusted with any responsibility, no matter how small.

But Aredann *wasn't* going to be abandoned. Jae was going to save it, even if she had to do it Lord Elan's way. She looked over at him and found him silent, watching Lord Desinn carefully.

"It isn't fair to waste water on a tiny estate like this, when others need it more," Lord Desinn said. "That is what the Highest have decided, and none of us has any right to question that."

Lady Shirrad looked down, cowed.

"We'll need to prepare for Lord Elthis's arrival, be as close to ready to leave as we can when he gets here. Aside from what remains in the reservoir, what is there to bring to Danardae?" Lord Desinn continued. He glanced at the room's largest mosaic, which had already been removed from the wall and sat leaning up against it. "Is there anything else of value?"

"Aredann has value," Lady Shirrad said.

Lord Desinn rolled his eyes. "The artwork, the furnishings. Things that matter."

Jae seethed at that, for the first time appreciating something the Lady had said. Aredann was their home. The people had value.

"The fountain," one of the other Avowed ventured. "It was mage-crafted by Lord Aredann himself."

"There's no way to move that," Lady Shirrad said.

Jae frowned, that familiar feeling of a memory just out of reach hitting her again. The fountain—mage-crafted. But *not* by Lord Aredann. It had been sculpted by a woman, Jae was certain of that, someone tied to the Well. . . .

She stared at the door that led to the corridor, as if she'd be able to gaze through the walls and into the courtyard.

"It is a shame, though, to leave it," Lord Elan said, finally contributing something to the conversation. He glanced at Jae, then away. "If it could be moved, it would be worth more than any artwork. It isn't just mage-crafted; it's a piece of Aredann's history. Lord Aredann won the War here. It's something we should never forget."

Jae swallowed her disdain. Of course the Highest needed monuments to remember the War. The Closest remembered it with every cursed breath they took. They were the ones who'd lost and been punished, and whose ancestors had forced the Highest to impose their ruthless caste system on the world, just to control the Well's reservoirs.

But the Well's gifts hadn't been meant to be restricted. The Well was meant to belong to everyone.

To everyone.

The voice echoed through her mind, a woman talking to a man, her son. Jae *had* seen it, but not in a dream. In some kind of vision, when she'd first unlocked magic in the fountain. The woman—*Janna*, Jae remembered—had crafted the fountain as part of her legacy. But her son had been sure her real legacy would be the Well, which she had needed help to create but which had been her idea. And Janna had meant for it to serve everyone.

Jae shut her eyes, trying to remember if she'd ever heard a legend of a mage named Janna. Surely the Highest would celebrate the ancestor who had brought them together to build the Well. But Jae couldn't remember her name from any story, any legend, any history. Janna or her son—Tandan.

But Janna had also thought about Tandan's children. Jae knew *their* names well enough. Lord Aredann, and his twin brother. Taesann, the great traitor.

Glowing energy pulsed around Jae when she opened her eyes. The Curse pounded in her head, but the magic was everywhere. She hadn't called for it, wasn't trying to do anything with it, but there it was, practically singing to her, and the fountain in the distance shone brighter and louder than anything else.

Jae could remember now, as if she were Janna and she'd built the fountain only minutes ago, but she was sure so much more had happened, and she *needed* to know what. If there was more magic in the fountain than just what she'd already discovered, she had to find it. It might be something that could help her save Aredann—or help her resist the Curse.

It would be a while before Jae could look at the fountain, but she could examine it from where she was sitting now, with magic. Except, as soon as she thought that, the Curse slammed into her skull, and the bursts of pain grew stronger. She wasn't supposed to use magic without Lord Elan's permission, even though the magic surrounded her like sunlight.

She forced herself to return to her mending, but it was a good thing none of the Avowed called on her to do anything else. She wouldn't have heard them, with her mind already outside.

Most of the Avowed seemed happy enough with their lot when their gathering ended. Only Lady Shirrad scowled as she stalked out. Jae stayed huddled in her corner, waiting until everyone else had followed Lady Shirrad, and the room was empty. No one summoned Jae, not even Lord Elan, so as soon as they were gone, she took the chance to dart out to the courtyard.

She grabbed the fountain's rim. She couldn't use magic without Lord Elan there, but she wasn't going to, not really. She was just looking.

That was all she did. She stared at the fountain, leaning over the basin, letting her eyes go wide and unfocused until they watered. Then she shut them—and *then* she saw it again, the radiant light she'd seen before.

She reached out with her mind and her hands, and the light consumed her. This time, she didn't scream. She just *saw*.

Chapter 9

The magic wouldn't keep Aredann back for long. He was too powerful, now that he'd found others like him. They were so desperate, hungry for things Taesann could never give them. Could never, and would never. Grandmother Janna and all the mages of the Bloodlines had decided when they'd founded the Well that it was meant for everyone—everyone had a right to drink from its reservoirs, and the Wellspring Bloodlines would build more reservoirs wherever people needed them. But Aredann and his allies wanted to seize the Well's power and use it to control the world, wielding access to water as a tool more deadly than any weapon. Taesann couldn't allow that to happen.

A wave of power hit Taesann, driving him down to his

knees. Whatever Aredann and the others were trying, this was it, their last attempt. There was too much power behind the blast for one mage to hold off, even one as strong as Taesann, and he couldn't feel the rest of the Bloodlines anymore. It was as if they'd all vanished.

That was impossible. The Well drew power from the Wellspring Bloodlines, the descendants of the mages his grandmother had bound together—surely Aredann wouldn't try to gain control by killing all of them. Even he wasn't mad enough to do that. Aredann's allies' goal was to seize control of the magic that commanded the Well, not to destroy it.

Taesann dragged himself toward the fountain on his hands and knees. When he shut his eyes and looked at the world with other-vision, the fountain shone more brightly than anything else at his grandmother's home. His father had told him she'd crafted the fountain herself, and that was obvious in other-vision. The energy inside it felt like the Well—like Grandmother.

Another wave of Aredann's power hit Taesann, and he screamed, clutching the smooth stone. With no one else to help him, they'd break through his barriers in a few minutes, and then . . .

No. He wouldn't let them have what they wanted. Grandmother had charged their father with protecting the Well and the fragile balance it brought to the world, and Taesann's father had entrusted that to him. He was still a stronger mage than Aredann—but Aredann had allies, children and grandchildren of the mages who hadn't joined the Bloodlines. They called themselves the Highest, and they'd lent their power to Aredann, making him stronger than he'd ever be alone. But *only the Wellspring Bloodlines could command the Well. Tae-sann would die before he'd let the Highest and Aredann wrest that magic away.*

Taesann grabbed the knife he carried with him. Blood had more energy than anything else nearby, as it bound earth and water together. The knife was small and ceremonial; it would never help him in a fight, but it wasn't meant for that. It was for this.

Taesann slashed his arm and held it over the fountain's basin, ignoring the blinding pain of the cut. He reached out, seizing the power floating around him, and searched—

The Bloodlines were still there, weak and distant. They were spread across other battle sites through the world, but Taesann could sense them through the binding that held them together and powered the Well. But the battles they fought were minor skirmishes and distractions—the Highest mages were concentrating most of their power on trying to overtake Taesann himself.

Taesann couldn't save any of the other Bloodlines mages from where he was, stranded in isolation at Grandmother's estate, but he could protect the magic that commanded the Well. That was the most important thing—more important than any of their lives.

"Forgive me," he murmured, and rallied his energy. He wasn't as strong a mage as Grandmother had been, but he could touch all four elements, and he seized as much of their energy as he could. Then he reached out, found the Wellspring Bloodlines again, felt their magic all bound together, and yanked.

Somewhere across the desert, dozens of mages went weak, their power stolen through the binding of the Bloodlines. It left them defenseless, vulnerable to the mages who were attacking them. They would doubtlessly give their lives—but their families would carry on their blood, and the Well would be protected even if the mages themselves died. Taesann didn't have the time to mourn them or the energy to regret what he'd done.

He formed the image in his mind of what he needed. Two generations ago, these mages had linked themselves together with blood; now he imagined their magic as if it was the blood seeping out of his arm. He poured that blood not just into the fountain's water but into the fountain itself, hiding it as deep in the stone as he could.

Grandmother had wanted this fountain to last forever, to be her legacy. She'd bound it, so it would run as long as there was enough water to sustain it, and it would gleam and glisten whether there was water or not. It was that binding magic that glowed so brightly when he looked at the fountain with other-vision—brightly enough to hide the Bloodlines' power buried underneath it.

When this cursed war was over and done, any of the Wellspring Bloodlines descendants would be able to reclaim their power. Even Aredann himself, if he could find it.

Taesann had no choice but to hope he wouldn't.

But he needed to leave something, some clue, so someone would. Taesann was weak now, as if the gash up his arm had sapped his life along with his blood, but he had just enough left in him to add a single, faint shape on the fountain. A handprint. A blood drop.

He pulled his hand back and stared into the fountain, using the last of his energy to will away all traces of what he'd done. The stone and the water glistened, undisturbed, as if *nothing had happened at all. The impression he'd left was subtle enough that no one was likely to see it unless they truly looked for something.*

Dizzy and exhausted, Taesann staggered inside and refused to look back. Aredann would find him soon. Taesann no longer hoped his brother had mercy—no longer believed his brother even had sanity. Taesann had given a death sentence to the other mages of the Bloodlines, but he would join them as soon as Aredann found him. Preserving the Well was more important than any of their lives, so surely preserving their magic was better than letting it die with them.

It had to be.

The Curse throbbing in her head brought Jae back to herself. The vision had been too much, skirted too close to breaking Lord Elan's order not to use magic. But it had been enough.

Jae didn't understand all of it yet, but one piece was very clear. Taesann had died defending the Well from usurpers, including his own brother, Aredann. Aredann had allied himself with the group that had eventually won the War of the Well—the Highest. Which meant that the Highest were the usurpers who had started the War.

They hadn't created the Well, as they'd claimed. They'd stolen it from the group Taesann had thought of as the Wellspring Bloodlines, who had lost the War. The Closest *were* the Wellspring Bloodlines, cursed for the crimes their ancestors had committed.

Except they hadn't.

Taesann wasn't a traitor. The Highest hadn't created the Well. Everything Jae had ever known was a lie.

Duty called her back sooner than she'd have liked, before she had a chance to finish turning it all over in her mind. She went through the motions of work, barely thinking about what she was doing. Fetching water, mending, helping in the kitchen. None of it was enough to distract her.

How long had it taken for the Closest to forget the truth? Maybe they'd been forbidden to speak of it, silenced like they were so often. Maybe the Highest had forgotten, too; maybe Lord Elan didn't even know the truth.

She seethed. Taesann's sacrifice had kept the Well's power out of the Highest's hands, and any time they said otherwise, claimed to command the Well, they were lying. The Highest said it took a great work of magic to change how the Well's water flowed between reservoirs—but that was a lie, because the Highest had no control over the Well's magic at all.

No wonder the Highest families had decided to abandon some estates. It was all they *could* do, since they were as helpless to save the Well as everyone else. The population being too large—if Jae was right, that was nothing but an excuse.

As she served dinner, she wondered how long it would take before the Avowed figured out they'd been lied to for generations. When people started dying from thirst and the Highest didn't stop it, there would be riots in the cities, shattering the Highest's precious social order. Imagining it brought a grim smile to her lips. Once people got angry enough, the Highest would be torn down, dragged through the streets. The riots wouldn't solve the problems, but tearing the Highest down would be a vicious kind of justice. The Highest families would pay for the crimes they'd committed and covered up, including the slaughter of so many Closest.

The future was chaos, war and blood and thirst, ending with everyone's bones bleached white in the desert. The sand would bury their buildings and bodies, and eventually it would be impossible to tell that anyone had lived in the desert at all. Unless the Well was saved. Jae didn't know what had happened to it, why its power was failing if it *wasn't* about the population, but there had to be a way to save it.

But if the Well was saved, so were the Highest, and the Curse would continue. Jae's people, the rightful owners of the Well, would still be enslaved.

As Jae watched Lady Shirrad drink her fill, she decided that she would *never* help the Highest maintain their lies. She would help Lord Elan save Aredann and the Closest who lived on it, but then . . . then she'd find a way. The Curse had been cast by mages, and a mage could end it. Jae would figure out how, and she would free the Closest and reclaim the Well that was rightfully theirs.

She didn't know yet how she'd resist Lord Elan's orders. But after so many generations of lies and sorrow, she would either end the Curse or she'd end *everything*.

After dinner, Lord Elan told Lady Shirrad he wanted to retire to his rooms to rest. Jae followed him, anticipation and anger warring under her skin. She shut the door behind them, and for a moment, fear colored everything around her. Being alone with him in his chambers . . .

He tossed himself down onto his cushion and gestured to her to sit. She made herself as comfortable as she could on the flat bench of the windowsill. There was no breeze coming in, but she liked the feeling of the empty air behind her, and knowing that the garden and fountain were below.

"I want to find the Well," Lord Elan said. "You said you can sense water. See if you can sense that."

Jae nodded, resenting the order even as she shut her eyes. But the Curse started thrumming in the base of her skull — despite her immediately obeying the order. She'd had plenty of practice at ignoring pain, but the Curse *shouldn't* have punished obedience.

When she opened her eyes, the world was glowing. It only took her a few moments to separate out the brighter shine that she knew was water. The cistern in the corner was lit like the sun. She stared at it until her stomach dropped and she was seeing double, until she adjusted and let her mind float above the estate. From there, she could see the jugs in the basement and the kitchen, and when she widened her gaze, she could see the reservoir.

"Are you doing something?" Elan demanded.

It sounded as if he were calling from far away. When Jae looked at him, she barely saw him at all, just a ghostly glow where he was sitting. Her stomach swooped again as she saw both with her eyes and with this other-vision. The Curse echoed in her mind, pulling her back and compelling her to answer. She snapped, "I *was*. I need to concentrate!"

If he was angry that she dared yell at him, she couldn't tell. She couldn't make out his expression like this, only the Curse in her head. Even that felt distant, like fingers tapping against her skull instead of its usual hammer.

A faint glow pulled her attention not to the reservoir itself but under it, to the aqueduct that connected the reservoir to the Well. The reservoir was bright with water, even if it had run low, but the aqueduct was barely damp. There were traces—Jae could *feel* the power that had once run through it—but the magic had faded almost entirely. No wonder the reservoir hadn't filled, if the magic that called water to it was so dim.

There was still enough magic for her to follow with her mind. She let the remnants of power pull her out into the desert, where she saw almost nothing at all. There was a different kind of energy out here in the sand and in the few scraggly plants that held on despite the drought. There were even animals, foxes and reptiles and insects that looked like glowing specks.

Finally the trail she followed brightened, widened, and joined up with another trail—another aqueduct. It must have come from another estate, branching off from the main duct Jae was following toward the Well. If she followed it, she might be able to find the central cities, or at least another estate.

But instead of following the branch, she continued along the main duct, farther out in the desert. Away from civilization, toward the Well. It was easier to track now that there was more water, and she skimmed along it quickly, out of breath, as if she were running. Another branch joined up, and she knew she had to be *close*, with this much water. More water than she'd ever seen before, than she'd ever imagined existed—

Searing pain hit her.

She was used to the Curse feeling like a hammer to her skull, but this was more like something trying to pull her apart. She gasped, barely able to get a breath, and tried to pull away, but it gripped her, yanking, as if it wanted to pull her mind out of her body entirely. She toppled forward but couldn't catch herself. The Curse still pulled, ripping her, tearing her apart, but there was something *beyond* it. She spread her hands on the floor, fingernails scraping stone as she grasped for something just out of reach—

The sense of whatever was near faded, her mind too awash with pain to latch on to whatever it had been.

The agony was too much. She gave up and let go of her other-vision, crashing back into her body. She was staring up at Lord Elan. Not a glowing imprint of him but his face, eyes dark and full of concern. He knelt next to her, a hand on her shoulder.

She recoiled reflexively, and the world kept spinning even after she'd gone still. She shut her eyes to it, heaved, and vomited. Some of the pain began to fade. Not much, not *enough*, but it dulled around the edges. She opened her eyes slowly, letting them adjust to the late-evening light.

"What happened?" Lord Elan asked.

The question set the Curse off, focused it into a throb at the base of her skull. At least that focus freed up the rest of her body. She panted, her chest still aching a little, and managed to say "I was following an aqueduct, looking for more water, but . . . the Curse, it . . . it was too much."

She pushed herself up until she was sitting, facing away from the pool of vomit, and wiped her mouth with her hand. Elan screwed up his face and gestured to the cistern. "Take a drink— No, wait. You look like you'll faint. Sit; I'll get it."

She dragged herself farther away from where she'd been

sick, sure she'd be the one who'd have to clean it up, and sat against the wall. Elan dipped his mug into the cistern and carried it to her, pressed it into her hands. It was damp against her chapped skin, and she drank gratefully, reveling in how it cooled her throat and washed away the taste of vomit.

She caught her breath as the Curse's throbbing tapered off. Elan's face had gone red by the time she'd finished drinking and could breathe easily again. He didn't say anything, just stared at the mug in her hand, and she realized slowly that the Highest probably never fetched their own water. They certainly didn't serve it to other people—it was given to them as a gift, a sign of respect to the families who maintained order. This might have been the first time one of the Highest had ever fetched water for a Closest.

"Thank you," she mumbled, pushing up to her feet slowly.

Elan nodded, then cleared his throat and demanded, "Tell me everything."

Jae groped for an answer before the Curse could force one out of her. "I *can* sense water," she explained. "I could feel where the aqueduct is buried. I followed it— It's hard to explain— It was as if I was flying, but I could still see every detail. Smell everything, taste it. And then I reached some kind of barrier. . . ."

"Did you find the Well?"

"No, but I think I could. I know where it *is*," she said. "The aqueducts that serve the reservoirs, they all come together out in the desert. All I'd have to do is follow them. But the barrier . . ."

"Tell me about it."

She gestured uselessly, her hand painting nonsense in the

air. "It felt like hitting a wall—not quite like the Curse, and even stronger. I couldn't cross it, couldn't even see beyond it. When I tried, the Curse punished me. It wouldn't let me pass."

He frowned. "I've never heard of anything like that. I don't know why anything like that would happen."

"I don't, either," she said, but she was groping for an idea on the edge of her mind, one that hadn't quite taken shape yet. If the Highest were the ones who had stolen control of the Well, and there was some magical barrier keeping her away from it, then . . .

He looked at her expectantly and finally prompted, "What?"

"I don't *know*." She glowered as the Curse ripped it from her. "I almost had it, but . . . I think it had to do with the War, and the Closest, and the Curse. It felt like I had been ordered not to cross that barrier and was fighting against it."

Lord Elan considered that for a moment, then nodded. "During the War, that might have made sense. If the Closest were trying to steal control of the Well, of course my ancestors would have found a way to keep them away from it."

She examined Lord Elan for a moment, but it didn't seem like he was lying. She wasn't sure she'd be able to tell—she had never needed to consider if someone was telling her the truth before. Anything coming from the Avowed was an order; anything coming from the Closest could only be honest. It sounded as if Lord Elan really believed the Highest had crafted the Well.

But they hadn't, so they weren't trying to keep control of it with that barrier.

"You look thoughtful," Lord Elan said.

"I'm trying to figure it out," Jae said when he looked at her expectantly.

"How to get past it?"

She shook her head and was forced to admit the truth: "Where the barrier really came from."

"You don't think it was the Highest?"

"I *know* it was the Highest," she said carefully, measured.

"Then . . . what?"

It was maddening to have him ask her so many questions, pull the truth out of her no matter how hard she tried to twist her words, and though she tried to bite her tongue, the Curse pulled from her, "I'm trying to figure out why the Highest created it, when they *didn't* craft the Well, weren't trying to protect it from the Closest."

Elan laughed. *"What?"*

Helpless, Jae repeated herself. "The Highest didn't craft the Well. The Closest did. But they weren't called that yet."

His laughter faded, leaving him staring at her in disbelief. "That's madness. That's even more ridiculous than a Closest with magic!"

"I'm cursed," she reminded him, the words bitter in her mouth. "It's the truth."

"You're *wrong.*" Disbelief gave way to anger, his voice going low. "My ancestors crafted the Well. Even a Closest must know that."

She didn't answer—she didn't dare contradict him, not when he was glaring like that. But anger sparked in her chest, because she *knew*. Everything she'd seen, the way her mind had opened to magic, *everything* only made sense if she was right and the Closest had crafted the Well. Which meant the Highest had started a war over it.

Daring and angry, she looked up and met his gaze.

He clenched a fist and then let it go again, his hand still tense. "My ancestors built the Well, and saved this world—including *your* traitorous caste. Without them, none of us would be here. *You* would not be here to be so—so ungrateful. I've made allowances for your rudeness, I've shown you every kindness. And this is how you repay me, with—"

"If you don't like the truth I'm telling, that's your own cursed problem," Jae snapped, her anger spilling out like water from the mug. "I know what I've seen, and I *saw* my ancestors crafting the Well, and defending it. All I know for certain about *your* ancestors is that they cursed me—they cursed *us*, and now you're leaving us all for dead."

She didn't bother to hide her sneer, too angry to care what he did to her for it, because she knew the truth. The Closest's ancestors, the Wellspring mages, had crafted the Well, and it was their bloodlines that kept its magic bound. If their descendants died out, the Well would die with them. Abandoning Closest to die at Aredann and other estates would weaken the Well, not strengthen it, until it went entirely dry. The Highest's bloodthirsty lies would finally be revealed when they did nothing to save the Well or the world, because there was nothing they could do. Killing the Closest cursed the whole world.

Lord Elan could punish her. He could kill her. But he couldn't change that fact.

"I ought to— I ought to—" he sputtered. "I don't know why I bothered trying to reason with you. You never deserved a moment of my time."

She glared right back at him. She didn't *want* a moment of his time. She only wanted him to leave, to take the Avowed with him. Elemental energy sparked around her, brilliant and flashing. She didn't know what she'd do with it if he truly threatened her. If she tried to fight back, the Curse would crush her—but she'd rather take the pain of fighting than the hopeless, endless pain of obedience.

But all Lord Elan said was "Get out."

For a change, she didn't wait for a pulse of pain from the Curse to remind her that it was an order. She turned and strode out, slamming the door behind her.

Chapter 10

JAE WAS SURPRISED THE NEXT MORNING WHEN SHE DIDN'T RECEIVE any new instructions from Firran. She didn't want to go anywhere near Lord Elan and had half expected him to order her back to her grunt work in the garden, but maybe he was so far above her that he didn't even care that she'd snapped at him. Or maybe he wanted her under even closer control, now that she'd shown she wouldn't just give him everything he wanted, swallow all of his lies.

Either way, she still woke before dawn to take a quick look outdoors with Gali, and then to set about waking the Avowed. Jae shuddered her way through the task of waking Lady Shirrad and then the minor Avowed, like her advisor, Lord Hannim, and then Lord Rannith. The sight of him on his sleeping mat made her even more anxious, and she quaked as she retreated toward the master chambers.

Lord Elan woke slowly and fixed her with a long, flat stare once he realized who'd been calling his name. He ordered her to help him dress, to fix his hair, and he ran a critical hand over his chin before turning away from the mirror. "Tell them I'll be down for breakfast soon," he added, dismissing her.

His voice was cold, devoid of the fury he'd shown last night. As Jae hurried to the kitchen, she realized she trusted that even less than anger. Anger came with punishment, but coldness was *calculating*. A mask that covered everything else as he figured out what to do with her.

Elan didn't even look at her as she served breakfast. He just drank his morning tea and nodded politely at the subdued breakfast discussions. After, he let himself be pulled into the study with Lady Shirrad and her advisors, no doubt discussing his father's impending arrival. Lord Elan's father, Highest Lord Elthis, was the one who would choose where each of the Avowed would go, what estates they'd be assigned to.

It was a grimly satisfying thought. Lady Shirrad and the other Avowed were used to having power, not being at its mercy. When Lord Elthis told them to leave Aredann and where to go, they'd be just as helpless to refuse as any of the Closest. Except, unlike the Closest, they'd still be alive.

As Jae worked on the tedious, pointless mending, something stirred in her chest. An ember of anger. Nothing as bright and hot as her fury the previous evening—it wasn't about Lord Elan or the Well or their history. Not really. Instead it was about the lifetime of work she'd given Aredann.

No, it hadn't been by choice. She didn't care at all about Lady Shirrad or any of the others, or want to serve their meals or mend their clothes. But Aredann was her home. She'd spent countless hours tending the garden and the lawns, fighting a never-ending battle to keep the grounds beautiful. Maybe Aredann belonged to Lady Shirrad in name, but it was Jae's, too, by virtue of the work she'd put into it. When it was abandoned, that work would count for nothing. None of the Closest's work would mean anything, and it would be as if they'd never lived at all.

Lord Elan tried to reassure the Avowed that they'd be given good positions in the central cities, while Lady Shirrad watched with a sour expression, no longer bothering with a polite smile, and Jae stewed. It was a relief when she was called away for other chores and didn't have to listen to their conversation anymore. Preparing lunch was a hot, unpleasant task—tending a fire in the middle of the day, when the sun turned the whole kitchen into an oven—but it was still better than listening to the Avowed.

Lunch, usually more boisterous than breakfast, was subdued, too. Jae made her way through it, serving olive-topped platters and staying out of sight as much as she could. She hoped that Lord Elan would send her away to work on anything else during the afternoon so she wouldn't have to listen to the Avowed's petty, selfish conversation anymore.

The meal was finally ending when Rannith grabbed her arm as she picked up his empty plate. "You, Closest," he said, gaze flicking up to her face for a moment, "come to my chamber this evening after dinner."

The Curse settled around her, weighed her down, choked

her like a yoke around her neck, and all she could do was nod.

The first time she'd been called to Rannith's room, she'd been thirteen. Her mother had just died, but before she'd passed, she'd warned Jae, Gali, and Tal about the Avowed and their roaming eyes and hands. She'd told them what to expect, that the girls might bleed the first time, that taking certain herbs would make pregnancy impossible. Even back then, Gali, with her sweet smile and curving figure, had already caught several Avowed's eyes, and Lady Shirrad had already been too fond of Tal, in a girlish and innocent sort of way. No one had looked twice at Jae, the dirt-covered gardener.

No one until Rannith.

Her mother's warnings hadn't really prepared her. Her skin crawled from the second she walked into his chamber, even before he stripped her clothes off her. She'd stood there shaking, and he'd smiled at the sight. She'd shied away when he touched her—she couldn't help herself. His hands had wrapped around her wrists like manacles, pulling her close. She'd bitten her tongue until it bled, tried to keep quiet, but he'd lost his patience with her. Ordered her to lie still and be silent.

The Curse had taken over, forced her to obey. She'd tried to accept the compulsion, let it sweep her along while she shut her eyes and pretended to be anywhere else at all. She'd needed so badly to scream and run, to rake his face with her jagged nails and push him away, but the most resistance she could put up was trying to push him away as she quaked, and that brought the wrath of the Curse down on her.

The agony spread through her body, but the Curse's ache wasn't enough to block the pain. When she still fought, hands clenching the sheets against the urge to shove him away, the Curse had finally taken over her body entirely.

It didn't matter that she tried to scream, tried to run. Her body went limp and pliant, the Curse still burning her from the inside out, until Rannith finished with her. He laughed, he stroked her cheek. She wanted to cry but couldn't even do that. Not until he sent her on her way with an order to return the next night.

She'd fled to the relative safety of the back wall, hidden by trees, let their shadows wrap around her like blankets. Even so, she tried to swallow her misery and cry quietly, afraid someone would hear and find out. She didn't want to think about it, to talk about it. Not with anyone.

Tal had found her anyway. She hadn't told him anything, and he hadn't asked, just seemed to know. She'd flinched away from his supportive hand on her elbow, and he'd let her. He didn't speak, just comforted her by being there with her. And somehow he always knew when Rannith called her to his room and she needed Tal's strength. He always found a way to come be with her until she calmed down, the overwhelming misery shriveled to just a small ember of anger.

Rannith didn't call Jae to his room very often. He hadn't in months.

She *hated* him.

The afternoon was more of the same pointless, unending chores that the morning had been. Mending and fixing, serving, running errands. Every time Jae had to leave the room, something in the back of her mind cried out at her to run. To run out of the house, off the grounds, into the desert. Better to die of sunsickness on her own than find herself trapped on Rannith's mat. But she never took a single step toward the gate. The Curse wouldn't allow it.

The house was stuffy. The heat, the Curse, the fact that Lord Elan still didn't even look at her, all weighed her down until she could barely lift her head. Every step felt as if bricks had been tied to her feet. Her stomach churned and the scents from the kitchen made her ill, and she was still breathing around the ember in her chest, smoldering with anger and dread.

Dinner was as quiet as lunch, with only the most polite, quick conversations. When the meal ended, Jae found herself clearing dishes and watching Lord Elan. Part of her hoped desperately he'd call for her, demand that she follow him. He was one of the Highest, after all, and his orders were more important than Rannith's. If he wanted her to attempt to use her magic again, she'd *have* to obey, and Rannith could curse himself. But Lord Elan just left the dining room.

Rannith glanced at her, smiled, let his gaze linger. Jae felt as if she'd turned to stone, unable to look away, her hand still clutching the plates she'd gathered. Then Rannith left, too, and she had to get back to work before the Curse forced her.

Dizzy with dread, every step a chore, she willed herself to move. To finish the cleaning from dinner, and then, step after step echoing in her mind, to walk to Rannith's room. He called for her to enter when she knocked, and she let herself in. Shut the door behind her. Then it was just the two of them.

Her heart beat too fast, her chest aching with the effort of keeping herself under control. She didn't look up at him, but that didn't matter. He took her arm, pulled it down from where she'd held it crossed over her chest, and she swallowed and dropped both arms to her sides. He circled her once, then stood in front of her, smiling.

"Well, you aren't beautiful," he told her, and reached up to run a thumb across her cheekbone. "You ought to smile more, like your brother." His hand skimmed lower, fingers brushing her neck. "Smile, Jae."

The Curse thrummed in her head as she tried. Maybe it was enough—she knew it didn't look happy, didn't look *beautiful* like he wanted. He hummed his approval, pushed the neckline of her dress aside, and traced the U-shape at the base of her collarbone with his thumb. He reached around behind her, nudged her to turn so her back was to him.

Then he undid the lacing at the top of her dress.

She gasped, couldn't stop the sound from escaping.

"Shhh, shhh," he murmured, as if he were soothing an infant, as he carefully untied the rest of it. She ground her teeth, keeping her lips shut tight as he worked, but she couldn't stop herself from trembling. She shut her eyes and told herself to be good—be calm, be obedient—and it would be over soon.

When he pushed the dress from her shoulders, skimmed his hands down to her breasts, she still flinched, then froze, waiting for the order to stand still. It didn't come, but he stood too close to her, his hands roaming her skin. She clenched her own hands into useless fists, her arms tense as she resisted the urge to stagger away from him. He'd never allow that, and she didn't want the Curse to take control of her body—but she didn't want to be *in* her body, either. Not like this, not with him touching her.

He turned her around again and pressed his lips against hers. They were just as chapped and rough as her own, and the ember of anger in her chest sparked a little.

He stepped back, but only so he could strip off his own clothing. She didn't watch, didn't want to see his naked body. She never had, really. He'd ordered her to lie still, but never to look at him. Never to open her eyes.

"There," he said, as if stripping had been satisfying in and of itself. He took her arm again and tugged her toward the blankets and the mat on the floor.

She followed him, stiff but obedient, and sat on the edge of the blankets, then lay down when he nudged her to. When he didn't settle on top of her immediately, she made the mistake of opening her eyes to see where he was. He was just looking down at her, smiling. And glowing.

He and the rest of the room were swimming with light, energy. *Magic*. She'd been forbidden to use it, so the Curse wouldn't allow her to without Lord Elan there to give permission and supervise. Even so, the way everything gleamed, so bright after the darkness of her closed eyes, was almost comforting. It was there, it was *hers*, she could do anything with it—if not for the order Lord Elan had given her.

Rannith finally moved toward her, shining with a twisted, horrible aura. She shut her eyes against it as his hand skimmed down her body. She swallowed a whimper, her face hot with humiliation because she didn't dare resist him. There was nothing she could do, and she felt like nothing, like she was no one—

The ember of anger caught fire, rage burning inside her, overwhelming her. She twisted, trying to shove his hands away from her, to do *something*. He was stronger than she was, and already on top of her. She couldn't move far enough or fast enough. His hand seized her wrist, pinned it down on the mat, and he snapped, "Stop that."

The Curse hit her, a jolt of pain in her skull. Punishment for rebelling, even from unspoken orders; a warning not to do it again. But she couldn't stop herself, not now. She couldn't move after being ordered not to, but the pulsing, bright energy called to her. As Rannith reached for her again, she reached for the energy, grasped it with her mind, and *pulled*.

Suddenly she was outside her body, like she had been the previous night, with the whole estate spread out beneath her. She saw everyone, saw herself and Rannith. Blazing with anger, she ignored the throbbing Curse pain and seized more energy, *threw* it at him. He fell back, staring around in bewilderment, then reached for her again.

Her body was shaking now. Not with fear but with rage, defiance. The Curse punished her, throbbing pain echoing down her body and pulling her back to it when she'd rather be floating above. Even when she stared up through her own eyes, she could still see and feel the magic. See it, feel it, *use* it.

She shook, and so did the ground.

The ground shifted, the world trembling as if her nerves had run out of her body, down into the sleeping mat and the floor. Rannith let out a short, startled noise, and *now* Jae smiled, despite the pain. The Curse raged inside her, tearing, pulling her apart for disobeying Lord Elan's order—but she was white-hot with anger, and with *power*. The Wellspring Bloodlines' power, not just to control the Well but to touch the elements and use their energy. She pulled all the Bloodlines' power toward her, drinking it in greedily, letting it quench her the way water did. There was so much, the power of dozens of families, hundreds of people, all their magic now at her beck and call. It was so much, *enough*. It drowned out the pain, boiled inside her, and bled out. The room shook with her rage—the room and all of Aredann. Somewhere outside where she lay trapped, people screamed. Furniture crashed as it toppled over, sand and dust cascaded from the ceiling as the brick walls shook with her anger.

"What's . . . what's happening?" Rannith gasped, scrambling for a sheet to cover himself as he stared around, trying to keep his balance.

"It's me," Jae said, answering the question gladly. She looked up at the ceiling and could feel each individual brick.

"Stop it!" he screamed. "*Stop it all!*"

The Curse reared up again, making her deaf and blind from pain. It stabbed at her skull, raced down her spine. The whole world was agony—

Agony, and *power*. Teeth gritted, she reached for all that power. The Curse ripped at her, stabbed and screamed and tried to wrestle control back, but even when it took over her body, she could still control her mind. She couldn't see properly, couldn't open her eyes unless she surrendered to the Curse's authority, but she didn't need to.

Instead she reached for her magic and struck *back*, throwing energy at the Curse. Even with her eyes shut, she could sense the Curse around her, almost see it. It was enormous, invisible, but everywhere, like the air itself. She'd inhaled it, moved through it, lived with it her entire life, but now she could *see* it, see how it gathered around her, choking her and demanding she submit. She wouldn't, wouldn't, *wouldn't*. She threw magic back at it, all the energy she could find. She wedged the magic inside herself and pushed *out*, tried to throw the Curse back, but it wasn't enough. The Curse rushed into any space she created, too much, too huge. She needed to see more, to see it completely. She pushed past the Curse until she was outside herself entirely, able to see everything in the strange other-vision that was just energy.

The Wellspring Bloodlines were tangled together, each life a strand within ropes, the ropes making up a braid. They were stronger together, but another thread ran through the rope with them. Bloody and burning, it twisted between them, around them, stifling any hint of resistance. The Curse, part of them, destroying them.

When Jae tried to pluck it away, to unravel the Curse from the Bloodlines, another wave of agony hit. The pain struck everywhere at once, in her body and her mind, and more—not just hers. She sensed every Closest in the world screaming as the Curse came down on them all. She retreated, back into its agonizing embrace—

But no, no. Rannith knew she was the one shaking the world. Lord Elan would know she'd tried to disobey him. She *had* disobeyed him, just by holding the Curse off for so long. They'd never let that stand; they would kill her unless there was a way out. But how could there be, when she was one of the threads tangled up in the Bloodlines, in the Curse?

The world pulsed black and red around her as she fought to stay out of her body and in this magic realm. She searched and found *herself* inside the rope of Bloodlines. She was one tiny, glowing thread, but she pulled at it—plucked herself away from the outside. The Curse rushed in, but only in on her, and she didn't care, even as the Curse stabbed and tore, trying to keep her in her place. It hurt, but the pain didn't matter, because she'd rather die than live as one of the Closest any longer. Not when she knew all this magic belonged to them, and not the Highest. She'd never give in to the Highest again—

She pulled with all her strength, with all the Bloodlines' magic, with all the energy she could reach. For a moment it *was* too much, stretching her in every direction, as the Curse tried to pull her apart—

A *snap* echoed above everything else. The pain stopped, and she slammed back into her body so hard that the sleeping mat skittered to the side. Energy still glowed brightly around her as she opened her eyes, but she didn't see the Curse clinging to her. It still pulsed nearby, but it ignored her, the same way it ignored Rannith—

Rannith.

Jae laughed as she sat up, staring at him. He seemed so small, suddenly, puny and pathetic as he cowered. The ground still shook faintly, and the air was hot and dry. When Jae moved, the blanket crackled with energy, as if it was going to shock her. She could sense each individual brick in the ceiling, felt for their energy, and tugged. The bricks above

Rannith fell, the ceiling collapsing, rubble piling over half the room while she watched.

Rannith screamed once, and then there was nothing but the sound of bricks tumbling into a pile as they hit the floor. Jae tried to catch her breath, looked down at her handiwork. It was impossible to see Rannith under all that, but she *could* see the pool of blood leaking its way across the floor.

She exhaled and leaned back on the sleeping mat. There was still too much energy in the room around her, so much that it was stifling, and she was exhausted. She could barely breathe as it all tried to escape back to where it belonged, rushing away from her. She let it go, knowing she could call it back when she needed it, use it whenever she wanted, however she wanted. She was free of the Curse—she was *free*—and all that power was hers.

It swept away, and she let it, let the room go black around her, let the exhaustion catch up to her. Shut her eyes, unconscious but free.

Chapter 11

DINNER OVER, ELAN RETIRED TO LADY SHIRRAD'S STUDY. SHE and Desinn both followed him and settled around the table. The empty wall stretched above him, the bricks that had been behind the mosaic darker than those around them, untouched by the sun for so long. The mosaic itself leaned against the base of the wall, clean and ready to be packed away.

"My message should reach Highest Lord Elthis soon," Desinn said. "We'll want the estate to be ready for abandonment when he arrives. The less time he has to spend here, the better."

Lady Shirrad scowled. "The Well might still provide." She didn't sound hopeful, though. Just angry.

Elan took a moment to examine her. When he'd first arrived, she'd been made up beautifully, carefully. He'd seen through the facade quickly enough, the paint on her face and the fraying embroidery on her recently dyed dress. Now she didn't seem to care anymore. Instead of an artful arrangement, she'd pulled the thick coils of her hair back into a simple knot. Her face was clean of everything but sweat, and her clothes were as dull and unwashed as everyone else's. She stank of perfume—but so did everyone, even Elan. His skin itched with how much he wanted a bath, but there simply wasn't water for it. No wonder Shirrad had looked so pained when he'd demanded a bath that first night.

"Lady, enough," Desinn said. "The Highest have decided Aredann must be abandoned, for the good of everyone—even you, whether you want to admit that or not."

"It's *not* for my good," she snapped, then looked stricken and turned to Elan. "I—I didn't mean that, Highest. I *do* understand. It's just—Aredann is my home. The idea of abandoning it to the desert . . ."

"I understand, Lady," Elan said gently, and for a moment he thought of Jae, the grim look on her face when she'd said she was determined to save Aredann. He hesitated, wanting to tell them the truth. "Lady, the mage-crafted fountain in the garden, the one in that mosaic . . ."

"What about it?" Lady Shirrad asked.

"I think . . . I think there may be something unusual about it. Do you know if it was really built by Lord Aredann?"

"I have no idea, Highest," Lady Shirrad said. "I think so, but I'm not sure."

"It doesn't matter," Desinn said. "We can't move it, we can't take it with us. It's a tragedy to lose an artifact like that, but there are plenty of other mage-crafted sculptures back in Danardae."

"Yes, but . . . It's just that . . ." Elan trailed off, still not quite at ease with the idea of telling them. Yes, Jae could find them the Well; he was sure of that now. But she was so angry and volatile. With the Curse to control her, it shouldn't matter, but something inside him twisted when he remembered her bitter claims about the Well's founding. She had to truly believe she was right in order to make those claims at all—but if she said something like that to his father, or even Desinn, their reaction would be swift and violent.

No one questioned the Highest or their history. Especially not some Closest girl. Even if she'd been driven to believe madness by whatever magic had consumed her, she didn't deserve his father's wrath.

"What?" Desinn demanded again.

Elan started to reply, crafting a nonanswer, but the ground shook suddenly, shifting and lurching like a drunkard staggering. Desinn went silent, mouth still open, shocked.

"What was . . . ," Elan started, jumping to his feet, but he trailed off as the floor trembled and then shook, tremors sending the table skidding from side to side. He crouched, trying to keep his balance, as the mosaic propped against the wall crashed to the floor. Lady Shirrad shrieked, stumbling, her arms flailing at the air. Elan grabbed one of her hands as another tremor hit. The floor buckled, knocking ancient bricks out of place and sending them skidding across the floor.

He looked up. The floor was moving and sending the walls shaking with it. The ceiling was made of the same bricks as the floor, but if the walls were knocked over like the mosaic had been—

A steady rush of dust, ancient mortar knocked out of place, cascaded down. "Quick!" Elan shouted, pulling Shirrad with him as he dove under the table and braced it, trying to hold it still above him.

"What's *happening?*" Shirrad screamed as Desinn came to cower under the table with them.

"I don't know," Elan managed. He gestured Desinn toward the table leg. "Hold that! If the ceiling comes down . . ."

A brick banged against the table. Shirrad screamed again, and Desinn scrambled to do as Elan had said, to hold the table in place even as the floor kept shaking back and forth.

"This is impossible!" Desinn yelled above the din of groaning bricks and crashes and screams from across the household. "The ground can't— Nothing like this has ever— not since the War!"

Elan's gasp was lost to the storm of sounds around them as he realized what was happening. Legends said that during the War, mages had turned the ground into a weapon, had used it to swallow up whole armies. They'd called down lightning and fire, and sandstorms that had buried entire estates. Every battle had been fought with magic, won by the side with stronger mages. Now there was only one person at Aredann who could use magic—but he'd ordered her not to.

A scream rose above the rest of the clatter, but not from any of them. It took Elan a second to realize that the scream wasn't one person's alone. He couldn't tell how many, but the scream echoed through the whole room and left him ill. It sounded like someone being crushed to death—maybe dozens of people.

The scream went silent as abruptly as it had started, and the ground fell still. Elan could hear his heart beating in the sudden quiet, and had managed to take a real breath, to open his mouth, when the ground started seizing again. He grabbed for the table leg, but the whole table skittered across the floor, dragging him and Desinn with it. Shirrad shrieked as a brick crashed down next to her. She scrambled and rolled away, unable to get her footing. The table hit the wall and shuddered from the impact.

"We're going to be crushed!" Shirrad yelled, scurrying in a half crawl toward them. "If the wall comes down on the table—"

"The whole ceiling will come with it!" Desinn interrupted.

Desinn was right. Whether it was the wall or the ceiling that came down, they were dead unless this stopped. "Stay here," Elan said to both of them. He took a moment to gather himself and then ducked out from under the table. He couldn't quite get his footing as he tried to make it toward the door, but if this was Jae, he had to stop her. He didn't know how she was doing this despite his order, but he'd use the Curse to *force* her to stop.

He scurried toward the garden out of habit, but before he reached it, the ground stilled again. He paused, waiting, counting his own heartbeats. When the world didn't show any more signs of upending itself at the count of fifteen, he started walking again. At thirty he started running.

He surveyed the garden. It was in better shape than the study had been. Dirt and sand were everywhere, and a few bricks had fallen out of the building walls, but there hadn't been much else in it to be destroyed. Even the fountain was heavy enough to stay upright, its base holding it in place.

A girl lay next to it, hard to see in the long, dusky shadows. Elan jogged toward her, afraid of what he'd find. If she'd hit her head against the fountain when she'd fallen, there was no telling what shape she'd be in. There was no blood on her, though, and she was breathing. Judging from her simple, dirty shift and bare feet, she was one of the Closest, but he didn't know her name.

Crouching next to her, he rolled her onto her back. She gasped, her eyes open and blinking rapidly.

"Are you all right?" he asked.

"No— I—I don't know, Highest," she gasped, the words barely more than a murmur. "Everything started shaking, and then the Curse, it, it, I don't know, but . . ." She started to sob, her body heaving.

"Does it still hurt?"

"Yes, Highest," she said as he helped her sit up. She leaned back against the fountain, pulling her knees up to her chest.

"All right. Then—then sit here until you feel better. But I need to know, where's Jae? Do you know where she is?"

"She's—she— Lord Rannith summoned her," the girl said.

He nodded and stood, headed back inside. The whole hallway was strewn with debris, bricks that had fallen or been knocked out of place on the floor. The art on the walls, mosaics and woven hangings, were all askew or had fallen entirely, and he sneezed as the dust and sand hit him.

When he reached the study, Desinn was helping Lady Shirrad to her feet. "What happened, Highest?" she asked.

"I need you to take me to Rannith's room."

"Rannith? Why?" she asked, then backtracked. "Of course, Highest. I just don't understand. . . ."

He didn't bother to clarify, just followed her through the wrecked, messy hallways toward the wing where the Avowed had rooms. Desinn followed them, stumbling. There weren't many footprints in the dust yet, though around them, people slowly appeared in the halls, helping each other.

"We'll need someone to check every room for people," Elan said, glancing back at Desinn. "To make sure no one is hurt too badly to move. Desinn, take care of it."

"Highest—"

"Or find someone else to do it," Elan said, turning back toward Lady Shirrad. He'd been debating whether he should tell Shirrad and Desinn about Jae before, but now he didn't dare until he knew she was under control. She shouldn't have been able to do any of this, not after he'd ordered her not to use magic without permission, unless for some reason, magic didn't always obey the rules of the Curse. If that was the case, then things might get bad again, and he didn't want Desinn or Shirrad to make them even worse.

The closer they got to the sleeping quarters where Rannith had his room, the worse the destruction got. The hall was nearly blocked off with debris at one point, and Elan had to climb across and then help Shirrad follow.

Finally they reached the right room. Shirrad hesitated. "I don't understand why you need Lord Rannith, but . . ."

"Wait out here," he said, and tried to open the door. It didn't move, blocked by more destruction. He leaned his shoulder against it and shoved, heard a pile of rubble give way. The door opened slowly, and he pushed his way in as soon as the gap was wide enough.

A patch of sky showed overhead, where half the ceiling had fallen in. Nearly everything in the room had crashed over, and the sleeping mat had slid away from the wall. Jae lay on it, unmoving. He rushed toward her, terrified for one second that she was dead, that the magic had somehow been released by her death, but no. Her chest was rising and falling slowly. He shook her shoulder, but she didn't stir, didn't move at all. It wasn't until he gave up and dropped her arm that he realized she was naked.

She was naked on the sleeping mat—but where was Rannith?

Elan scanned the room again. The whole house was a wreck, but the rubble was much worse in here, piled everywhere except on the sleeping mat itself. If Jae had done this, she must have protected herself, but anyone else in the room . . .

Blood seeped from under the wreckage of the ceiling, and Elan's stomach churned. He gingerly stepped closer, pausing between each movement, afraid another piece of roof would crash down on him. The ceiling held, and he crouched in the midst of the bricks and began pulling pieces out of the pile.

He found more blood, then a hand. He moved a few more bricks to uncover the arm, found the shoulder, and then—

Rannith's whole body had been crushed, and his skull was smashed open. Elan turned away from it, heaving, and lost his dinner on the debris he'd piled next to him.

"Lord Elan? Are you well?" Lady Shirrad called from the hall.

He wiped his mouth with his hand, pulled himself up, and took a breath. He didn't want to let anyone else in until he knew for sure what had happened.

"I'm fine," he assured Shirrad, though his voice came out thin and shaky. He made his way back to the door and stood in the entrance, careful to block the view in case Lady Shirrad leaned in. "Something happened in here. I need . . ." He glanced back at the sleeping mat, then decided. "There's a Closest boy—the groundskeeper's brother."

"Tal?" Shirrad asked, surprised. "What—"

"Find him and bring him here. Quickly," Elan ordered.

Lady Shirrad hesitated, mouth opening as if she wanted to object. But she snapped it closed and nodded, turned away, and hurried down the hall. Elan turned back to Jae.

She didn't look injured, and the bedroll was still mostly made, though the thick blankets covering the mat had been pulled loose. Jae lay on top of them. He glanced around until he saw her clothing among the debris on the floor.

Jae was naked, and Rannith was dead.

He shuddered, carefully pulled the top blanket out from under Jae, and laid it over her. He sat down, stared at the rubble, and tried to think. He didn't know how she'd used magic despite his order, but what had happened was easy enough to guess.

She'd have to be held responsible for all of this, but that

didn't feel quite right somehow. Being ordered onto some-one's sleeping mat wasn't the same as being ordered to work in the kitchen or a field. Elan couldn't imagine what it was like for the Closest, forced to obey absolutely every order; he'd never even thought about it. If it had been him lying there, if he hadn't wanted Rannith . . .

Still, she'd killed him, and Elan didn't even know yet if anyone else had been hurt. That couldn't be allowed; he'd have to use the Curse to do something about it. Except that the Curse shouldn't have let Jae do this in the first place. It shouldn't have let her disobey him, let alone kill anyone, and if she could do that, then maybe she could do anything. If that was true, then no matter what Elan ordered, they'd all be at her mercy.

He glanced back at the rubble, at Rannith's remains, un-sure if Jae even possessed mercy. Maybe she hadn't intended to kill Rannith, but then again, maybe she had. Elan had never thought about that, either, but the Closest probably weren't happy about their lot. He'd never heard of them com-plaining, but how could they? Even if they wanted to object, the Closest could only ever bite their tongues and do as they were told. He'd never even met one of them until coming to Aredann.

Not that it mattered. Whether she'd meant to kill Ran-nith or not, Jae was dangerous. If she'd kept the quake going longer, she could have shaken Aredann to the ground, taken it apart brick by brick. If the Curse couldn't control her fully, there had to be another way.

"Highest?"

He looked at the open door. Lady Shirrad was back, with

Jae's brother—Tal, Shirrad had said—and he was staring at Jae on the sleeping mat. Elan stood and glanced at Tal for a moment, then back at Jae.

"Lady, we have much to discuss," he said.

"Is . . . is Lord Rannith in there?" she asked, edging her way in carefully, but Elan hurried to meet her and block her view.

"He's dead," Elan said, then looked at Tal. "Was this the first time he ordered Jae to his room?"

"No, Highest," Tal said softly, still studying Jae's form.

"Do you think she'd have killed him, if she ever had the chance?"

"Lord Elan—" Shirrad started, but Tal interrupted her, compelled to answer.

"Yes, Highest."

"Lord Elan, surely you don't think— Jae couldn't have had anything to do with . . . could she?"

He nodded, and Shirrad gasped, her hand coming up to her mouth. Before she could say anything else, Elan ordered Tal, "Take Jae to my room. Carefully."

Tal made his way to the sleeping mat. He picked Jae up gently. She didn't stir at all. He kept the blanket wrapped around her as he found a way to hold her. They were about the same size—she was tall for a woman, but lithe and thin—and he carried her out.

Elan followed, Lady Shirrad at his side. Jae still didn't wake as they moved, but that was for the best. Elan watched Tal carefully, the way he cradled her, the way he shifted to keep her as steady as possible, even when he had to climb through rubble in the halls. Jae was his sister, after all, and it was obvious that he worried about her, that he loved her.

For the first time, Elan wondered what life was really like for the Closest. To care and worry and want to help—but to be at everyone else's mercy, unable to even speak. Elan would do anything for his own sister. Surely Jae and Tal wouldn't do any less for each other, if the Curse allowed them. But he *couldn't* imagine what it would be like, not really, to be cursed, to have to stand by and watch, and never be able to help at all.

Chapter 12

Jae woke, feeling as light as steam. The Curse had been a weight on her body her whole life; every morning had meant waking to lingering pain and exhaustion. Waking to dread settling over her like a blanket as she thought about the long day and excruciating heat in front of her. Now, instead of her pulse echoing with the Curse, all she woke to was sunlight streaming in through curtains. She braced herself as she pushed up onto her elbows, but there was no familiar pounding. No Curse dragging her down. There was no pain.

Everything in the room seemed to be dimly lit from within, shining with energy, so bright and inviting that it took her a few moments to realize she was in Elan's chambers.

They were a wreck: overturned furniture, art fallen from the walls, bricks strewn across the floor, with a layer of dust coating it all. She could make out footprints in it, heavy steps treading from the door to the sleeping mat, where they grew too messy to follow, and then back to the door.

Someone had carried her in. Carried her in, and dressed her, because her last clear memory was of Rannith on the mat, and she'd been nude. Now she was wearing a long, loose shirt and her underclothes. The shirt was deep green, more vivid than anything anyone at Aredann owned. Elan's, then, the cleanest and softest thing she'd ever worn.

She took a deep breath and sneezed at the dust, then almost laughed. Everything came back to her in an onslaught of memories, a rush of feelings more than images. She'd fought off the Curse, she'd beaten it, and then Rannith . . .

Her lips curled up into an unkind smile. She was free now—and that meant free to use her magic however she chose. No one could stop her, not even Elan, and she would *never* allow anyone to hurt her again.

The door opened, sliding until it hit a small pile of rubble. Tal walked in, saw her sitting, and hurried to her side.

"You're awake," he breathed.

"I am. And I'm— Tal, I'm *free*." She grabbed his hand and pulled him down to sit on the edge of the mat. "I fought against the Curse, and I *won*. And it feels like—"

"Jae—"

"I feel so *light*. I can do anything," she said, the energy around her shining and enticing. "The magic is everywhere. I can see it so much more clearly now. I can feel it, and once I'm better at using it, I'll free you, too—"

"*Jae.*" He squeezed her hand, and when she fell silent, he continued, "You killed Rannith."

"Yes," she agreed. "I did."

He stared at her, as if she could deny it even if she wanted to—but the Curse didn't control her anymore. She *could* lie if she wanted to, but why would she bother lying about Rannith? She wasn't sorry, and it was no more than Rannith had deserved. She smiled again, until she saw Tal's expression. No longer shocked, just frowning.

"You can't blame me," she said.

"I . . ." He trailed off, pulled his hand away from hers. The Curse still controlled *him*. She could see what was happening, had felt it too many times herself. She hadn't asked him a question, so he wasn't compelled to speak, but he was trying to find a way to shape the truth in his response anyway. "I don't blame you. But, Jae, you *killed* someone."

"I'm not sorry," she said. That truth was easy, even without the Curse to force it. "He raped me. He was trying to rape me again."

"I know," Tal said, and his hand was back, a tether binding them together. "I understand. It's just . . . you *destroyed* him. His entire body was broken, and there . . . there was so much blood."

"Good."

"*Good?*" he echoed, the incredulity turning it into a question.

"He deserved that, and—and more. When I find a way to free you, you'll understand. The way Lady Shirrad treats you is—"

"But I don't want to kill her!" His voice hadn't risen above its usual hushed tone, but the words were harsher, carved from stone and left unsmoothed. "She's not . . . She uses me, and I use her." Tal shook his head. "I'd find another way if I could, but I wouldn't kill her."

"Then I won't," Jae agreed quickly. "But I won't let her touch you again. Or else . . ."

"Or else what?"

That question had to be on purpose. He stared at her, and she started to answer automatically, but there was no push from the Curse to force her. She had nothing to say, no *or else* to give him, and he sighed.

"You nearly killed her anyway. Look around." He gestured with his free hand. "The whole estate is like this. We're repairing the damage, but it's a mess. And when the bricks fell, people got hurt. It's lucky no one else died."

"I didn't want to kill anyone else," she said. "I just wanted him to stop touching me."

"I know," Tal said, and he squeezed her hand. The Curse let him say it, so it couldn't be a lie. Somehow, it didn't make her feel any better. "I know, but you could have killed all of us."

"I wasn't trying to—"

"But you could have. You have all this power." His voice was back to normal, calm and kind. "I can't even imagine it. And now there's nothing to stop you from using it. But the very first thing you did was kill someone, and—and really *look* at all of this." He gestured around again. "Did you mean to do so much damage? Did you have any control at all?"

"You don't understand!" She pulled her hand free and scrambled away, stunned to have him turn questions on her, grateful that there was no Curse compulsion to answer. Because he was right, she *had* killed Rannith, and she wasn't sorry. She never would be. She just hated the way Tal was watching her, looking at her with that sad frown, dancing around whatever he wanted to say. As if he was afraid of her. As if she was one of *them,* as if she would ever hurt him.

She wouldn't. But the room *was* in ruins, the beautiful designs in the walls missing pieces, cracked and marred. They'd be all but impossible to repair. She *hadn't* meant to do that. She hadn't thought at all about the house outside Rannith's room, or the people in it. She hadn't meant to hurt anyone but Rannith, but she could have—she could have hurt Tal.

Her throat burned, and she braced herself, squeezed her eyes shut. She'd spent the last seventeen years careful not to cry, to never let anyone except Tal see that she was hurt, but with Tal staring at her like this . . .

A hot tear splashed down onto her cheek, and he sighed, made a soothing *shhh* noise. He reached for her, and she let him, let him hold her and stroke her back.

"Oh, Jae. I didn't mean to . . . It's not like that at all. I know why you did it, and I . . . I wouldn't have asked you not to. It's just that you scared me."

She clutched his shoulders and mumbled against his skin, "I'd never hurt you. Never."

"I know," he said, still stroking a soothing line up and down her back. "But you would hurt *them,* and they know it. They're scared, too. What you did to Rannith . . . it was gruesome, and they're terrified. I'm sorry for the question, but what do you think they'll do to you for that?"

"They can't hurt me anymore," she said, and straightened

up enough to mop at her face. "I'm free, and this magic . . . They *can't* hurt me."

"But they'll try," he said. "Lord Elan's father is already on his way to Aredann, and when he finds out what happened here . . . Even if you didn't have magic, even if you'd just been some Twill who'd killed an Avowed . . . They won't just leave that be. If they can't control you, they'll try to kill you. And when you defend yourself . . ."

"What?" Jae asked.

"I'm scared," he said simply, not hesitating or flinching from the compulsion to answer. "I want to help you. I don't want anyone to hurt you, either. But, Jae . . . if you defend yourself like this again, a lot of people *will* get hurt."

❖❖❖

Elan shuddered, peeling himself off the wall where he'd been listening. Tal's words echoed in his mind. *A lot of people will get hurt.* If Jae lost her temper, if anyone threatened her, she *could* destroy Aredann, just like mages during the War had disposed of whole armies.

Now that she was free of the Curse, there was no telling what she might do. He could only hope that she'd see reason, that she'd listen to Tal—he was the key to keeping her calm. Tal might only be a Closest, but Jae cared about what he said, and he'd already spoken to protect Lady Shirrad.

Which meant that Jae wasn't *entirely* unreasonable. She was just angry. He couldn't blame her for that, not knowing what Rannith had done to her. He couldn't imagine being in her position, helpless to defend herself against a monster—in her place, he might have reacted the same way. And whether he would have or not, he *understood* why she'd done it. He just needed to make sure she knew that.

She didn't like him much, either, but he wasn't like Rannith. He wouldn't hurt her; he never had. They could work together. In the end, they were on the same side. They both wanted to save Aredann from being abandoned, and to save the lives of the Closest who lived there.

He knocked on the door, and Jae and Tal both went silent inside. He didn't wait for them to answer, just let himself in. He walked slowly, hands raised in front of him. Open, honest. Not a threat.

"Jae, I'd like to talk to you, if that's all right," he said carefully. "Tal, wait outside, please."

Tal patted his sister's shoulder once, then stood. He bowed to Elan, then scurried by and shut the door after himself.

"May I sit?" Elan asked, pointing at one of the cushions near the sleeping mat. It had been shaken free of dust and sand. Tal must have sat there, waiting for her to wake.

Jae shrugged and arranged herself on the sleeping mat, blanket pulled up to her waist, his shirt pulled down firmly. She ran a hand over her hair, which was still too short for her gesture to have much effect—but then again, it was also too short to be messed up by sleep.

"I wanted to talk to you about . . . I wanted to say," he began carefully, contemplating every word before speaking it, "that I understand what you did to Rannith. It was brutal, yes, but deserved. I know that."

She gave him a long, wary look, and finally said, "I doubt that, Elan."

He blinked, shocked for a moment that she hadn't used any honorific with his name. Even the Avowed did—but she wasn't Avowed, or Closest, or even Twill. She wasn't like anyone else in the world.

"I know what he . . . what he planned to do to you. That it wasn't the first time. I can't blame you for defending yourself," Elan continued once he recovered. "Anyone would have, and no one civilized would ever take advantage of the Closest like Rannith did."

"I doubt that, too."

"It's true. Rannith was a monster. No one else would even *think* to order someone to lie with them. The very idea is ridiculous. It's as much as admitting that no one would want to, given the choice."

Jae's narrow-eyed expression didn't waver. "I suppose that would be your concern. How embarrassing it would be to rape someone."

"No! I didn't mean—didn't mean it like *that*," he said hastily, not sure where he'd gone wrong. He only wanted to tell her that he *understood*. "It's wrong, of course it's wrong." He paused, trying to think of a way to continue, but he found himself just staring at Jae. She was watching him back, not flinching from his gaze, all her features sharp and jagged, striking and fierce.

Looking at her like that, he could understand Rannith's fascination with her, but the thought turned his stomach. "Does that . . . What Rannith did," he said, not quite able to name it like she had, "does it happen often out here?"

"Yes." Jae tipped her head back, as if she was considering him, then continued, "It's not as if Tal *wants* to spend his nights at Lady Shirrad's side. There's no difference, except she's kinder to him afterward."

Elan shook his head a little. Not disagreeing, just amazed—appalled. "It isn't like this at home," he assured her. "We're civilized there. No one in my father's court would ever stoop to this."

"Are you sure?" she asked him. *She* sounded sure that he was wrong.

"Yes," he said.

Her eyebrows raised just a little, a slight smile tugging at her lips. It was eerily reminiscent of the way his father and Desinn looked at him, as if he was stupid. Which he *wasn't.*

"No one in my father's court abuses power like that," he repeated.

"Of course they do," she said. "And if you've never noticed, it's because no one's ever taken advantage of *you.*"

"Plenty of people have tried," he said. "They want my favor. They'd use me if they could."

"Just like you wanted to use me and my power to find the Well," she said.

"I didn't want to use— I mean . . ." He tapped his fingers against his leg. This was what he'd come to talk to her about. "Of course I wanted to use your power to find the Well, because that's how to save Aredann. That's what you wanted, too."

"I wanted to do it without your interference," she said.

"But we wanted the same thing. You were going to help—"

"You *ordered* me to help," she interrupted, her voice sharp and thorny. "I had no choice, but now I do."

"And that makes it more important than ever for you to see that we are on the same side," he pressed.

"We will never be on the same side," she said, voice stony. "You—your family—your whole caste are *liars*. The Well was never yours, and it never will be. I will *never* help you."

Elan gaped at her, shaking his head slightly. "You have to know that that's not true, that they didn't . . . My ancestors would never have cast the Curse if that was true."

She said nothing, but her expression spoke for her. She thought *he* was a fool. Naïve, like his father had called him before exiling him to Aredann. But she was wrong, she had to be wrong, no matter how much she believed what she said. Maybe the magic had driven her to madness, or maybe now that she was free of the Curse, she was determined to believe the Highest had been in the wrong during the War. But it didn't matter what she believed, because now that she was free, he couldn't order her to help—and he still needed her. The whole world needed her.

He took a moment to compose himself and finally said, "This isn't just about Aredann. Other estates, other *Closest*, are being abandoned, too. If you can save Aredann, you can save them all."

"I can do almost anything I want," she said, and something like a smile flitted across her face. "And don't bother to pretend that you care at all about the Closest—at Aredann or anywhere else. *You* were going to leave us all for dead."

"But I didn't want to! I never liked the idea," Elan said, his gut twisting. It was true enough. Once he'd really thought about it, the idea had horrified him. He just hadn't thought about it, not until she'd yelled at him. "But it's what's necessary—*was* necessary. Before you had magic. But now, now everything is different. All we have to do is convince my father of that."

"*We* don't have to do anything."

"Yes, we . . ." He trailed off, regrouped, tried again. "You don't know my father. You have magic—power—but he has power, too. He'll think you're a threat, but I can convince him you're not."

Jae let out a scoffing laugh. "But I am. You have no idea what kind of power I have. I *will* save Aredann, and if your father stands in my way, I will do to him exactly what I did to Rannith."

It took him a moment to understand, for what she'd said to sink in. She *could.* If his father angered her or tried to stop her, she could really kill him. And of course his father *would* do anything to stop her. Even though allowing Jae to find the Well and save Aredann would benefit them all, his father wouldn't stand for being threatened—and wouldn't allow his decisions to be undermined. He'd all but disavowed Elan for even *asking* him if there was another way to end the drought. Having one of the Closest directly challenge him . . . He wouldn't allow that. And when he tried to control Jae, she might very well kill him. That would only make things worse, not just for Elan's family but for the world. It would cause a war.

If Elan's father died, the other three Highest families would see the threat Jae posed to all of them. They'd send their guards to Aredann to stop her. Elan didn't know how many people it would take to overwhelm Jae's magic, but he *did* know that people would die in the process. A lot of them. But first, she'd kill his father.

"You can't," Elan said, voice softer than he'd meant it to be. "The chaos it would cause . . . Please, Jae. Let me smooth the way for you to save Aredann without his interference. Let me help you. At least let me try."

"I won't stop you from trying," she said. "But I am going to save Aredann, and I am going to save the other Closest, whether you smooth the way or not. I will do *anything* I need to. Don't ever forget that."

Elan swallowed, nodded.

He was *never* going to forget that.

Chapter 13

Sunlight cascaded through the corridors, illuminating damage from the quake. Elan picked his way through the rubble and around the people who were dragging broken bricks and tiles out of the halls, sweeping and clearing the floors. Most of them were Closest, and though this main hall was starting to look better, it was only one small part of the house. Even if the other servants and the Avowed who lived there deigned to help, it was an overwhelming job.

Elan paused to watch the Closest at work, and couldn't help but notice every time someone's gaze slipped over toward him. It was always wary, waiting. Suspicious. Jae always looked at him like that. Now he saw that they all did. They all knew who he was and what he could do; he didn't even know how many of them there were. He'd only learned two of their names.

He turned and walked on, toward the guest quarters he'd claimed for his own after settling Jae in the master rooms, where she'd be isolated from everyone, Closest and Avowed alike. The damage was worse here, nearer to the center of the quake. He dragged himself through it carefully, and sagged when he finally reached his room. The conversation with Jae hadn't been easy. He needed time to think, to figure out how he'd handle his father, but Desinn was already waiting when Elan walked in.

"We need to talk about this," Desinn said.

"Later," Elan answered.

"Now. It's too important to put off; you must know that."

Elan swallowed a groan but didn't disagree. Desinn was right—convincing him that Jae and her magic were under control would be the first step toward convincing his father. Nothing was more important than that. He sank onto a cushion and nodded. "Yes, fine."

"That girl—you knew something." Desinn squinted at him. "You ran off like you could stop the quake, and you knew exactly where to look for her."

"I asked one of the Closest."

"You knew what was happening."

"Yes." Elan took a breath, but couldn't force the tension out of his body. Everything in him had been pulled too tight, stretched out and then tied into a knot. "I was about to tell you, when it started. We can't abandon Aredann, because there's magic here. It was linked to that fountain. Jae—the Closest girl—she unlocked it somehow, and now she controls it. But I controlled her, and she wasn't supposed to . . ." He shook his head.

"A Closest? Then we can order—"

"No," Elan interrupted. "She's *not* Closest any longer. I don't know what she is, but she freed herself. Otherwise this would never have happened. I ordered her not to use magic without permission—I'm not stupid enough to let her do anything she wanted with it. Then Rannith raped her, and she found the power to break the compulsion. Now she might do anything."

Desinn frowned. "How long has this been going on?"

"A few days."

"And you didn't tell—"

"You wouldn't have helped me!" Elan snapped. "Jae is powerful—even when she was cursed, she was. And she's so angry. She requires a careful hand, and you wouldn't understand her at all."

"I wouldn't need to, if she was cursed!" Desinn snapped back at him. "You are supposed to be your father's warden, and this girl is definitely a threat to the Well. You should have sent word to him immediately."

Elan fell quiet. Desinn was right about that much, at least. Elan reached up with one hand, pressed it to his rumpled robe, over the brand on his chest. He had vowed to obey his father, and to always act in the Highest families' interests. Yes, he should have sent word as soon as he'd discovered magic. It didn't matter that he'd planned to eventually, that he'd only waited so he could be careful with how he revealed Jae and her magic. Now it was obvious he'd mishandled everything, that maybe he was unworthy of his title after all.

Eventually he sighed. "Not telling you probably saved your life. Jae doesn't like anyone Avowed. If you'd tried to order her around, she would have lashed out at you instead of at Rannith."

Desinn recoiled. "I wouldn't have dirtied myself like that."

"She's not dirty. She's— Never mind." Elan sagged on his cushion again, his shoulders curling forward. "Look. She doesn't trust me, but she's willing to let me try to keep things calm when my father arrives."

"That's nothing but your duty," Desinn said.

"I know," Elan said. "But without some kind of go-between . . . Desinn, she could kill him. She told me she would."

Desinn stared. "You can't be serious. No one is that foolish."

"I don't think she thinks it's foolish at all," Elan said. "But if I can keep them from trying to kill each other, then with the power she has . . . if she'll use it *for* us, there's so much she could do. She could find the Well."

"And do exactly what her ancestors did—try to take control of it from the Highest. Better to leave it lost," Desinn said.

Elan nodded. Especially given Jae's delusions about who had crafted the Well. If she believed it was supposed to belong to the Closest in the first place, it would almost make sense for her to try to reclaim it. But this wasn't just about controlling the Well—there were people dying from the drought. Hundreds of Closest had been abandoned already. "But what if she could protect the outlying estates? They wouldn't have to be deserted."

"If that was possible, the Highest would have already done

it," Desinn said. "Whatever this girl can do, though . . . you need to keep her calm until your father arrives. He'll know what to do with her. If you'd written to him in the first place, we might still have control of her—which I intend to tell him as soon as he arrives."

Desinn pushed up to his feet and walked out, and Elan buried his head in his hand. The worst part was that Desinn was right. His father would have known exactly what to do, how to handle Jae. If anyone could find a way to keep her under control now, it was Elan's father.

But anything he did to try to control her would just make Jae angry, and if she got angry enough . . .

Elan forced himself to his feet, but only so he could cross the room to his mat and collapse. He'd managed to place himself in the middle of a precarious situation, stranded between his father's power and Jae's, the only buffer between two forces that wanted nothing more than to destroy each other.

❈ ❈ ❈

Jae wasn't accustomed to sitting idly. In her whole life, she'd never gone a waking hour without work—mending, gardening, cleaning. Closest were *never* allowed to be idle for long. But Elan wanted her to stay in his room resting, and she saw no real reason to argue with him about it.

Firran brought her dinner that evening. He moved silently, deposited the tray on the table, looked over at her, and shrank from her gaze.

Her breath caught as she realized: She was free, and Firran was still cursed. She wasn't Avowed. He wouldn't be compelled to obey her, not exactly. But the Closest were still expected to do as they were told by anyone, even the Twill, and didn't dare resist orders. Just like she had always scurried to follow the cook's instructions even though he wasn't Avowed, she knew Firran would do what *she* said.

She narrowed her eyes a little. Firran hated her and Tal—

He took a quick breath and retreated a step before recovering and waiting, perfectly still. Just like she always had when she'd known Lady Shirrad was angry with her and she'd braced herself for Shirrad's temper. Or maybe Firran was even more scared. Jae always knew what Shirrad would do, how bad it would be. Jae herself could do *anything*.

Whatever anger she felt toward Firran crumbled. He'd put her near Rannith, and she would never stop loathing him for that. But she would never be like Lady Shirrad, either, or any of the rest of them, lashing out at people who were powerless to defend themselves. So all she said was "Thank you."

He bobbed his head and fled, practically running out of the room.

The next time Elan stopped in to check on her, she informed him she only wanted to see Tal or Gali. Elan agreed, and after that, Tal brought her meals, and no one but Tal, Gali, and Elan set foot inside the room with her.

As it turned out, lying around without leaving a single room was boring. After two days shut in, she couldn't stand it anymore. She started pacing the room and let herself bask in the magic she sensed around her. It still shone brightly no matter where she looked, glistening and twinkling, and without the Curse fettering her, she was able to tell different kinds of energy apart more easily.

One, a darker and steadier glow, felt like what she'd grabbed for when she'd set off the earthquake. She could see it under her, under the estate, spreading off into the distance — the energy of the earth, the land itself. By contrast, water's energy was bright and glistening, like the surface of the reservoir. There were other energies she couldn't separate as well, one that jangled and clanged more like a sound than a glow, and still another that shimmered around people.

The power left her humming, vibrating with energy, and with it, she could see beyond her room. She stood still and let her mind drift *up*, looked down at the whole estate. When she'd practiced with magic before Elan had ordered her not to, she'd learned how to tell who was who when she looked at the world like this. It was as easy as breathing, now that she was unfettered by the Curse.

Some people felt familiar to her, like Gali and Firran — but she didn't know Firran well, and Shirrad, who she knew much better, felt strangely *different*. The Closest all seemed to shine with the same glow, and everyone else was alien to her.

Like this, she could find and follow anyone, but the only person she really cared about was Tal. He moved through his day as usual — he worked with the teams that were clearing out rubble and replacing bricks and tiles, smoothing cracks in the walls and floors. Hovering over him was soothing. She couldn't make out any of the actual words said around him, but she could watch over him and know he was safe.

She found Elan, too, though it took her some time to realize what she was watching. Elan spent the morning with Shirrad and Desinn, lost in a conversation Jae couldn't hear and didn't care about. After that, he spoke with the other

Avowed at Aredann—and formed them into another work crew, one that he joined. She watched in amazement as they began work on another section of the estate, cleaning and clearing.

Tal brought Jae lunch and a handful of dates to share, which she doubted had originally been intended for the two of them. But she didn't ask, and it wasn't likely that anyone would notice they'd gone missing during the chaos of cleaning up the estate.

He sat to eat with her, his knees knocking against hers, leaning in close so they could talk. "You should have seen it," he said, and laughed, mouth full. "Of course, no one had a choice. When Lord Elan gave the order, they all *had* to do it. None of them were too happy about that—especially not since they're leaving Aredann soon. But then he said he'd be working, too. He stripped off his robe and started hauling bricks—and, Jae, I thought Lady Shirrad was going to swoon at the sight."

"She doesn't care for him," Jae said.

"No, but I think she took it as a sign. There are rumors that the quake was magic, and some people think . . . some people are starting to say, if there's magic, the Highest won't abandon Aredann," Tal said. "Lady Shirrad believes them. And she believes Lord Elan will make that case to his father. Even *you* might appreciate that."

"I'd rather he just left, and took the others with him," Jae said.

"Me too—but if he wants to repair the house before he goes, I suppose I don't mind," Tal said, smiling a little.

Jae rolled her eyes, but smiled back. It was nice to sit with

Tal and let him tease her. It was *safe*, as if nothing had ever changed at all. Not that she wanted to step back in time to before Elan had arrived and upended her world. She'd never go back to being powerless. But back then, she'd always known what to expect, and now she had no idea what was going to happen next. When she sat with Tal, things still felt easy and normal.

Unfortunately, meals were the only times when the work crews could spare Tal. Spending the rest of her time alone left Jae itchy with a need to use magic. All evening, she let herself drift into her other-vision, watching the estate and the people in it.

After dinner, Elan broke away from the workers to sit with Shirrad and Desinn again, while Tal and Gali finally crossed paths for the first time since dawn. Jae shifted her vision elsewhere when they kissed, but it was only moments later that they were both off again, working on different areas of the grounds.

Jae frowned when Elan's meeting ended and he and Shirrad started walking together, inspecting all the work that had been done—and sweeping closer to Tal with every step. She couldn't hear them, but sure enough, when they stepped into the room where Tal was cleaning out the last of the debris, Lady Shirrad drifted toward him, put a hand on his side.

A fierce drumbeat of magic thrummed in Jae's veins. Tal smiled, but Jae felt the dread underneath it. If Shirrad wrapped an arm around him, if she ordered Tal to her room, Jae would—

Elan stepped between them, his expression just as smiling and placid as Tal's. He patted Tal's shoulder as he spoke, and Tal nodded and headed out of the room, his careful walk speeding up as he left them farther behind. In the study, Elan smiled at Shirrad and offered his arm. They resumed their inspection—and they walked away from wherever Tal had been sent.

Jae released her breath, and some of the bright glow of magic around her dimmed. Tal was still busy, but whatever order he'd been given, it had saved him from Shirrad for the night. It should have been a relief, but it wasn't really.

The next morning, Jae made up her mind. When Tal brought her breakfast, she asked him to stay and sit with her as she paced across the room. "I want to try to free you."

"And you really think you can," he said, fingers splaying open against the floor.

"I think so," Jae said. With as much power as she could sense now, it would be easier than when she'd freed herself. She'd attack it the same way, plucking Tal away from the Curse, pulling until he was free from the binding of the Wellspring Bloodlines.

"Then . . . all right," he agreed. He tapped his fingers against the floor. "Tell me what you need me to do."

"Just sit," she said. She pulled a cushion around to face him, sat down, and reached for his hand. When she looked at them in other-vision, she couldn't see where his glow ended and hers began. Taking a deep breath, she searched for the visions she'd had the night she'd killed Rannith, the way she'd seen the Closest all bound together. Once she found that braided rope of energies, it was easy to see the Curse, inside and around the Bloodlines, staining their every breath.

She reached into the rope of energies with her mind,

sifting through the feeling of familiarity until she found several that felt more like her than all the others, and realized they were the Closest of Aredann. It made sense: Closest were tied to the estates where they were born, so the same groups had been intermarrying for generations. Each individual was related to some of the others *somewhere* back in their history. The Closest were all bound together as the Bloodlines, but the ones at Aredann shared more of her blood than the Closest anywhere else did.

Even at Aredann, there were dozens of people she didn't know, though one felt so much like her that she thought it was Tal for a moment. But no, because she found Tal, too, at last. Which meant the other person had to be related closely to them—their father. Jae had never met him, since he hadn't been brought into the household when her mother had, but it made sense that he was out there somewhere, too.

Her mother had never talked about him. Jae didn't know if they'd chosen each other or been chosen *for* each other, told to produce a child. Someday, once Aredann was safe, she'd find him. For now, all she really cared about was Tal. Tal, whose blood and energy were all but identical to hers, easy to focus on once she found them.

She plucked at the thread that represented him, and he gasped.

"It's the magic," she explained, trying not to lose her focus on what she'd found. "Brace yourself."

"Sure," he agreed, and she dug back into other-vision and began to work.

The Curse pulsated around his thread, wrapping around and strangling it as she tried to pry him free. Something peculiar seemed to wrap around her throat while she worked—then she felt it, like a light touch against her skull. The pounding of the Curse, but miles away. Reaching for her, but not able to hurt her.

She braced herself, just like she'd told Tal to do. She plucked at Tal's thread again, pulling it closer to herself—pulling herself closer to the Bloodlines, closer to the Curse.

She jerked out of other-vision, her hands pulling free from Tal's, the room rushing back around her. Tal stared, wide-eyed. "That wasn't . . . ," he said, not quite a question.

She shook her head. "Not yet. It was . . . the Curse. . . ."

"If you can't, Jae, it's . . . I'll be fine," he said, and she didn't miss how he hesitated as he groped for a truth to placate her. "I'll be all right for now."

"No," she said, and took a breath. The Curse was gone from her body, there was no pain in her head, but she could swear she could still sense an echo of it. "I can do this, I'm sure. The Curse just . . . wanted me back."

"Then don't be stupid," he said. "If you can't free me without cursing yourself—"

"I *can*," she said. "I just need to be careful."

He didn't look thrilled at the idea, but nodded. She took his hand again, braced herself, and fell back into other-vision. It was much easier to find him this time, but the Curse was still waiting.

Gritting her teeth, she reached for Tal's thread and *yanked*. Tal screamed, jerking away from her and falling off his cushion. His thread almost got away from her, too, and as she fumbled for it, the Curse rushed in on her. Pain pulsed in her skull, and Tal was still screaming. Guilt twisted up inside her as she ignored that, pulling and pulling while she pushed back against the Curse, trying to keep it away from her. The pain in her head receded a little, but Tal was still writhing on the floor.

She pulled again—almost there—

"*Jae!*" He yanked her arm, and she saw him in real vision, eyes blown wide and glassy with tears. "Stop, please, please, *stop!*"

She stopped.

The power flowed away from her, and Tal climbed back onto the cushion, trembling, and wiped at his eyes.

"I'm sorry," she mumbled, sagging. "I was so close. I was so *sure.*"

"It's . . ." Tal broke off. He couldn't say it was fine when it wasn't. She knew how hard the Curse must have hit him, and even if it hadn't, to be so close to freedom and lose it . . . That wasn't fine.

"I'll find another way," she murmured, but she didn't know how. She could see so much energy, feel so much power, but she barely knew how to use it. And if she couldn't even save Tal, there was no way she could save all of Aredann.

"I know you will," Tal said. Then, as if he'd read her mind, he continued, "I'll help. And if you can free me, then you can free Gali and the others, too, and bring water back to Aredann. We'll find a way."

He smiled at her, and she nodded, letting some of his confidence seep under her skin. They *would* find a way. As long as he was there to help her, she could do anything.

Chapter 14

THREE DAYS LATER, AN ADVANCE MESSENGER ARRIVED JUST PAST dawn to warn them: Highest Lord Elthis was on his way and would arrive after lunch. Elan thanked the messenger and exchanged anxious looks with Shirrad.

Aredann was still in a sorry state. Though teams of Closest and others had been working almost nonstop to clean and repair the damage, there was only so much they could do. The kitchen had been the first area cleaned, and the teams had fanned out from there. Now the dining hall and the study were somewhat repaired, too. They'd been emptied of all debris, with furniture pulled back into place, all cushions and mats cleaned, but the rooms still had missing tiles and cracks across the ceilings and walls. The corridors were the same. The estate house had been built by a mage, and while work crews could replace tiles, the beautiful, intricate patterns would never look as smooth and well crafted again. Not unless a mage did the repairs, and Jae didn't seem all that inclined to help.

It was just as well she didn't. Elan didn't want her wandering around, terrifying everyone—or worse, losing her temper and lashing out with magic. He couldn't hide what had happened, and there were dozens of rumors about the quake's cause, but he didn't want anyone to know too much about the truth. So, once they knew for sure Elthis would be there within a few hours, Elan asked Jae to stay out of sight as much as possible. His father would doubtlessly want to see Jae eventually, but Elan wanted to put off that clash as long as he could. He first needed to make sure his father understood what Jae was capable of and how careful they had to be.

Sure enough, within an hour after they'd finished lunch, word came in from the yard that a group had been spotted in the distance, drawing closer. Lady Shirrad sent word around the house—the cleanup crews were to get out of sight, though they should keep working anywhere they could, and the Avowed got ready to gather.

Lady Shirrad met Elan at the front gate a few minutes later. She'd changed from a shapeless, stained shift into the same deep red dress she'd had on to meet Elan originally. It was a little shabby, but not tattered, and the gold belt and embroidery were a nice reminder that whatever state Aredann was in now, there had been a time when Shirrad's family had been wealthy and prosperous.

Lord Elthis's travel party approached the gate. There were

at least a dozen of them, led by Elthis himself, clad in pale tan travel robes over green garments. His features were obscured behind the mesh that protected his face from the sun, but he was tall and broad-shouldered, a large man with an even larger presence. Two Avowed rode behind him, followed by servants who led camels laden with jugs.

"*Water*," one of the Avowed murmured behind Elan.

"They have plenty in the central cities," another said. "They can spare some for us."

Elan shook his head a little but didn't bother to say anything. The water wasn't for anyone at Aredann—it would only ensure that his father's visit would be comfortable.

Elthis dismounted, and one of his servants trotted over to take his horse's reins. The Lord faced the gathered crowd expectantly, and Lady Shirrad stepped forward with the same elegant water cup she'd used to greet Elan. She looked away as she handed it to him, and Elan saw a faint tremble in her arm, but Elthis just drank and nodded in satisfaction.

"Thank you, Lady Shirrad."

"Of course, Highest," she said, her voice almost as quiet as a Closest's. "Please, come in and be welcome."

Elthis didn't move to enter the house. Instead his gaze caught on Elan, who stepped forward and bowed his head, saying, "Welcome, Father."

His father nodded a little, but instead of answering him said, "Desinn?"

Desinn joined them, nodding back.

"Lord Elthis, would you care to come inside?" Shirrad asked again.

"No." Elthis brushed his hands together, wiping off sand

and dust. "Don't think me too impolite, Lady, but the letters I've received have spoken of a crisis—and I can certainly see it around me. Before I take off my riding gear, I'd like to visit your reservoir."

"Oh," Lady Shirrad said. "I— Of course, Highest."

Elan helped Shirrad mount, and Elthis dismissed the rest of the travel party. Shirrad rode out to take the lead, since it was her reservoir. She set a slow pace. Even so, it didn't take them long to get there. The riding trail itself was next to a dry streambed that had once served the estate house, as well as irrigating the fields and orchard. Now it was riddled with debris, stones, and cracks from the quake.

The reservoir still seemed tiny to Elan—at least a dozen of them would have fit into the Danardae reservoir. But despite its size, it was still an eye-grabbing, glittering oasis; a beautiful lake in the midst of the drought-ridden fields and endless, endless sand. Just looking at it helped Elan recover some fortitude. Shirrad, too, squared her shoulders as they all dismounted.

"This is it?" Elthis asked.

"Yes, Highest," Shirrad answered. "I know it doesn't look like much, but it has served Aredann very well, even through this drought."

"Not well enough, I gather," Elthis said.

Shirrad pressed her lips together in a forced smile.

"Elan, Desinn," Elthis said, and Elan obediently made his way to his father's side. The four of them began to walk around the reservoir's perimeter, far enough out that the mud was dried and cracked, not wet. His father's riding boots would be dirty but not damp. "What happened to this place?"

"An earthquake," Elan said.

"Yes, I know *that*." His father pointedly looked over at Shirrad. "Has anything like that ever happened before, Lady?"

"No, Highest," she said. "Not that I can recall."

"Then why now?" Elthis asked. "Desinn, you made it sound as if it were magic."

"It was, Highest," Desinn said. "I assure you of that."

"Magic," Elthis repeated.

"Yes, Highest," Desinn said. "Lord Elan . . . discovered it."

When Elthis glanced at him, Elan nodded. "Yes, Father."

This was the true reason they were here at the reservoir, Elan realized. To talk about it without being overheard.

"Tell me everything," Elthis demanded.

Elan explained as they slowly circled the reservoir. The fields were on the far side. When he looked for them, he could see Closest moving around them, still working despite everything, as if nothing had changed. But then, nothing *had* changed for them. No one had given them any new orders. He wondered if they even knew about their impending abandonment.

Elan willed his voice not to falter when he described everything that had happened with Jae. He hated having to bring her up at all, knowing his father would see her as a threat, but he had no choice except to describe how she'd unlocked magic, and everything that had happened afterward.

His father listened attentively, which was enough to make Elan uncomfortable in and of itself. Elthis had only ever given him so much attention when he was in trouble—like the last time they'd seen each other, when Elan had been banished to Aredann. His father rarely forgave and never forgot anything, which meant that now he was gathering ideas, weighing them. Deciding if Elan had handled things well enough to make up for his mistake weeks ago, or if this was another in a series of disasters that were his fault.

He knew which his father was thinking when he said, "You should have sent me word immediately."

"I . . . Yes," Elan agreed. He opened his mouth to explain why he hadn't, then thought better of it. His father wouldn't want to hear any kind of excuses.

"At the very least, you should have alerted Desinn," Elthis said, and Desinn practically preened.

"I *was* telling Desinn when the earthquake happened," Elan said quickly. "And would have sent word when I finished explaining it to him."

"But you could have told me a day sooner," Desinn said, "and the quake would never have happened."

"I was only waiting until I understood Jae's powers!" Elan snapped. Then, recovering himself, he said, "I didn't want to waste your time with a fool's errand, Father. I wanted to be sure she'd be useful before I sent for you."

"So instead of alerting me, you bided your time and cost us control of her entirely," his father answered, voice cold.

Elan had no response to that at all, which was just as well. His father had made up his mind that Elan had been in the wrong, and nothing would change it.

Finally his father said, "I'm here now. Shirrad, tell me everything you know about this Closest girl."

Shirrad spoke up: "I know this will sound odd to you, Highest, but we . . . well, things have been difficult at Aredann for many years, and we've had a hard time enticing Twill to stay out here. So when my mother died, and there were no Avowed women ready to be my nurse, my father selected one of the Closest to do it. Jae's mother—Jae and her brother had just been born. They're Closest, but they're not . . . they grew up in the house; they're almost like servants, really."

"She has a brother?" Elthis asked.

"Yes, Highest," Shirrad said. "A twin, Tal."

Elan frowned, and Elthis continued, "The brother, is he still cursed, or has she freed him as well?"

"Still cursed," Shirrad said.

They had almost made their way back around to where they'd tied the horses. Elthis nodded. "Very well, then. We'll head back to the house now, and I will handle this. I will count on you—all *three* of you—to help me keep order. Things here are too dangerous. Another quake could destroy Aredann entirely, kill all of us and everyone else. And a Closest with magic . . .

"Listen to me very carefully. My duty is to protect everyone. To protect our society," Elthis said. His shoulders were stiff and his voice was deep, commanding. "I am not worried about this Closest's magic. I know how to control her, and she will be an asset if we handle this well. But if anything else goes wrong, the danger isn't from her magic. It's from what will happen when word of it spreads. If people believe there's a Closest capable of rebelling, there will be panic. *That* is what causes riots—and war. I will not allow that. Do you understand?"

"Yes, Highest," Desinn and Shirrad said in unison.

He gave Elan a sharp look.

"Yes, Father," Elan said, ducking his head. Because he

knew his father was right—that was why his father had all but disavowed him. Elan had questioned him, and it could have led to confusion and chaos. The Highest would do anything to prevent that. Threats to the social order were the only reason Highest ever disavowed their followers.

Elan had come perilously close once already. His father wouldn't let it happen again. It didn't matter that Elan was his son. If Elan forced Elthis to choose between family and order, his father would choose order, every time, especially with the ongoing drought scaring all of the Avowed. Which meant that no matter what his father decided to do with Jae, Elan was going to have to be careful. Careful to keep Jae calm, so she didn't use magic against them, and careful to obey his father and keep the world as a whole calm. If Elan couldn't manage that, then whether or not Jae could end the drought wouldn't matter. People doubting the Highest's control would tear the world apart.

Chapter 15

JAE COULD FEEL IT WHEN ELTHIS FINALLY ARRIVED. THE ENERGY around the estate was frantic, and when she used other-vision to look into the distance, she could see the group of people approaching. Gali brought her lunch, but was too nervous and jumpy to stay with her while she ate. Not that Jae blamed her. Elthis's arrival meant the beginning of the end for Aredann. When he left, Jae assumed, he'd take the Avowed with him — and leave the Closest to their fate.

Jae hoped the Closest had heard the rumors about her and her magic, and realized she would save them. But if she were in Gali's place, she wouldn't believe anything like that. It seemed impossible that even magic could stand up against the Highest. But Jae could and would.

To her surprise, Elthis left the estate almost as soon as he arrived, with only Shirrad, Desinn, and Elan accompanying him. She followed their path around the reservoir and back to Aredann slowly. Elan and Shirrad walked off together, finding other Avowed and sending them scurrying, while Desinn and Elthis made their way toward the largest hall.

People began to gather there quickly, Shirrad and Elan joining them after a few minutes. Jae decided she'd been stuck in this room long enough. If Elthis was going to make Aredann's abandonment official, she was going to hear it for herself. She made her way downstairs and gave Firran a wry look as she walked past him into the hall. He flinched and darted to another corner, farther from her. She didn't push her way through the crowd, though, just stood at the back and waited.

Elan stood at his father's side at the front of the room, facing the crowd. Jae knew the moment when he spotted her by the way his eyes widened, but she just stared him down. His expression smoothed quickly, morphing into the same polite, bored smile he'd worn throughout the first days of his visit.

"My friends, my beloved Avowed," Elthis finally began. He was a large man, and Jae could see how much Elan resembled him. They were both handsome, with warm brown skin and loose dark curls, but Elthis's eyes were darker and more narrow, his chin not quite as square. And he was more *commanding*. He stood as if he owned the room, because he did. The room, and everyone in it. Except Jae.

"My advisor has written to me about Aredann again and again over the past weeks. He and my son have told me how much the drought has affected you all—how much you've

suffered, how hard you've all worked. But I did not understand the enormity of it until I saw it with my own eyes.

"I've been told of your earthquake. I can see the evi-
dence of it around me, from the patched walls to the chaos
of the streets outside. And I know what it means." His gaze
swept across the crowd. Jae waited for it to stop on her, but it
didn't—he didn't seem to notice her at all. "The more people in our world, the less water for each. So we have begun
changing the way the Well flows—moving people away from
outlying estates, and then sending the water itself to other reservoirs. We must do this with Aredann now. It has been a hard
decision to reach, and changing the Well's flow takes a great
deal of magic. The process has begun—and unfortunately,
you experienced the results as an earthquake. But don't fear.
We will *all* leave Aredann within a few days. With any luck,
none of you will suffer such a fright again."

He smiled at them, calm and paternal. People around
her murmured in relief, but Jae stepped forward. Elthis had
lied to them. It was a grain of sand compared to the desert of
the Highest's lies, but Jae knew better now. And she could
prove it.

"That is not true," Jae said, already reaching for the magic
around her.

Elthis's gaze swept down her frame. He glanced at Elan,
and Elan gave him a slight, tiny nod. When he looked back
at her, he smiled again.

"You must all forgive this girl. My son granted her permission to speak on behalf of her people—but now you hear
for yourselves why we keep the Closest in silence. They are,
as they always have been, mad—and traitorous." He shook

his head a little, as if he was bemused. "We'll discuss this in private."

"There is nothing to discuss," Jae said, but it was obvious from the smirks and stifled amusement of the Avowed around her that none of them believed her. Elthis's explanation for the earthquake was so much more comfortable. They would never believe anything else, not unless she made them.

Elthis began walking toward her—toward the door. Shirrad, Elan, and Desinn followed in his wake.

"You *know* it's a lie, Elan. You know it," she said, but it was hard to speak loudly enough to be heard over the crowd, and he wouldn't meet her gaze. He just gestured her toward the door.

She had no choice but to follow, the moment lost. Not that it mattered. Maybe the Avowed believed Elthis—but of course they would. What they thought didn't matter. *Elthis* knew the truth, that magic made her as powerful and dangerous as he was. So fine, she'd discuss this in private. She would inform Lord Elthis that even his power had limits—and tell him what she was prepared to do if he forced her hand.

They made their way to Lady Shirrad's private study, a smaller room where one of the mosaics had been pried off the wall. The table had been pushed back into position after the quake, but the missing bricks in the wall hadn't been replaced, and the cracks in the ceiling hadn't been repaired. Elthis threw it all a disdainful look, but gestured Shirrad down onto one of the cushions.

"Desinn, have someone fetch us water," he said calmly.

Desinn nodded and hurried out. Elthis turned to Jae and added, "So this is the Closest who has caused so much trouble. What is her name?"

"Jae, Highest," Lady Shirrad said quickly.

"Jae," he repeated. "I have to admit, I'm fascinated by everything I've heard about you. A Closest who is *not* a Closest, who dares speak in front of me. Who, I'm told, has magic. I'd accuse my son of making it all up, but even Desinn seems to believe it."

"Because it's true." Jae stood up as tall as she could.

"You shook Aredann to its foundation," he continued. "Nearly knocked the whole place down. And Lord Rannith, you killed him in cold blood."

"No," she said. "There was nothing cold about it. I killed him to protect myself."

"But you *admit* that you killed him."

"Yes," she said. There was no point in lying, and she wasn't ashamed, or sorry, or afraid.

Desinn came back into the room, Tal trailing behind him, carrying mugs and a water jug. He placed them on the table and poured, but before he could leave, Desinn grabbed him by the sleeve.

"If you are free from the Curse," Elthis said, his tone almost entertained, "then you are nothing but a pesky Twill and should be dealt with as one. You murdered one of Lady Shirrad's Avowed, and have confessed to it. That's a crime, and it's punishable by death. Why shouldn't I simply see you hanged?"

"Father, she—" Elan started, but Jae interrupted him.

"Because if you so much as touch me, I will do to you the same as I did to Rannith." She met his gaze with a stony glare, certain that he, alone among the Avowed, understood how insulting it had been to ask her a question.

"Do not threaten me, Closest," he said. "You may think you have power, but you have no idea what I can do. You have no right to even speak to me."

"*You* have no right," Jae spat back, allowing the truth to spill freely from her lips. "You can lie to the Avowed, but *I* know the truth. Abandoning Aredann won't change anything, because you *can't* change anything. You say it takes great magic to change the Well's flow—but you *can't.*"

"Jae—" Elan started, but she ignored him.

"You don't control the Well, and you never did," she said. "It always belonged to me—to my ancestors. They crafted it, they controlled it, and *I* will use it to save Aredann."

"Enough," Elthis said. "Be silent, and I will be merciful."

"Once Aredann is safe, I will break the Curse," she continued, staring him down. "And I will show everyone the truth—that Aredann was the traitor, not Taesann, and that the Highest started the War."

"No one will ever believe that," Elthis said, but his bored expression had crumbled. He was glaring at her now, hatred etched in every line of his body.

"But *you* believe it," she said. "You know it—know that the Highest were the usurpers, the rebels, the thieves and liars. You *know*—"

"*Enough!*" Elthis finally gave in to his fury, and in that moment she was certain she was right. Elan might not have known the truth about his caste, but Elthis did. He took a breath, but it was too late for him to pretend.

She smiled into the silence.

Elthis turned away from her entirely—and toward Tal. His voice was calm again when he finally spoke. "You, Closest—Tal. You are her brother, aren't you?"

"Yes, Highest," Tal said immediately, standing statue-still, Desinn's hand still on his arm.

"Come here."

Tal trotted over to him obediently, but his expression was wide-eyed with terror, and he winced away when Elthis produced a knife from his belt. The Curse wouldn't let Tal go far, and he only fell a step back before stilling again, unable to move.

"What are you doing?" Jae demanded, gaze fixing on the knife. It had a long, sharp blade that glinted in the light as he turned it in his hand, until he was holding it by the blade, offering it to Tal.

"Proving a point. Tal, take this."

Hand trembling, Tal reached out to take the knife from him, and his fingers closed around the hilt.

"Your hair." Elthis nodded toward him. "Cut it off."

Jae swallowed, her throat dry and her stomach dropping. Tal's hands both shook as he pulled the twist of hair at the back of his neck taut and sawed into it with the knife. Tal's hair was thick, and while the knife was sharp, it wasn't made for this, especially not with the awkward angle he had to cut at. He sliced his hand on one stroke and gasped in pain, face screwed up in agony, but he couldn't stop cutting until it was done and he held the knife in one hand and the severed clump of hair in the other.

Elthis gestured toward the corner. "You can wait over there now."

Tal moved jerkily, the Curse carrying him while he still clutched the knife. He retreated to the corner and stood so still and scared that he didn't even try to stop the bleeding. Trembling, Jae turned to face Elthis.

"It's very simple, *Closest*," he said, neutral expression dropping again. His voice was dark and loud, powerful and terrifying, like the one thunderstorm Jae could remember from her youth. "You may control magic, but I control your brother. You will do as I tell you, you will never speak a word of your mad story again, or the next order I give him will be to slit his own throat."

Lady Shirrad gasped, hand going to her mouth. Elan stared, eyes wide and mouth open, his hand pressed to his shoulder. Even Desinn looked down at the floor. But Elthis's gaze never wavered.

"Do you understand?" Elthis asked.

"Father—" Elan started, but Elthis silenced him with a wave of his hand.

"Do you understand?" he repeated.

Jae looked over at Tal, whose eyes were wide, bright saucers in the dark. He was still trembling, still bleeding. Still holding the knife.

She could see it now, as if it was happening already. Tal was a genius at twisting orders, at interpreting them to meet his own ends in ways the Curse could never punish him for. But there would be no arguing with Elthis, no way around it. He would give a direct order, and Tal's body would carry it out, no matter how much his mind screamed and rebelled. Without so much as a whimper, he'd draw the blade along his neck—

"Yes," Jae whispered, staring at Tal. The righteous anger she'd felt burned out, a flame extinguished suddenly, replaced by the cold stones of terror she'd always known. "I understand."

Chapter 16

ELAN DIDN'T WANT TO WATCH, BUT HE COULDN'T CLOSE HIS EYES to the sight, either. Tal stood in the corner, the hank of his hair in his bloody hand, the knife in his other. The blade gleamed, wisps of hair sticking to it. It was nothing, Tal was barely hurt, his hair shouldn't matter. But his free will . . .

Elan was sick to his stomach. He knew Jae had been violated by Rannith, but that had been almost too much to think about. What Rannith had done was its own kind of evil, something Elan had thought was separate. It had happened because Rannith had been wrong in the head, not because Jae was a Closest. But *this*—the look of terror on Tal's face, the silent plea in his eyes that he could never speak out loud, and the crushing, heavy knowledge that he was helpless. His death would be nothing to Elthis, but Tal himself wouldn't be able to beg for his life, to say goodbye to Jae, to fight back. It was — it was horrific.

It was all the more so because Elan had never seen his father like this before. He'd never seen his father caught off guard, never seen his father let slip any hint of emotion he didn't want the world to know about. His rage at Jae's accusations was beyond anger at any insult. It had lasted only a heartbeat, but Elan had never seen his father look so murderous.

And his father had lied about the earthquake. If Elan hadn't seen the truth with his own eyes, he'd have believed everything his father had said. He understood why his father had done it — keeping order was vital — but it had seemed to come to his father so easily. He'd been so convincing. Jae had said the Highest were all liars, and his father *was*. For the greater good, yes, but . . .

Cursing the Closest had been for the greater good, too, and Jae believed the Highest had lied about that. And the War, and the Well, and everything else. For just a moment, with his father losing control and lying so easily, Elan thought maybe she was right.

But that was impossible.

"See that you don't forget," Elthis snarled at Jae, and Elan forced himself to push those impossible thoughts aside as much as he could.

He swallowed, his throat as dry as the air outside, despite the mug of water he'd just downed. Still, he forced himself to try to ease the tension in the room. "Father, that wasn't . . . that won't be . . . it won't be necessary."

His father fixed a knife-edge glare on him. "Saving the peace is necessary. No Closest's life is worth more than that. And you *will not* question me."

Elan's protest died in his throat. He didn't know what else he'd have said, anyway. Jae knew a secret that his father wanted kept. She was a threat—to Elthis, to all of the Highest, to the order and peace they protected. Neither her life nor Tal's meant anything to Elthis, compared to that.

"You said you will use the Well to save Aredann—and that means you think you can control the Well," Elthis said to Jae. "And I know my son was planning to use your magic to find it in the desert. Can you do that?"

Jae nodded, not looking up or meeting his gaze.

"Good. Then you will. Accompanied by Elan and several of my guards," Elthis continued. He glanced at Elan, who didn't meet his gaze, either. Yes, he'd wanted Jae to help him find the Well. But not like this.

"Aredann must still be abandoned—too much has happened here. I will return to Danardae with your brother." He turned his attention back to Jae. "And I'll expect you all to return with the Well's location, and a way to control it, within six months. If you don't come back, your brother's life is forfeit. Do you understand?"

Jae nodded stiltedly, her jaw trembling. But across the table, Shirrad gasped.

It took Elan a moment, and then he understood what his father had said, too. Jae was to return with a way to control the Well—which meant Elthis *didn't* have that. And if he had no control over the Well, then . . . then Jae *had* been telling the truth all along.

The Well, the War, the Curse. Everything Elan knew about them, all of it, was a lie. His father commanded such loyalty and fear that he wasn't afraid of this group knowing. There was no way any of them would speak up, speak out. Tal couldn't, Desinn and Shirrad would never even think to, and Elan had already learned his lesson once. If he dared question his father ever again, he'd be disavowed. Given the secret he now knew, he might even be killed.

Elan swallowed, sick to his stomach. He said, "Then that's . . . that's settled, and it's enough for tonight."

Not that it would matter what Elan said, unless his father agreed. Jae didn't bother moving until Elthis said, "Indeed. You two may go"—he waved his hand at Jae and Shirrad—"wherever. And you"—to Tal—"will stay with Lord Desinn until you are told otherwise. And that knife—you'll keep it with you. Just in case."

Tal nodded too, but since Desinn made no move to leave, he couldn't, either. Lady Shirrad's eyes were damp, and she strode out quickly. Jae gave Tal one last look before she fled, and it made Elan ache. He had hoped his father would triumph, bring Jae back under his control somehow, yes, but he'd thought his father and Jae would come to some kind of agreement—that Elan could help them do it.

His father was right. He *was* a fool. Elthis would never, never agree to anything less than total command and control, and Elan hadn't wanted to admit that, because he hadn't wanted to think of what it would do to Jae. Even before she'd freed herself, she'd always been so angry, defiant, but now she looked weak and scared.

It shouldn't have mattered to Elan at all. None of it should have. But Jae had been fighting for a reason, she'd been *right*, and he couldn't stand the sight of her looking so hopeless.

Elan wasn't sure he'd ever be able to look his father in the eye again, now that he knew the truth. And Aredann . . . Aredann would still be abandoned, even though Jae had the power to save it. Dozens of Closest would be left to die, just to keep a secret.

Elan found his voice again, against his better judgment. "If you think Jae can control the Well, why not allow her to save Aredann's Closest?"

His father's shoulders went stiff, his back straight. He glanced at Desinn. "I'd like to speak with my son in private."

"Yes, of course, Highest." Desinn hurried toward the door, and Tal followed him, stiff and awkward, as if he were pulled along by an invisible cord. Elthis shut the door firmly after them and turned back to Elan.

"It is not your place to question me," he repeated, voice low and angry. "You've taken vows of loyalty to me, and you are my *son*. I will not allow you to undermine me."

Vows. Elan could only nod dumbly. He'd made vows, and he'd meant them. As his father's warden—grand warden, because he was from one of the Highest families—Elan held a position of honor and power. That had always meant everything to him. He searched his father's face for a modicum of mercy or understanding, empathy for the people he'd consigned to death, for Elan for trying to help them. Maybe his father had always been a liar, but it wasn't as if he'd started all this. Elthis knew the Closest weren't the traitors everyone believed them to be.

But his father said, "I told the Avowed that the Well's

magic will cause more destruction at Aredann, and I won't have that questioned. If the girl really can do everything she claims—*you* claim—then at least this will be the last estate to be abandoned."

"But . . ." Elan trailed off. Nothing he could say would change his father's mind, and he was skirting close to disloyalty. "I'm sorry. It's just—it's all so messy. And Tal has never done anything wrong at all."

"Only because he's never had the chance. He's a Closest, with traitors' blood. Do not be squeamish when it comes to your vows—or your duty. I will not have a warden who won't do his job."

"Yes, sir." As a warden, he'd sworn to uphold his father's will, which in turn protected the world. Nothing else was supposed to matter. Not even the truth. And it was better that the unrest end here and now, with his father controlling Jae and the Well both, for the good of everyone.

Everyone except the Closest, because they were schemers and liars. Traitors, just like their ancestors had been.

Just like *his* ancestors had been.

He hung his head, not able to look at his father anymore, bowed over by the weight of history and lies and vows.

Elthis, his stewards, Lady Shirrad and her Avowed advisors, and Elan all met in the larger study midmorning the next day to discuss preparations for the trek to the Well and for Aredann's abandonment. Elan sat near his father at the head of the table. One of the stewards was taking careful notes, listing everything they'd need for the trip into the desert, as all Shirrad's advisors offered their expertise. Shirrad herself sat at the other end of the table, nearly silent, her painted lips pulled down at the corners.

She knew the truth, too. And she must have realized what Elan had, that Jae could save Aredann—her home. But instead Lady Shirrad would be forced to leave it behind, sent away to live on someone else's estate. At Aredann, she was the most important Avowed, its guardian, the highest authority outside of Elthis and Elan himself. Soon she'd be just another member of someone's court, holding no particular power or respect, too young to be taken seriously but old enough to be seen as a failure.

Desinn was at Elthis's other side, which meant Tal sat shadowed in a corner, still, silent, and alone. His hair was wild around his face, too short for him to bind anymore, and when Elan glanced at him, he wondered if that was what Jae would look like if she allowed her hair to grow out. Their features were similar enough, after all, with high cheekbones and sharp noses, and now that Tal was no longer smiling, the resemblance was even more obvious.

Jae herself wasn't there. She hadn't left the master room since the previous night, and though she'd let that other Closest girl in with food and clean clothes, no one else had checked on her. Elan knew he should, but he couldn't stand the thought of how she'd look at him, knowing he knew the truth but wouldn't do anything about it.

Elan shivered, something cold building in his core as he thought about leaving Aredann to turn to dust. Not just for the sake of the Closest who'd die, but because if there was any proof of the truth, it had to be here. If there were any more mysteries in the estate's mosaics and garden, no one would ever discover them. If there was any more magic . . .

Jae's magic and her history were all tied up together, and tied to this place. Jae and her magic, Aredann and the Well, were all a tangled rope that was now starting to fray, one his father would never allow to come undone. It was the rope that tied their world together.

As the afternoon hour grew later, Elthis finally seemed satisfied with their plans, and dismissed most of the observers to go on with their evening. He motioned to Desinn as he stood. "I'll be in the private study, preparing letters to send to the other Highest. Elan, you will keep an eye on . . ." He nodded sideways at Tal's corner. "And do not flinch from your duty."

"Yes, Father," Elan agreed, still not able to look directly at Elthis as he spoke.

Elthis and Desinn strode out, which left Elan alone with Shirrad and Tal. She stood and wiped her face. When she dropped her hand, a black smear covered her cheek, and her eyes were rimmed with red.

"Lady," Elan murmured. "I'm so sorry about Aredann. About—everything."

She took an audible breath. "I'm grateful for your father's kindness and his wisdom."

He met her gaze. She was even more helpless than he was. "I know," Elan said. "But I'm still sorry. You worked hard to keep Aredann alive for so long, and I . . . I can't imagine losing my home, or . . ."

She started to answer, but pressed her hand to her mouth instead as fat tears began to fall. She sank back onto her cushion, turning away from him, her breath coming in gasps and pants. "I'll lose everything," she finally managed. "Everything."

He didn't know what to say to that, but before he could think of a reply, Tal was on his feet. He walked to Shirrad, placed a hand on her shoulder. She didn't shake him off, didn't order him to do anything at all, and he began to slowly rub her back. Elan watched, amazed, as she turned toward him to bury her face in his side. He stroked her hair, put an arm around her.

No one had given him any order. She hadn't demanded this of him. And when she had said she would lose everything . . . She'd lose Tal, too. Just like Jae would.

She cared for him—and he seemed to care for her, too. Even though she'd had to stand there helplessly as his life had been threatened, as the rest of the Closest had been condemned. Maybe she didn't care for every Closest like this, but she was responsible for them.

"Tal," Elan said softly. Tal looked up at him, eyes wide and scared, but Elan forced himself to smile as kindly as he could. "It's all right. I only wanted to say, you may speak. If you wish to. That's all."

"Thank you," Tal mumbled, and pulled a cushion over to Shirrad's side. Elan looked away from them, embarrassed to see something obviously not meant for his eyes, but given his father's order, he couldn't leave. So he listened but didn't watch as Tal said, "Don't worry for me, Lady. You've done all you can, I know you have. I will swear to it when they ask me."

They. The other Closest. If Tal even got to see them again.

"Can you ever forgive me?" Shirrad asked.

"Yes, Lady. You tried to save Aredann. You've tried for years."

"Is there anything else I can do to help you?" she asked.

Elan glanced up and saw their hands linked together on the table.

"I . . . I don't know, Lady. I'd like a chance to see Jae before she leaves. But . . ." He glanced over at Elan. "I don't know if that can happen."

Elan's father wouldn't want that. The farther Elthis could keep them from each other, the easier they would be to control. But if his father was willing to keep secrets, so was Elan, especially since this small kindness was the only one he could grant them. "It can. I'll see to it. But not just now. My father might ask where you are, might come looking for me. Later, after he's gone to sleep."

"Thank you," Tal said.

Elan nodded, because he couldn't imagine at all what Tal would say to Jae. Elan had a sister, too, after all, and though Erra had always been the heir—the heir, and their father's favorite—she'd still looked after him. When they'd been young enough to play together and she'd gotten them both in trouble, she'd never left him alone to face the consequences. Even now that they were both adults and she was so busy with her responsibilities—her children, the husband she'd been forced to marry, and the lady she loved on the side—Erra still looked after him when she could. She was the one who'd made sure Elan had a plan when he came to Aredann, a way to redeem himself. Elan loved her, and his niece and nephew, and he'd do anything for them.

Tal and Jae felt the same for each other. Jae would do anything to save Tal, even give away her freedom, and Tal . . .

Elan realized what Tal would tell Jae after all: that his life wasn't worth it, that she shouldn't worry about him, that she should never bow to Elthis and let him abuse her magic. Tal would tell her that she should do anything she could to fight back and save Aredann—and break the Curse. Even if it cost Tal his life.

Elan wondered if Jae would do it, allow Tal to die so she could be free to rearrange the world into a new order. Elan would never let Erra die, if it came to that.

But Elthis would sacrifice Tal no matter what, to get what he wanted. So why shouldn't Tal be allowed to sacrifice himself instead, for what *he* wanted? At least then it would be his decision to make. Elan could prevent that, simply by going back on his word, by not letting Tal pass Jae any sort of message. That was what his vow to his father demanded, and anything that risked the hold his father had over Jae was as good as breaking that vow.

Elan pressed his palm against the brand on his chest.

He didn't *want* to betray his father. Even now, knowing the truth, it was still all but unthinkable to break his vows intentionally. Not just accidentally asking questions that his father didn't want to answer, but to act directly against his father's interests.

But the Highest made vows, too. Vows to protect the world, and everyone in it. Yet his father was willing to murder hundreds of Closest to protect his secrets.

At least Elan wouldn't be the only vow-breaker in his family.

Chapter 17

JAE SPENT THE DAY CURLED UP IN LADY SHIRRAD'S OLD QUARTERS, miserable and unmoving. All she could think about was Tal and that madman, and how she'd failed to protect her brother. How she'd let herself believe, for the first time in her life, that she'd had any sort of power over anything, that she'd been safe.

She was a fool, and she deserved every moment of misery for it. She would even have welcomed the Curse's steady, unrelenting pain as punishment, because her idiocy was going to get Tal killed. Now she would never make any difference, she wouldn't be able to save Aredann, and nothing would change—except that if she dared breathe wrong, Elthis would slaughter her brother.

A tiny voice in her mind rebelled, asking: *Would they really kill him? If he's dead, they lose all their power over you.*

But Tal's life was worth more than water to her. If he died, she'd be able to take revenge, but she could never, never let him die. The thought of revenge was sweet, though. She'd deal with Elthis the way she had with Rannith, but maybe not so quickly. She thought of the garden, of the cactus spines she used to imagine as weapons. They still could be. It would be nasty, brutal. Deserved.

Gali brought her dinner. At Jae's questioning look, she volunteered, "I haven't seen him all day." She handed Jae the plate. "They aren't even allowing him to work, just keeping him in the study with them. He wasn't in the Closest's quarters last night. Jae . . ."

"I won't let them hurt him," Jae said.

Gali nodded but said, "You should . . . you should do what you think is right."

"Saving Tal is right," Jae said, but Gali wouldn't look at her.

Jae wilted. Cooperating with Elthis meant abandoning Aredann, and that meant *Gali* would die, along with all the Closest except Tal. The idea of choosing between them, weighing Tal's life against all of theirs, made her stomach churn, and the meal became even less appealing. But she still knew, deep down, that Tal's life outweighed everything else. The other Closest, the Well, the Curse. He was her brother, her twin, the only one who'd ever tried to protect her. She'd endure anything if it meant saving him.

There were no right answers, and there was nothing she could do. Gali left, shutting the door behind her, and Jae pushed the plate away. Her stomach rumbled, but she didn't mind the ache. She'd been hungry countless times in her life, and physical pain was better than letting herself get lost in thoughts again. When she shut her eyes, all she could picture were the Closest she'd known her whole life. Her mother, who'd passed away years ago. Gali, Firran, Asra, and the others she saw every day. All of them would die because she'd chosen Tal over them.

She couldn't stop her mind from wandering toward him. She glanced at the room with her other-vision, let the world glow softly, and followed the lights through Aredann's corridors. Elthis was in his borrowed set of rooms, with servants helping him prepare to sleep. Shirrad was nearby, alone. And farther down the hall, Tal sat cross-legged in Elan's room. Elan was pacing, while Tal watched him warily. Elan was talking, like he'd always talked at Jae.

At least it looked like Tal was safe, for the moment.

Shirrad stirred in her quarters. She moved slowly, pausing every few feet, and headed toward Elan's room. Jae sat up straight, the room around her fading farther away as she concentrated. She could make out Shirrad's expression, the tension in her as she moved toward Elan and Tal.

When Shirrad reached Elan's room, she didn't venture in. Instead the three of them slipped out. Elan took the lead, moving just as slowly as Shirrad had, and back in the direction she'd come from. Not toward Lady Shirrad's room and Elthis's but toward the main hall and the center of the house. From there, they could go anywhere.

Jae watched, confused. They were obviously trying not to be seen, but she couldn't imagine why—what they could be doing that would be so secretive. She widened her other-vision gaze and saw that only a few people were still in the halls, and though a couple were near Elan, none of them seemed headed toward him.

Elan reached the main hall and hesitated, looking back at Shirrad and Tal. But as Elan started forward, another presence came into her view: Elthis, heading toward them.

She didn't know what they were doing, but it was clearly meant to be stealthy, and there was no one else on the estate they'd need to hide from. She ran for the door to her chamber, but it was locked. She could see them moving again, and Elthis getting closer. She grabbed for the energy she'd used during the quake and shoved it at the door.

It rattled, shook, and fell. It wasn't quiet or subtle, and everyone she could see in other-vision froze, startled, but that was fine. It gave her more time. She ran toward her brother, down the halls she knew so well. Elthis finally caught up to them in a large, domed atrium where several halls converged. He came to a stop on one side as they were about to exit out the other and demanded, "Shirrad, Elan—what are you doing?"

Jae stopped just shy of the atrium, in the hallway that Elan, Tal, and Shirrad would have turned down if they'd continued. Instead, the three of them all turned back toward Elthis.

Jae crept closer to them, staying in the shadows. She could just make out their backs and Elthis's face, but he didn't seem to notice her.

"Nothing," Elan said. "Just taking a walk around the grounds."

"Why? There's nothing worth seeing," Elthis said, and

snorted. Then he looked back and forth between Elan and Shirrad. His eyebrows climbed his forehead. "Unless—you and this girl?"

Shirrad clenched a fist but said nothing, despite the sneer in Elthis's voice. Elan answered, "What? No, of course not. Lady Shirrad and I were only chatting."

"About what?" Elthis demanded.

"About . . ." Elan squared his shoulders. "About this estate and what's to become of it. Will it truly turn to sand in time? Or will it still be here, abandoned?"

"What does that matter?"

"There's so much history here," Elan said. "So many secrets. I hope it stands up to the desert and someone will rediscover it, someday."

Elthis frowned. Elan's voice had been hard and heavy. Not meek, like yesterday, when he'd heard the truth from Elthis's own lips.

Elthis peered at him, and then at Tal, and said, "What are you doing with him?"

"You ordered him to stay with me," Elan said. "I went for a walk. He had to follow."

"I *ordered* you to *deal* with him," Elthis said. "Not take him for a stroll. Do not lie to me, Elan. Closest, what is going on?"

"I . . ." Tal cast a helpless look at them, then said, "They were taking me to Jae, Highest."

Jae swallowed heavily. Taking him to *her*. Elthis asked the question for her: "Why?"

"I asked them to—"

"To say goodbye," Elan interrupted. "A kindness—

because Tal hasn't done anything to deserve his treatment. Not any more than his ancestors did—because they didn't, either, did they, Father?"

"How dare you?" Elthis spat, and Jae grabbed for the wall, needing something solid to cling to as the world shifted around her. Elan knew the truth—and it *mattered* to him. She'd thought he was as much a liar as his father, when Elan had said he would save Aredann and that he wanted to help, but maybe she'd been wrong. Maybe he really just hadn't known.

"Elan." Elthis stood like he was built out of the bricks they'd used to patch the wall. He nodded toward Tal, but when he spoke, it was to Elan. "Stop this nonsense, and send *him* over to me immediately."

Tal didn't move, looking back and forth between them. No order had been given to him. Jae clutched the wall harder, realizing. It wasn't about Tal at that moment—it was about Elan, and whether or not he'd obey his father. She didn't dare hope, but—

"I can't do that," Elan said.

"Elan—"

"He's done nothing wrong. I *won't*," Elan repeated.

His father stared at him for a long moment, and so did Jae. "Is that your final decision?" Elthis asked.

Elan's shoulders heaved with a single deep breath, and he said, "Yes."

"Then you are no son of mine any longer," Elthis said. Shirrad gasped, hand going to her mouth, but Elthis continued. "And you have broken your vows."

Elan fell back, letting out a strangled shout as he staggered. His hands both went to his heart, and he winced, falling against the wall. Jae's skin tingled as the energy around her *changed*. Something snapped, like it had when she'd freed herself. Elthis was still shining, bright and steady, tendrils of magic connecting him and Shirrad, but the glow around Elan pulsated and rippled, while Elan's features twisted with pain.

Jae's head swam as she pulled herself off the wall. Elan believed her. He'd stood up to his father. And now he'd lost everything for it. Jae's skin tingled, magic building, energy glowing all around her.

"You, Closest," Elthis barked. "Come here."

"*No!*" Jae screamed, years of silence falling away from her in a heartbeat. Tal couldn't stop, but everyone else turned toward her. As she broke into the atrium, she grasped for all the magical energy she could. "Let Tal go. Let him go!"

"I will not," Elthis said, reaching out to grab Tal's arm as soon as he was near enough. "And you will be silent."

Jae clenched her jaw, teeth shutting with a snap, but she didn't need to speak. Instead she poured the energy she'd gathered into the floor and walls until they shook. This time it was no slow, confused build, and no accident. She flung her arms out for balance as she stared at the spot under Elthis's feet, willing the stones to slide apart. They rumbled, and Shirrad screamed. Even Elthis looked scared, staring around with wild eyes, but he didn't relinquish his grip on Tal.

"Stop this! Stop it now!" he shouted.

Jae sent a brick that had been knocked loose skittering across the room toward him. Elthis jumped, avoiding it easily, but he had to shove Tal away to do it—and as Elthis danced backward to avoid more debris, he yelled, "Closest, the knife. Cut your throat!"

Jae screamed again, and so did Shirrad, as Tal reached for the knife in his belt, his arm jerking and shaking. Jae let all her fury and rage loose, hurled it at the ceiling above Elthis—

Elan threw himself forward, narrowly missing a brick that had come dislodged from above, and landed on Tal. He scrambled, reaching for Tal's knife hand, while Tal fought back against Elan to carry out the order he'd been given. Jae poured more and more magic into the floor and ceiling as Elan wrestled with Tal. Elthis backed away, but the floor buckled, bricks crashed down, and he staggered and fell. He landed badly on a pile of rubble, his head slamming into one of the bricks. A spray of blood coated the floor, bright red that turned dark where it hit the ground.

Jae reached her magic toward the bricks above Elthis, ready to end him, but Shirrad shrieked, "*Stop this!* Tal, listen to me! *I order you to be still!*" Tal's body convulsed under Elan's, and Shirrad yelled, "I am the highest authority at Aredann now, and you *will* stop!"

Tal's body jerked again, trying to throw Elan off, and Elan grunted as he struggled to keep his hold on Tal. Then, remarkably, Tal fell still. His chest was heaving, but he leaned back against the shaking floor, and Jae let the room's trembling dwindle and die. She didn't know if what Shirrad had said was really true—it was if Elthis was dead, but he was only unconscious. Maybe that was enough, or maybe Tal had just believed her enough that the Curse had, too, but either way, Jae was grateful.

Elan scrambled off Tal and landed on his knees among the downed bricks, hands pressed to a dark spot on his chest. Jae ran over to them and knelt next to Tal. She took his hand, and he stared at her, dropped the knife, and let her drag him up into her arms.

Shirrad crouched next to Elthis and pressed a hand to his chest. A moment later she said, "He's alive. You need to go *now*. Do you understand that, Tal? I *order* you to go with your sister into the desert."

Tal nodded.

"Shirrad—" Elan started, but she cut him off.

"They were gathering supplies. Take what you can and go. Jae, I know you can save Aredann. I *know* you can." She stared at Jae, her eyes wide white saucers in the dark room. "I've given you your brother, and I will give you anything else in my power if you protect this place. *Please*. It's your home, too."

Jae swallowed. She didn't owe Shirrad anything at all— Shirrad was one of *them*. Lady Shirrad had only been able to help Tal *because* she was one of them—

"Do you know what Elthis will do to you for helping us?" Elan asked.

"It doesn't matter," Shirrad said. "Aredann is my home, and I won't abandon it. Not if there's even a chance to save it."

"Good," Jae said, and for the first time, she met Shirrad's gaze and held it. "Elthis is a liar. The Highest are *all* liars. They didn't craft the Well, and they can't control it. They never, ever could."

Shirrad looked from Elthis to Jae, and nodded. "But you can. Please. Go now, before—before anything else can stop you."

Jae hesitated, gaze falling on Elthis's unconscious form. This was her chance. She could finish what she'd started, kill Elthis now while he was helpless, and strike down anyone who challenged her. She could find the Well and make it her own, take revenge for her ancestors and all the generations since, force the Avowed into the same servitude the Closest had known. She could do anything, *anything* with her power.

But she looked at Tal, and remembered his unease with how she'd killed Rannith, and how scared Firran had been, and how Gali had still served Jac meals, even knowing she was going to be abandoned. Jac had so much power, and the very first thing she'd done with her freedom was kill.

But she'd grown flowers, too.

She could do anything.

Jae stood, offered Tal a hand up, and looked at Lady Shirrad. "We'll find the Well, and I'll save Aredann. When Elthis wakes, warn him that I will return. And if he has harmed any Closest here, I will kill him. I think he will believe me, this time."

Shirrad nodded, and when Jae looked at Elan and Tal, they both did, too.

"We have to go now," Elan said. "Hurry."

Jae started for the hallway, Tal at her heels, but despite his words, Elan didn't move. He stared down at the figure of his father for a long moment, then up at Jae. Then he squared his shoulders, walked away from the blood, and followed her out into the night.

Chapter 18

"I WONDER IF THEY CAME AFTER US," TAL SAID.

Elan looked back at the expanse of sand and scrub, even that slight stretch pulling at his wound, sending a pulse of pain through him. It was hard to make anything out through his mesh head covering, and with the moon having sunk to the horizon, but he didn't see anyone.

They'd run just before midnight, grabbing all the supplies they could carry or load onto a groaning camel. Most of it was water: several jugs, plus large satchels strapped onto Tal's and Elan's backs, and individual water skins to drink from while they traveled. This far out in the desert, water was life. They'd also taken food, a low tent, a few changes of clothes, and supplies in case one of them got injured. That was all.

They hadn't even taken his father's horses—they'd need too much water in the desert, especially considering even Jae didn't know exactly how long the trek would be.

Dawn hovered at the edge of the sky. Elan sagged in place, catching his breath for a minute, just long enough for the night chill to raise bumps on his neck. He welcomed it, wishing there was a way to bundle it, hold it against his skin. He hadn't told the others about the wound on his chest yet—they seemed to think Tal had gotten him with the knife, and he'd assured them he was fine. He'd wrapped bandages around his torso while they'd loaded the camel, so they hadn't seen.

He hadn't been stabbed. The brand on his chest had turned into a raw, fresh burn, searing his skin the moment his father had declared him disavowed. The initial flash of pain had only lasted a few seconds, but the wound remained. Every movement that had jostled his body had ached, until they'd walked so far that he'd gone entirely numb.

He nodded at Tal. "My father brought guards to keep the order as they abandon Aredann. He'll probably send at least a few of them to look for us. He'll have to."

Jae looked over at him, the whites of her eyes all he could make out under her hood. She cocked her head a little.

"No one can raise a hand to the Highest and live," Elan explained. "It ruins the order of things. And disavowing me . . ." He swallowed, throat tightening as he tried to explain. He fought to keep his voice steady, to ignore the betrayal that ached just as much as his chest. "Disavowing me would be humiliating for him, admitting he couldn't even keep his own son in line. The Highest can't afford weakness in their ranks, and between your magic, and me challenging him, and even Lady Shirrad . . . he'll have to do something."

"I wonder if we've come far enough to rest," Tal said, his voice lilting up into something that was almost a question. He was leading the camel with one hand. The other reached up toward his neck, his fingers alighting on the back of his hood for a moment, where his ponytail had been. His hand jerked away quickly, dropping to his side.

"I think so," Jae said, turning back toward the open desert to the west, away from Aredann, long out of sight though it was. "There's so little life out here. I'll be able to feel anyone coming."

"I'd appreciate it if you'd check," Tal said.

"Let's settle first," Jae said. "I don't want to be in the open when the sun comes up."

Elan spotted a boulder a little way off. It wasn't enormous, but hopefully it would be big enough to cast a shadow. His body protested as they walked toward it, limbs exhausted from overuse, but he'd be glad to have the shade during the day. Even though the tent they'd brought was designed to keep as much heat out as it could, it would still get cursed hot.

The boulder came up to his rib cage and was wider than it was high. He and Tal unloaded the tent, which sent more jolts of pain across his chest and shoulder. He grimaced but didn't say anything—it was no worse than Jae and Tal had dealt with their whole lives.

Elan had never actually put a tent up himself before, but he was the only one who had even seen what it was supposed to look like, so when Tal and Jae both gave him questioning looks, he did his best. It took all three of them to figure it out—there were cut wooden poles of different lengths that tied to the fabric, and they had to experiment to figure out which pole tied where. In the end, Elan wasn't actually sure they got it right. It was lower to the ground than he expected, and it looked like a strong gust would knock it over. It would have to do, though, because the sun was creeping up and exhaustion was creeping in.

Tal tied the camel outside, and they all filled their water skins, then crawled in. The sleeping mats were thin, barely protecting them from the sandy desert floor, and there was just enough room for them to set up shoulder to shoulder. Elan laid his mat out to one side, with Tal between him and Jae.

Elan groaned as he sat, amazed at how silent both Tal and Jae were. They were more used to pain and physical labor, he knew, but he doubted they'd been prepared for hours of a forced march like this. People said "as quiet as the Closest" for a reason, and a lifetime of silence would have to be a hard habit to break.

Tal pulled off his boots in jerky, awkward motions, and blanched at the sight of his own feet. They were blistered, bloody, and raw. "Are you all right?" Elan asked.

"It hurts," Tal answered.

"Don't ask him questions," Jae said, shucking off her own boots. Her feet were in bad shape, too. "It's rude."

"Oh," Elan said. "I—I didn't know that."

Tal shrugged a little. "I don't mind all that much. But I *am* compelled to answer—that's why it's rude. To force a Closest like that."

"Oh," Elan said again. That made sense, and he'd never even thought about it.

"Well, no harm done." Tal gave him a friendly smile and began digging through one of the packs. "We've never been anything but barefoot."

Of course. Elan looked away as he lowered his hood and shrugged off the thick travel robe. He'd grown up wearing sandals and travel boots. His feet ached from the long walk, but the calluses on his heels had protected him from blisters. But the Closest had been given that name because they went barefoot; they were the closest to the land they were bound to work. Tal grabbed clean rags from the bag and dampened them with water. Without even asking, he reached for Jae's feet first and dabbed the blood off.

After they'd finished cleaning their feet and wrapping them in gauze, Tal turned to Elan. "Let me see your wound. Running all night can't have been good for it."

Elan shook his head. "It's fine."

Tal glanced over at Jae, and Elan had the disconcerting feeling that they were having a conversation without ever speaking a single word. Finally Tal said, "You're not fine; you were stabbed. It'll get infected if we don't take care of it."

Elan hesitated. He didn't know what it would look like and didn't want them to have to deal with it. But the burn could get infected just as easily as a stab wound, so finally he stripped off his shirt. Jae looked away, pulling her knees to her chest and staring down at the sand and her mat, but Tal scooted closer and began peeling away Elan's clumsily tied bandages.

"You didn't stab me," Elan said uselessly as Tal gaped. Jae looked up sharply, and her eyes went wide.

"I don't understand," Tal said, sinking back to get a better view.

Elan turned away, uncomfortable with their scrutiny. His rib cage felt tight with anxiety as he explained, "It's the brand from my vows."

Jae frowned, and Tal said, "Lady Shirrad has one, too. But . . ."

"All Avowed do," Elan explained. "They do it when you say your vows, and the vows protect you. It doesn't hurt at all, and it heals instantly. But . . ."

"But when you were disavowed, the magic left your body," Jae said. "So the burn reappeared."

"Oh," Elan said. He hadn't thought about it in detail; all he'd known was that it hurt, so he'd imagined it was some sort of punishment for vow breaking. Jae's idea made more sense.

"So it'll heal," Tal said.

"With time," Jae confirmed.

"Then I'll clean it." Tal reached for the damp rags again. "While I do that, Jae, I'd love to know if you can sense anyone coming from Aredann."

Elan did his best to hold still as Tal carefully pressed the rag against his skin. It was cool and damp, but the pressure had Elan gritting his teeth against the pain. Tal gave him a sympathetic look, but he didn't say anything. Elan didn't, either, just waited for it to be done and for Tal to rewrap the bandages.

By the time Tal had finished, Jae had crossed her legs and shut her eyes, and her body was now perfectly still. She didn't respond when Tal pressed a water skin into Elan's hands, a silent order to drink. That would help the burn, and Elan *was* thirsty. As he finished drinking, Jae opened her eyes again.

"No one is in the desert between here and Aredann. I'm too far away to see much clearly, but the whole estate feels . . . frantic."

"Can you sense the Well?" Elan asked. "Are you sure we're going in the right direction?"

"Questions," Tal reminded him gently.

Elan almost winced. He'd forgotten already. "I'm sorry. I didn't—"

"I can follow the aqueduct toward the Well. I can sense the water easily enough," Jae said, interrupting his apology. "But . . ."

The question—*But what?*—was on the tip of his tongue. He swallowed it, waiting, and she finally continued.

"The barrier." She shuddered, and her eyes blinked back to normal. She hunched over her knees again. "I still can't see beyond it, and it still feels . . . cursed."

"Is it . . ." He caught himself this time. "I'd like to know how far it is. If you don't mind."

"A few days, I think."

"Nights. We'll want to travel at night," he decided. "It's easier to move in the cold than the heat."

"Don't tell us what to do," Jae snapped.

"Jae, he's right," Tal said, stretching forward toward his feet. He grimaced, but stretching probably wasn't a bad idea, after all the walking and running they'd done. Elan reached out to do the same, but the burn throbbed, and he gave up, relaxing his body instead.

"He doesn't get to give us orders anymore," Jae said.

"He *can't* give me orders anymore," Tal answered.

"Nothing he's said has set off the Curse. He's not . . ." Tal shot him an apologetic look but continued. "Since he's not Avowed anymore, neither of you can order me to do anything."

Tal grinned a little as he said it, but his hand drifted up toward the nape of his neck again. His fingers twitched for a moment, catching the loose end of a curl, and then he dropped his hand into his lap.

"I don't want to give you any orders," Elan said, fighting an urge to brush his fingers against the brand, his throat aching as if it had gone dry again. No one had been disavowed in years, and Elan had *never* heard of a Highest being disowned. But of course not. He knew now that disavowal wasn't just about protecting the social order—it was about keeping the Highest's secrets, defending the lies at the foundation of their world.

Disavowal meant he'd lost everything. Not just his family, his status, and his power, but everything he'd known. It was as if the sun had changed directions in the sky. Nothing was as he'd thought, and now, as far as the world was concerned, *he* was nothing. No one at all.

"Let's rest," Tal said, voice so soft that Elan could barely hear it. "We'll figure out travel when we wake."

It was nearly impossible to sleep, even with the shelter of the tent. Though the coarse fabric blocked out the worst of the sun and the heat, it was still stifling inside, especially with the three of them in such close quarters. Elan rolled over and over, unable to get comfortable, constantly jostling his burn and setting off cascades of pain. Finally he just lay still on his back, one arm draped over his eyes to block out the light.

After the sun peaked and began its evening descent, Tal sat up. Elan followed slowly, disoriented, and took a long drink from his water skin. Now his chest not only ached; it *itched*.

They folded the tent messily, not able to get the packs back into the neat order they'd been in before. It was good enough, though. After a quick meal of bread and dried meat, tasteless even compared to what he'd been eating at Aredann, they started walking again. Tal was the one who took the lead, urging them on even though the sun wasn't down yet, and Jae didn't argue with him about it.

The sun was directly in front of them on the horizon, lighting the desert with red and orange as if it were on fire. It was uncomfortably warm to walk, and the sky stretched above them, endless and cloudless, an expanse of perfect blue. This far out, there were hardly even any scrub bushes poking up through the sand, just dune after dune, patterned by the wind.

If every step the previous evening had ached, then this was agony for the first hour. Finally, as the sun dropped out of sight at last, Elan found the rhythm of it. Maybe walking so much more stretched the soreness from his limbs, or maybe they went numb, but as long as he put one foot in front of the other without hesitating, he didn't stumble.

The moon was nearly as bright as the sun had been, silver instead of gold, but thankfully without the heat. It wasn't quite full yet, but it was bright enough to see by easily. The group took a single long break for something like lunch, a midnight meal instead of midday.

They ate quietly, the night silent and still around them, until Jae said, "Tell me everything you know about magic."

Elan almost choked, shocked by both the sudden sound

and being given an order like that. Not that it was anything like he imagined the Curse to be; there was nothing that would force him to answer Jae. Most likely, she hadn't even meant it like that, and just wasn't used to asking for anything at all. But it still took him a second to remember that and to beat down the feeling that she had no right to demand anything of him.

He must have needed more time to do that than he thought, because Tal said, "It's probably a good idea, Elan."

"I know. I just . . ." He couldn't explain why it had taken him by surprise. He thoughtlessly reached up to scratch the sore skin around his burn, winced, and then said, "Of course. I just don't know how much you already know."

"Not enough," Jae said.

"Then I'll start at the beginning, but I don't know all that much, either. I wish I'd brought some of my papers. . . ." There had been no time to retrieve them. He hoped someone would think to take them when Aredann was packed and abandoned. Erra had borrowed most of them from someone. She'd want them back, and he didn't want all that knowledge to be lost with Aredann if Jae failed to save it.

Tal and Jae were both waiting expectantly, so he tried to remember what he'd been able to glean from the few pages that hadn't been in that strange, other language. "The world and everything in it is built from the four elements—earth, wind, fire, and water—and each element has its own kind of energy. Mages can sense that energy and manipulate it, use it to craft almost anything they can imagine."

Jae nodded.

"'Craft' might not be the right word," Elan continued, mulling it over as he spoke. "They built the estate houses by each reservoir, they built the Well, but they can also *do* things. Like cause earthquakes."

"Or grow flowers," Jae said.

"Right. I don't really understand much about how it works. Those books said mages have their own way of seeing things."

"Other-vision," Jae said.

He didn't know where the phrase had come from, but it was as good as any. "Yes. But I don't have much more information than that—and there aren't any more mages to ask," Elan said.

"I'd love to know why that is," Tal said.

Elan gave him a confused look, and then realized: it was a question without *asking* a question. "I don't know," Elan confessed, hating that he couldn't even answer that. For all the research he'd done, all the ancient parchments he'd searched through, he felt as if he'd barely learned anything. Not even why no one in generations had been able to see or use magic except the Highest, and they weren't really mages. They'd just inherited the ability to command the Well.

Or so Elan had always believed. But that was a lie, too, which meant there had been no new magic in the world in generations—which made it even stranger that Jae had become a mage out of nowhere.

"There are no mages to do new magic, but old magic can still work, if it has a binding," Elan finally continued. Then he explained, "The mages would bind the magic to a physical object, something that would last for generations. That's the only way a spell can last beyond the initial casting, or beyond the life of the mage. I do know that when the Well was created, the last step was a binding so that it would last forever."

Jae said thoughtfully, "But the reservoirs are going dry."

Elan nodded, heart heavy. His father had sounded so sure when he'd said it was because there were too many people and not enough water to go around. And that made sense — except that the Well was magic. It had never failed before, no matter the size of the population, no matter how bad the drought. Looking back now, Elan could see that when he and the other Highest had effectively signed the death warrants for hundreds of Closest, it had been because it was the only thing they could do. Just walk away from the dry reservoirs and hope for the best. Because they didn't control the Well, and it shouldn't be running dry.

Jae had the thought just as he did. "If the Well is drying up, then . . . that might mean that something is weakening the binding, or that the binding is gone."

"Makes sense. But no one knows what the Well was bound to. If we did, we could figure out what's happening to it." Since he didn't have anything else to say about bindings, Elan changed subjects slightly. "The lore also said that most mages have an affinity for a particular element, or maybe two. It seemed as if it was very rare that they could use more than that. But some mages, the most powerful, thought there were other kinds of energies, too. That people have their own kind of energy, separate from the elements."

Jae's brow furrowed, and Tal said to her, "You can use earth, clearly. I'd love to know if there are others."

"I think . . . ," Jae started, then trailed off for a few seconds. "Yes, earth, strongest. And water, too. I had to work harder to pull water out of the plants, but I think it would get easier with practice."

Elan started to ask her about the others, but stopped himself before it came out.

His restraint was rewarded a moment later when she added, "I've *sensed* the air, but it doesn't feel right to me. And I don't think I can feel fire at all. I never have, anyway."

"Maybe you can try it sometime," Tal said.

"Maybe." She went quiet, staring up at the sky, then shook her head and pushed herself up to stand. "We should start moving again."

Tal nodded, stood, and gave Elan a hand up. Elan shook his head. Letting Tal haul him up would hurt his burn. Instead he stood slowly, carefully, and sighed. He was exhausted and achy, his chest itchy and sore from the burn, and the rest of his muscles were just tired from overuse. But the Well was still at least a few days away, and their water wouldn't last forever, so they couldn't dawdle.

As they started walking, Jae said softly, "Thank you. For telling me about the magic."

Elan glanced at her, surprised, and nodded. "Of course."

That was all. Walking didn't leave a lot of energy to chat, and once Elan fell back into the rhythm of it, his whole mind seemed to turn off, and only looking up at the moon in the sky made it feel like they had moved at all.

They walked until dawn, and couldn't find a boulder to shelter under this time. They pitched the tent at the bottom of a dune, ate quickly, and crawled inside just as the temperature started climbing again.

This time, despite the heat of the day, Elan fell into an exhausted, dreamless sleep.

The third night of walking was nearly as bad. Their water was warm, barely even soothing, and Elan's water skin had developed a sour taste. They stopped to drink more often, sweating off as much as they took in.

Elan found himself trying to imagine the Well they were walking toward. It would be like Danardae's reservoir, only much larger: an enormous, glittering oasis, surrounded by bushes and trees that lived off its water. They'd be able to eat and drink their fill, to bathe, to *relax*.

They just needed to find it.

"You're sure we're heading toward it?" he asked, breaking one of their long, tired silences.

"I'm sure," Jae said, shooting him a glare.

"How far—I mean—" He cleared his throat. "I'd like to know how far it is."

Tal made an amused noise, and Jae said, "I don't know. The barrier, though. We're close to that."

He frowned. She hadn't elaborated on what the barrier was, and didn't seem inclined to. So they just trudged onward, the sand dyed silver by the moon.

Shortly before sunup, Jae stopped walking so sharply that Elan almost crashed into her. Before the question finished forming on Elan's tongue, Tal screamed, impossibly loudly in the expanse of desert around them. He whirled toward Jae, grabbing for her, but missed and fell to his knees, hands clutching his head.

"Tal!" she shouted. "Tell me what's happening!"

Elan grabbed for Tal's arms, but Tal was moving now, scrambling back the way they'd come. He collapsed after a few feet, panting, and managed, "It's here. We can't— Jae, the Curse, you must be able to feel it." He stared at the horizon in terror. "It won't let me— I can't go any farther. I *can't*."

Elan held out his water skin. Tal took it, his hands shaking.

"Drink," Jae said, though Tal already was. "And breathe. Then tell me more, if you can."

Tal took a few gulps, then handed the skin back to Elan. His voice was still shaking as he said, "It was . . . One moment, I was fine, and the next, the Curse hit me. I couldn't move forward at all. It wouldn't let me. It's here. You must be able to feel it."

Elan shook his head. He'd been disavowed, but not cursed.

"The barrier," Jae said. She peered at the desert in front of them, frowning, her eyes going vacant again. "It's . . . enormous. It does feel like the Curse, but not . . . not quite. . . . Something is happening. It's in the air, but it's the land, too."

Elan had no idea what that meant, but peered in the direction she and Tal were staring. He didn't see any kind of barrier, just more sand in front of them, sky above.

Sky and . . . Oh.

He grabbed Jae's arm, and her eyes snapped back into focus. He pointed at what he'd seen: a dark spot in the sky, small but getting larger—closer. Coming out of nowhere, impossibly fast; deep brown, almost purple.

"A cloud," Tal said.

Elan shook his head and reached to haul Tal up. "No, no, we have to go. We have to find shelter. It's a storm."

"Rain . . . ," Jae started, but they were all realizing that wasn't it.

"No." Elan pushed Tal to start him moving, yanking on the camel's lead, panic so thick that he could taste it, and he admitted what they all knew and feared most: "A sandstorm."

Chapter 19

JAE STARED AT THE CLOUD IN HORROR. IT WAS DARK AGAINST THE horizon, growing larger as the wind howled in the distance. It hit them only moments later—innocent, small gusts that would grow stronger until they were large enough to knock her down. Sand was already pelting them, and the wind would bring more with it, dumping enough to bury all of them.

Jae had only ever seen one sandstorm before, and that had raged far out in the desert, only its edge reaching as far as Aredann. Even so, it had destroyed their fields. Lord Savann, Lady Shirrad's father, had been searching for the Well, and had died out in the desert.

Something tingled in the back of Jae's mind. Lord Savann searching for the Well, and a sandstorm—

"Run!" Elan screamed, pulling her out of her fear-induced daze. He grabbed her hand as Tal scrambled for the rope attached to the camel. Tal grasped her other hand, and they ran, clinging to each other, back the way they'd come. Everything else fell away as they ran, even the ache in her limbs. But it was useless; they had nowhere safe to go. There was no shelter around anywhere, nothing to protect them once the wind really hit.

Within a few minutes, it was on them. Jae clutched both of the hands in hers, stumbling as she ran, her limbs too tangled up with Tal's and Elan's, desperately trying to keep the group together. With no shelter, all they had was each other, and it would only take a heartbeat to lose even that.

The wind howled and shrieked around them, invisible hands trying to break them apart, battering their bodies. It shoved them forward and then sideways, pummeling them with so much sand that it felt more like rocks or bricks.

Jae faltered and barely caught herself, yanking at Tal's arm to get her footing back. As long as they kept moving, they couldn't get buried, but the moment they stopped—

Elan stumbled, tripped, his hand wrenching away from Jae's. She yanked Tal's arm, trying to stop him, but the camel broke away on Tal's other side. He dropped her hand to reach for the camel, and she fell, knocked off balance when Tal let go. She pushed up, trying to find her footing, but the wind smashed her back down, crushing the breath out of her lungs. Wind whipped the veil from her face, and she screamed, then coughed, inhaling sand. Eyes shut against it, she flung her arms up, trying to get the sand off her face and out of her mouth, but there was no way she could even stand up, let alone run.

Elan yelled something from nearby, but the wind was too loud for her to make it out. She turned toward him, groping in the air to try to find him, but it was useless. The wind itself was a blur of orange, as much sand as air, and she couldn't make out anything else. Not even the rising sun.

After that, all she knew was the ache in her lungs and the crushing wind and sand, pressing her down, and worse, starting to build up over her limbs. She thrashed, trying to pull herself free, and heard Elan shout again. He sounded farther away, but she made out a word this time — "magic" — and everything fell into place, clarity driving away the panic.

Lord Savann had been caught in a sandstorm when he'd searched for the Well, and this storm had hit only minutes after Tal's fit at the barrier. Both storms had been caused by magic, the *same* magic. Jae finally managed to get up to her knees, hands still blocking her face, and took the deepest breath she could manage. Then she fell into other-vision, and instead of the orange wind around her, she saw the pulsating glow of energy being twisted into magic.

If magic had created the storm, then magic could end it. Jae tried to shut out the wind's shrieking and instead concentrate only on other-vision. The storm around them was bright, active, but not the heart of the magic. That was closer to where Tal had fallen. Jae cast her mind out, trying to find it, and spotted a blinding line across the desert. It stretched farther than she could see in either direction, curving slowly. A long line, maybe wrapping all the way around the Well. But *how*?

She threw all her energy at it, and it stung, the buzzing prickles growing sharp and angry as she grabbed for them, tried to find a way to tear the streak in half. There were no weak points to attack. Giving up on that method, she sank deeper into its magic.

She plunged into it, but it felt—*different.* Something at its core was the same, almost identical to the earthquakes she'd caused, but infused with something strange that tingled like a limb left in one position too long. The two were tied together, the solid, familiar glow of land and the prickly energy of—

Air.

Elan had said that for magic to last, it had to be bound to a physical object. Someone had stitched the two elements together to create a sandstorm, binding them both somewhere so they would protect the Well for generations. Instinctively she searched for the binding object; that was the key to the storm.

The earth's energy was familiar, but it glowed with a feeling of foreignness; maybe this was her element, but it was not her magic, or magic crafted by the Wellspring mages. But she could still examine it. When she looked at its binding, the barrier wasn't one unbroken streak; it was a series of nodes, magic stretched between them. The nodes weren't only magic; they were physical. Rocks, enormous boulders, mostly buried under centuries' worth of sand, linked to enough magical energy to pull the very air down, give it direction. *They* were the binding. Without them . . .

Jae coughed again and tried to pull her robe up over her face without falling out of other-vision. It was caked with sand, but she managed to pull a few clumps off. Just enough so that she could press the cloth to her mouth and nose.

When she could finally breathe again, she cast out for

any spare energy she could feel, and pulled it toward her. It wasn't much—most of the energy she could sense was part of the barrier—but she could gather a little. It wasn't very strong, hardly enough for the kind of destruction she'd caused at Aredann, so she focused on only the nearest of the boulders.

When she tried to shatter it, it struck back, the magic infused in it protecting itself—but she could hit near it. She shook the ground, and a decade's worth of sand shifted, falling away, enough of it moving to make the boulder roll. The bright streak of the barrier dimmed, so she pushed harder. The streak didn't snap, but it frayed like twine. She moved to the next boulder, and instead of pushing, she pulled, drawing the land closer to her, yanking the boulder onto its side. Better still, it hit a natural slope and started rolling. She tugged and tugged while the streak frayed further, until the distance between the two giant stones was enough that the streak snapped and went dark.

The air crackled with energy as the magic lost focus, its binding broken, and the wind suddenly gushed in all directions at once. It hammered Jae until she fell flat onto her stomach, swallowing another mouthful of sand, bleeding where the wind and sand tore her skin open.

Jae ignored the pain and reached for the newly freed energy. Gathering the air's magical forces didn't come as easily as earth's. The energy prickled, jangling her until she had to clench her jaw to keep her teeth from rattling. But once she was immersed in it, she could feel its natural flow, and she sent it careening back to the way it flowed naturally, only diverting a tiny bit. That, she wrapped around the three of them, circling and catching the sand until they were in the middle of a whorl, sand and wind like a wall around them, but dawn in the sky above.

Panting hard, she looked up and found Elan half buried, trying to pull himself free. Tal had fared a little better—he was crawling toward them. The camel was nowhere to be seen. She pointed at Elan, didn't even have the energy to speak, but Tal understood and moved toward him instead.

While Tal struggled to dig Elan out, Jae reached for the water skin on her belt, swallowed everything that was in it, and then began her own slow crawl toward Elan. She didn't have the energy to help, though. Instead she just lay on the hot sand, head swimming as she kept the protective wind whipping around them, and waited for the larger sandstorm to die down.

She must have fallen asleep, because she woke to find Tal curled against her side, Elan sprawled less than an arm's length away. The wind still circled them sluggishly, but the sky was bright overhead. The storm had passed. She released her grip on the wind, and fell back to sleep, exhaustion claiming her.

She woke again, this time, if not refreshed, then at least no longer too exhausted to keep her eyes open. The night sky was dark now, and their campsite—if it could be called that—was even darker. Looking around, Jae almost laughed as she realized why. Her winds had been effective, and while they'd been safe from the storm, sand had piled up around them, high enough to block out the sun earlier and the moon now. The three of them were at the bottom of a cone made of sand, steep slopes all around them.

Tal and Elan were both nearby, their gear strewn around. Elan had his knees folded up to his chest, his arms wrapped around them. Tal was kneeling by their gear, stacking it, lips pressed shut in a grim line.

"Good morning," Jae murmured.

They both looked up. "I was starting to worry about you," Tal said. "We tried to wake you, but you barely stirred."

"Using that much magic is exhausting," Jae said.

"What—" Elan stopped. "I'd like to know what that was."

"A barrier," Jae said. "I think it must have been crafted during the War—and definitely by the Highest mages, because the magic felt just like the Curse. It must have been meant to keep the Closest away from the Well."

Elan nodded slowly. "If the Highest couldn't control the Well, then . . . they must have hoped that barrier would keep the Closest from controlling it, too. Maybe the Highest even hoped that it would force the Closest to give up control."

"But they didn't," Jae said. "They decided they'd rather die, and . . . I had a vision. They *did* die. Taesann somehow took all their magic and pushed it into the fountain to hide it, and he knew Aredann would kill him once he was defenseless." She shuddered. She remembered that as if she'd *felt* it, as if Taesann's memory was her own. Now she was the only one who remembered what had really happened, that he was not the traitor the Highest claimed he was.

"So if the Highest built a barrier to keep Closest out . . ." Tal tapped his fingers against his water skin as he thought it through. "Then I ran into it, and that's what started the storm. And when Lord Savann was caught out in the desert . . ."

"He must have had a Closest in his party," Jae agreed.

"But now the barrier is gone," Elan said, an almost-question as his voice quirked up. He cleared his throat.

"Yes," Jae agreed. "And thankfully, we're still alive."

"For the moment," Elan said.

Jae frowned. He was still slumped over, defeated, and when Jae looked at Tal, he wouldn't meet her gaze. Something else had happened while she'd been unconscious. "Please tell me what's going on."

"Our supplies," Tal explained. "The camel's gone—I lost it during the storm, which means we've lost the water and the tent and everything else. All we have left is what we were carrying. And that won't last long, no more than a day. So unless we're very close to the Well . . ."

Jae held up a finger, motioning for him to be quiet, and sank back into other-vision. Now that the barrier was gone, the desert's energy had returned to normal, the magic floating around them with no snarls. She soared, searching, until she found a bright speck on the horizon. Followed it, and—

The Well was enormous, glistening with energy and life, but it was dwarfed by something behind it. When Jae looked, she saw . . . mountains. They were like nothing she'd ever seen before: enormous peaks that blotted out the sky, infused with strange, dark magic. Something more powerful than she could imagine had created them, something powerful and *twisted*. They were wrong in a way she hadn't ever felt before, something not even the Curse's cruelty could compare to.

Shuddering, she slipped away, back to her own body. "I can find it now, but there's something else. . . ." She shook her head. The mountains didn't matter. She didn't want to go near them, but the Well sat near their base, so they had no choice. They had to reach the Well—not just to save Aredann, but also to save themselves from the desert. "Another two days, maybe three."

"Then unless you can find our supplies, we're in trouble," Tal said.

Jae barely had to glance in other-vision to find the camel. There was so little life in the desert that it stood out in sharp relief, bright and shining, remarkably still alive, and heading back to Aredann on its own. It was making good time, though it wasn't fast enough that they couldn't have caught it—but there was no reason to. There was no glow of water attached to its back. The jugs must have come loose and shattered somewhere in the storm.

"We're in trouble," Jae confirmed.

"We could head back, get more supplies," Elan said hesitantly, then shook his head. "No, never mind. If we tried, my father . . . It's too far, anyway."

"Then we should go," Tal said. "There's no point in putting it off. We'll ration the water, get as far as we can. . . . We can make it. We have no choice."

Jae nodded grimly and helped him gather what remained of their things. Everything was so much lighter now. It would be easier to move, but wandering through the desert with no reprieve . . .

It was like Tal had said: they had no choice.

Crawling up the sand wall Jae had accidentally built was no easy task, but they made it out and back to the desert floor.

There was no sign that they'd passed this way before, no sign that anyone had, ever. Nothing but endless sand in front of them, and silver-specked black overhead.

Any sense of renewed energy Jae had felt evaporated with her sweat. The desert itself was cold at night, but the travel robes were heavy, and marching forward kept the three of them from cooling down. Jae kept moving because she had no choice, the cursed boots weighing her feet down with every step, but staying still was worse. She couldn't stop picturing their bodies, lost forever in the desert. The wind and sand would beat against them. Their bones would be bleached white by the sun, then lie buried in the sand forever, or dry entirely and turn to dust.

"I can't," Tal finally panted as the sun came up. "We have to stop. I can't . . ."

Stopping was almost as frightening as continuing, especially when Tal opened his water skin with shaky hands. He drank for a moment, no more than a few swallows, and passed it on. She did the same, and Elan finished what little water it held. Now they were down to just the satchel. Meant for one person, to last one day, now it would have to serve all three of them for at least another day, if not more.

It wouldn't last. They wouldn't make it.

Their tent was gone, and the desert was an endless expanse of dunes. They settled at the base of one slope, which at least would be shadowed during the worst of the sun, and huddled together. Jae shut her eyes and in other-vision tried to imagine a solid stone behind them and hanging over them, providing shelter. She could feel the energy of the earth building and building around her, and released it slowly.

There was a scraping, rumbling sound, and solid stone appeared, growing out of the sand around them, giving them shade and shelter. She smiled, exhausted but pleased, and found Tal and Elan staring at her.

"That . . . that's really something," Elan murmured, pressing a hand to the smooth stone.

It wasn't exactly comfortable to sleep in the small shelter. It was still too hot, with only the hard rock floor beneath them, and there was no water. As the sun rose, it spilled in far enough that Jae had to hide her face in the crook of her elbow to avoid it, but the shelter she'd built was still better than nothing.

When the sun finally sank, they resumed their walk. The moon was high and bright by the time Tal said, "Maybe . . . maybe we should stop. I'm so tired, Jae."

Jae frowned, then reached for him, pushed his robe aside, and pressed a hand to his neck. It burned against her skin, but there was no dampness there, no sign of sweat. Which meant he didn't have enough water in him *to* sweat, which meant sunsickness—even at night, from heat and exhaustion alone. She shook her head. "Drink now, just a little. We'll have more before we camp in the morning."

So they did, and then went back to walking. When the sun finally started to come up, they found another dune and drank, then lay down, all three pressed together. Jae reached for the energy of the earth again, but she was so tired that she was dizzy, and she couldn't quite force it to take shape around them. The ground rumbled, but nothing else happened, and she sagged in place, shaking her head. Too tired to do magic, but still not quite able to sleep through the worst of the sun.

Jae started them walking before dusk, squinting at the horizon. By midnight, Tal was dazed, stumbling and staring aimlessly around them. He fell to his knees and dry heaved. "Drink something," Jae urged him, but he shook his head.

"Later," he promised. "When we rest."

After that, Jae kept their hands linked together, pulling Tal along with her. Otherwise, he trailed behind, his gaze vacant.

They gave in and drank at dawn, but this time, they didn't stop walking. Jae tore a strip from her ragged travel robe and tied it loosely over her eyes. Once she'd blinked the sand out of them, not even able to form real tears to wash the sand away, it wasn't bad. She couldn't see much, but there wasn't much *to* see, and the strip of fabric helped keep the glare of the sun from hurting her eyes.

Elan held his hand out to Jae to help guide her, and she pulled Tal with them. Her stomach churned with guilt, bile burning at her throat, because she knew the sun would just make Tal worse. She wanted to rest, to wait, but the Well was somewhere ahead, and their supplies wouldn't last. The Well was their only hope. Moving was hard, but they had to reach the Well. They *had* to.

Jae focused on the magic in the distance to make sure they were heading in the right direction. Tal vomited and was too dazed to resist when she handed him the water skin. Elan was starting to stumble now, too, and worse, to mumble to himself. She could only make out a little of his quiet rambling, but it sounded as if he didn't really understand where he was anymore, as he said something about his sister, Erra.

Later, as the sun set the sky on fire with late afternoon orange, Elan all but yelled, "I don't doubt you. I only . . . If there's another way, shouldn't we . . . But I *don't* doubt you!"

It was a conversation he'd already had, Jae realized. Something he'd said to his father, trying to convince himself as much as anyone else that he believed what he was told. But he didn't, not anymore. Or else he wouldn't be here, now. Maybe none of them would.

"Jae," Elan said abruptly, loudly.

She stumbled to a halt, and he turned around to look at her. He frowned.

"Jae?"

"I'm here," she said. "Tal and I both are."

"I don't know where we . . . Where are we? What happened to Shirrad?"

He sounded so confused that she couldn't even resent the question. "We left her behind—"

"She's so strange." He began wandering again. "So backward. I feel bad for her. My father will never understand Aredann. The people there are too odd. Even the Closest."

"Elan," she tried again.

"*You* are odd," he told her. "You're strange, and strong. I've never seen anyone so strong."

She tried to swallow, but her throat was too dry. He wasn't really talking to her anyway. He was talking to someone else, far away.

"I think there's magic at Aredann," he said. "It sounds mad, but there must be."

He repeated it over and over, and eventually Jae didn't even hear it anymore.

It was well after dark when Jae finally paused to rest. She'd taken the water skin from Tal, just to be safe, and there was barely anything sloshing inside it now. All she wanted was to lie down and sleep, but she didn't dare. She could *feel* how close the Well was. If they stopped, they might never manage to move again, but if they just kept going . . .

She pressed the skin into Elan's hands, guilt flaring up when she had to tear it away after a moment to give it to Tal, and again when she took it from him. She finished the few precious mouthfuls left in it.

"We have to keep going," she said out loud, even though neither Elan nor Tal was really listening to her. Forcing herself to start walking again was hard, and dragging the others forward, step after weary step, was harder. But this was their final push. Either they would make it to the Well or they would collapse.

The magic felt closer and closer, and the very air around them seemed different. Heavier. Thicker. She'd almost never felt air like that before, but something deep inside her *remembered*. She couldn't truly call the air damp, but the air was no longer so dry that it ached to inhale, and there were bushes around them now, clawing their way up through the sand and rocks.

"We're close," she said, stumbling, then dragging herself back to her feet. "We have to be close. We have to be."

It was Tal who finally fell and couldn't climb back up. Jae reached for him, tried to drag him to his feet, but he just shook his head and wouldn't move. She knelt on the ground next to him, shoulders shaking even though she didn't have enough left in her to cry. She felt far too brittle, her body ready to give out, her limbs like clay dried too fast.

But they had to keep moving, or they'd die here. So close to the Well.

Looking at Tal, thinking of him lost in the desert forever, drove her back to her feet. It took all her strength to haul him up, get him moving again. Tal had risked everything for her— Tal and Elan both—and she couldn't stop now. She *couldn't*.

We have to be close, we have to be. . . . Her steps echoed with the mantra, repeating over and over in her mind even when she could no longer speak.

Dawn found them. Jae wanted to sob, to curl up and let the heat take her and turn her to dust, but the magic was so near now. She didn't even need other-vision to feel it; she just had to look around. She just had to keep moving, to keep dragging Tal and Elan, and hoping.

She fell again, and this time she couldn't get up. She only managed to rise to her knees, to crawl forward—

The world fell open in front of her, revealing the edge of a cliff. And beneath it, down at its base, sheltered by cliffs as far as she could see, was the glittering blue jewel of the Well.

Chapter 20

SOMETHING IN THE THREE OF THEM CHANGED WITH THE SIGHT OF the Well. Jae could sense it in the way Elan went quiet, the way Tal went still. All of them just stared.

She had never seen so much water. The only scale she had to judge by was Aredann's reservoir. If that was a brick, then this was a wall, dozens of bricks high and hundreds of bricks long. She couldn't even see across it as she scanned the horizon and tried to follow its shore with her eyes. If there were mountains on the far side, she couldn't see them from here.

But she *could* see that there was a problem. The deep, glittering blue of the water nearest them, at the base of the cliff, met the pale shoreline almost cleanly, but farther away Jae could see shore that had turned to gray, chalkier tones. It was mud that should have been underwater but wasn't. Judging from just how much dried mud she could spot, the problem wasn't just that reservoirs at small, outlying estates were going dry. The Well itself was shrinking. There used to be much, much more water here, and something had happened to it.

Which meant it wasn't just Aredann and other estates like it that were in danger. It had nothing to do with population. Water was missing, and if this kept up and the Well continued to shrink the way Jae thought it would, eventually the central cities and *their* reservoirs would be dry, too.

"We can reach it," Elan said. "There has to be a way down."

"I'll find one," Jae said. She looked over at Elan, saw that his hair was now too long and tangled, and that he had the beginnings of a beard on his jaw. His gaze was fixed on the Well in front of them, and his voice was more alert than when he'd rambled to himself. Then she looked over at Tal and said, "I can barely believe it."

"Me either," Tal answered, soft and honest, and coherent. It was the first time he'd spoken in a day. They still needed water badly, but the sight of the Well had brought them back from the brink, at least for a moment.

She kept her grip on Tal's hand as she slid into other-vision. Using magic ached like her sore muscles, but after a moment she was able to look around.

The Well dominated everything, though she could still sense the mountains at the far shore, out of sight. Once she got a feel for the Well's magic, separating out different kinds of energy was easy enough. She let the Well's power draw her vision to bright points, important places—

A spot along the top of the cliff, far off to their right, glowed brightly, though distantly. It was tied to the Well, but not the same magic. Built by the same people, drawing slightly from the Well's power, the magic created . . .

The image struck her hard, and her mouth watered. It was magic that grew *food*. The mages who'd crafted the Well had spent weeks out here, maybe months. They'd needed to eat, so they'd made it easy for themselves. Jae fixed her mind on the place—an hour's march around the top of the cliff. Before they'd spotted the Well, she wouldn't have thought they could make it another hour. Now, more alert and motivated, they just might.

"Follow me," she said, tugging Tal with her as she made her body start moving. Elan followed them, looking over at the Well every few seconds as he walked.

Euphoria at the Well's existence could only last so long, and they had been marching with no supplies for two days. Jae sagged as she moved, staring down at her feet, trudging forward by sheer force of will.

Soon they could see it: an ancient, overgrown forest that had once been an orchard. Enormous trees had been grown by magic and fed by the Well, and every one had ripe fruit hanging from its branches. Gnarled, wild bushes grew thick between them, but Jae recognized those, too, once she saw them up close. The roots were edible—with water and a fire, they'd taste delicious. But the fruit was easier to grab and eat.

Elan, taller than she was, plucked several and handed them to her and Tal. They had thick skins that she needed her jagged, broken nails to tear through, and then scent exploded into the air. Fresh and wet and like nothing she'd ever smelled before, and when she brought the first section to her mouth, she couldn't help moaning. The fruit soothed her parched throat and grumbling stomach. She ate a second and a third before she felt even a little bit sated, and then felt sick—it was too much too quickly. She was still hungry and thirsty, her stomach unsure what to do with the food she'd eaten, but at least she no longer felt so desperate.

After they finished their frenzied meal, Jae couldn't bear the thought of getting up again. Instead they rested, sheltered from the sun by the thick canopy of trees, waiting for their stomachs to settle.

That evening, after they woke, Tal said, "We made it. We actually found it. Jae, *you* found it. And all this!"

"There used to be all kinds of plants, I think," Jae said. "Enough varieties that the mages didn't need to send for supplies constantly. If those all survived . . . They *should* all have survived. They're magic. And if they truly did, then we could stay out here for a very long time. As long as we wanted."

"We'll have to get water, though," Elan said. "And the Well is so close."

"But it's not going anywhere," Tal said. "Let's just relax for a while. I could sleep for a week."

Jae nodded and settled back down on the ground, in the shade of one of the enormous trees. Even after resting all day, she was still exhausted from the desert, and with food and juice surrounding them, there was no need to push on until they were recovered.

Tal joined her. Elan hesitated, then pulled down a few more of the brightly colored fruits and sat with Jae and Tal. Jae curled up with her head resting on the kind of soft grass she'd never been able to grow at Aredann. For the first time she could remember, she slept—neither unconscious nor afraid, with no duties demanding her attention—until she woke naturally.

When she did finally wake up, feeling refreshed after almost a full day and night of sleep, Elan was still asleep but Tal was up. He was pulling at the roots of the nearest bush as birds sang from deeper in the trees. Jae helped him, and they walked together, picking and shoving their way between the rich variety of trees and bushes. The farther they got, the more different fruit she could spot, and the bushes gave way to lower, weedier plants, with different roots and vegetables. Jae and Tal gathered armfuls, all they could carry, and it didn't matter what they dropped on their way back to Elan. There was so much more—enough to feed all of Aredann and then some, for a whole season. Maybe two. Maybe ten. They hadn't found the other side of the orchard yet.

Breakfast was even better than their previous meal, heartier and with more variety. When Elan finally woke up, he thanked them sheepishly, and they shared plenty of what they'd gathered.

After they ate, Jae used her other-vision again while Tal and Elan packed as much as they could. This time, she didn't need to look far: the mages had wanted their supplies close to where they worked. She suspected they'd camped up here, too, though probably not exactly where her group had collapsed. Either way, the mages had carved a staircase out of the stone. It was close enough that by early afternoon, she, Tal, and Elan made their way down to what had once been the edge of the Well.

It must have been a relatively deep section of the Well, since there wasn't much dried-out shore between the base of the cliff and the water. The mud felt different under her boots than walking across the sand had. Curious, she reached down to touch it, and though it was warm, it wasn't blazing hot like the sand. Jae stripped off her boots at last, exposing her scabbed, blistered feet to the air, and walked barefoot like she always had before. The smooth ground and slight breeze soothed her feet, after days of every step making them worse.

The ground grew tackier with each step, the mud thicker and damp, and that felt even better but didn't compare at all to the feeling as they reached the edge of the water. Jae paused, glancing at the others, then dropped her bags right on the mud and ran, rushing into the gentle waves. She had never in her life felt anything as amazing as this: sun-warm water, pleasant against her skin as it swallowed her. She dropped to her knees and scooped water up to her mouth to drink until she was sated at last, her stomach heavy with it. Then she ducked all the way under, came up for air, and laughed.

"Amazing," Tal breathed when he broke the surface not far away. "This is the best day of my life. It's *amazing.*"

"Clean at last," Elan chimed in, stripping off his water-logged robe. He headed back toward the shore, half walking and half using ungainly, awkward strokes to propel himself forward. He stripped off his shirt and boots and deposited them on the ground. The bandages wrapped around his torso were ragged, caked with sand and blood, and after a second he unwrapped them, revealing an ugly mess on the skin underneath.

Tal was shrugging out of his clothes, too. "It'll be easier

to get the sand out of them like this," he said to Jae. "They're disgusting. Yours, too."

He had a point. Jae ducked under again, and the heavy travel clothes pulled her down. It wasn't dangerous out here, where the water was shallow, but if she drifted any farther . . . It wasn't as if she knew how to swim. Even Elan, who'd probably been allowed to swim in the enormous reservoirs at the central cities, barely seemed to know what he was doing. Best to be safe, then, and it really *was* a relief when she pulled the soggy cloth over her head and off. Then her pants, still out in the shallows, more modest than Tal or Elan, who had already stripped down to his underclothes. It wasn't until she'd tossed them toward shore that she realized that now she would be standing there nearly naked in front of Elan, the son of the Highest—

But Elan had been disowned, the burns on his chest a testament to how much power he'd lost. Jae looked over at him, and found him glancing back at her. Not staring or gaping, just glancing to see where she was. He ducked his head, looking away embarrassedly, and for a moment her heartbeat sped up, blood pulsing with—something. Pride that for once she hadn't looked away first, or hunched down in fear. No, she didn't want him staring at her, but what did it matter? His power was gone, but it was more than that. She had power now, but it wasn't that, either.

Elan had never hurt her, back when she'd been helpless. He'd been disgusted with Rannith and the others. He understood why she'd killed Rannith—he seemed to understand that better than Tal, who'd been shocked and squeamish. She'd thought he was a liar, cruel like the rest of his caste, but he'd listened to her, and eventually believed her, and cared about the truth enough to break his vows. He could have obeyed his father and kept his position, his title, his family. Instead he'd given all of that up, and he'd followed her.

Elan didn't frighten her because she trusted him.

"Look, look," Tal called, and she turned her attention to him. "If you lie on your back, just gently, like . . ." He leaned back in the water and floated for a few moments before he shook a little, flailed to get his balance back, and sank under the surface.

Elan laughed and followed suit more successfully. Jae didn't bother to try, just made her way out a little farther, to where the water was up past her waist, and sank under it. She held her breath, shut her eyes.

The water was gentle around her. Warm, calming, and—

Familiar.

Sinking through the water was strange, the press of it all around her unlike anything she'd experienced before. She couldn't quite feel up or down, and when she unwrapped her arms from her torso, they moved slowly, awkwardly. Even so, the water sang to her, like a melody she'd heard years ago but had forgotten until now. If the barrier had been her element, but infused with alien magic, then this was the opposite. Water wasn't her strongest element, but the magic in it was the same as the magic in the fountain, the magic that made sense to her. It was magic crafted by her ancestors, the original Closest—the Wellspring Bloodlines.

She broke back through the surface and caught her breath, then said, "This is it, the middle of the Well's magic."

Tal looked out at the expanse of water and said, "That makes sense."

"I think I can learn more," Jae said. "I need to go under. I could practically hear it when I was under the surface."

"Anything you can learn will help," Elan said.

Jae thrashed her way out a little farther, until she could barely scrape her feet against the bottom and keep her face above the waves, not quite willing to go deeper. The magic might have been easier to sense if she had, but she'd never been underwater before. Even just ducking under had been disorienting, and the thought of moving past where she could stand made her heart beat a little faster and her chest tighten. This would have to be deep enough.

She could feel Elan and Tal watching her as she stared out at the endless waves, bracing herself. If she was going to help Aredann, she had to know more about the Well, and she'd felt magic when she'd gone under. So she would do it again.

She took a deep breath, then plugged her nose and picked up both of her feet. She curled her knees up to her chest and sank, reaching out with her senses, groping for the Well's magic—for its binding. There had to be one, something to keep the magic working all these generations after it had been crafted.

Power glowed all around her. She reached for it, and pain exploded in her head, shocking and familiar—

The knife's blade glowed dark red, unnatural and angry. Saize dropped it into the fire, and flames consumed it, sparking high in reaction. Then he stood back and waved, and felt the air rush in, too. The whole room vibrated; then everything went white hot as the binding took, sealing the air and fire that made up the Curse to the knife Aredann had so kindly handed the Highest. Saize winced and waited, and the stinging heat passed.

"That's it? The binding is done?"

"Oh, yes." Saize could feel it now, angry tendrils of magic bound to the knife, seeking out blood. Their Curse, settling across the world.

"And you're sure it worked?"

Saize didn't have much patience for questions, even from his allies—but he had no doubt that it had worked. The other Highest mages were waiting outside, though this was hardly a proper room. With open walls and a view of the reservoirs on all sides, it was more of a pavilion. And with no walls to muffle sound, he could hear it when Aredann screamed.

"It definitely worked." Aredann had been their ally, but he was a traitor to his people—he'd killed his own brother. Maybe the other Highest mages trusted him, but Saize never would. And now he'd never have to. Aredann had come from the Wellspring Bloodlines, after all. He'd known what they were doing here, but hadn't realized he'd end up as cursed as the rest of them.

The flames died down, and Saize reached for the knife, already cool enough to touch safely, and regarded its blade. It was ancient, made of a material he'd never seen before. "As long as we have this and our vows, the Curse will be bound forever."

Jae's eyes flew open, and she clawed at the water around her. She was disoriented and all too aware at the same time. She twisted, trying to shove the magic away, force the Curse's pounding out of her mind. The pain receded, but that didn't matter—she couldn't find up, couldn't see anything at all. A scream built in her chest as she tore at the water, her limbs moving slowly despite her chaotic motions.

Light began to shine around her in tiny pinpricks, energy suspended in the water. She could feel the faint presence of the Wellspring Bloodlines and reached for them, but she was too weak and totally lost. She needed to breathe but couldn't, with blood pounding in her ears as she thrashed against the water.

Her feet brushed something. Horribly dizzy, her head throbbing and her eyes unable to make sense of anything through the distortion of the water, she pushed off feebly, barely able to straighten her legs—

She broke through the surface, and a moment later strong hands grabbed her, hauled her toward the shore. She couldn't stop coughing and couldn't resist, so anxious that even having someone else drag her around while she was helpless couldn't make it worse.

It felt as if she'd spat out half the Well by the time she got a deep breath. She was hunched over on her hands and knees, her throat raw and her head spinning. But at least the Curse was fading. After that one burst, it was gone; the ache in her lungs was all from her near drowning.

Elan was the one who'd pulled her in, and he still crouched next to her in the shallows. Tal came to kneel in front of her. He touched her elbow, and when she didn't pull away, he helped her sit up on her knees, and straightening up made it easier to breathe.

"Jae, what happened? Are you all right?" Elan asked, looking ready to catch her if she collapsed again.

She shook her head, drawing away from both of them, grateful the Curse couldn't force her to answer anymore. She just wanted to sit until her chest and throat stopped aching, and she didn't understand what had happened.

It should have been the Well's binding in the water. She'd sensed it there, those tiny pinpricks of energy, but they were almost gone. Instead there had been the Curse, somehow tied to the Well's energy, overwhelming it. But as she thought about that, it made a twisted, horrible sort of sense. The Bloodlines had somehow bound the Well—and the Curse worked its horrible magic on the Bloodlines. Now the two were linked together, the Curse and Bloodlines tangled with one another, and where the Bloodlines' magic should have ruled, the Curse did instead.

Finally Jae found the strength to push to her feet. She staggered to the shore and collapsed onto her back. Sand prickled, sticking to her, sun-heated and uncomfortable, but at least she could breathe.

"Jae," Tal murmured, tentative, not quite a question. He sat near her—not too near, thankfully. Elan hung back even farther, eyeing them unsurely.

"I think I know what happened to the Well," Jae said when she could finally speak again without her lungs hurting. "I don't know *how*, but . . . but the Well's binding is almost gone. The Curse has eaten the whole binding away."

Chapter 21

Jae only had to tell Elan and Tal once that she needed to rest before she could explain more. Neither of them seemed too happy about waiting, but they didn't argue with her. Instead Tal dragged Elan back to the edge of the water and showed him how to begin scrubbing the sand and sweat out of their clothes. They didn't have anything to wash the clothes with, but rubbing layers of fabric against one another would get the worst of the dirt and sweat out.

When they finished, Tal was the one who brought Jae her damp travel robe. She spread the robe over the sand so she could sit on it instead of the damp ground. Tal found an outcropping of rock at the cliff's base, and he and Elan spread the rest of the clothes over it to finish drying.

Finally they filled the canteens and came over to sit with her. Jae gave Tal a grateful look, and he smiled back at her, understanding. Then she glanced over at Elan.

Elan was still wearing only his underclothes. Unlike Tal, who was lithe and wiry the way she was, Elan was larger and broader. Even stripped of his title and family, he still looked powerful and strong. There were whiskers on his chin now, long enough to be a proper beard, if an unkempt one, and his hair fell in loose curls down to his chin. But the scar on his chest was what drew her eye. His skin was already a lighter, more golden brown than hers, but around the scar it was paler still, shiny and pulled tight. The center was still too scabbed for her to make out the design of the brand.

Jae's cheeks heated up, and she looked away from him.

"Can you— It would be nice to talk now," Elan said eventually, catching himself. Of course. He was less used to silence than she and Tal were.

She nodded. "The Well's magic *is* centered there, bound somehow. I could sense the Wellspring Bloodlines—the Closest who crafted the Well. Their magic *is* still there. But so is the Curse, and the Curse has been . . . feeding on the binding. That was what I found instead. The Curse, where the Well's binding should be."

"I don't understand," Elan said.

Jae gestured around. "The Well is going dry, just like Aredann's reservoir, because its binding is eroding, and the binding . . . somehow it's linked to the Curse's binding. So I was looking for the Well's magic, and I saw the Curse's instead. I *saw* it, like I was watching. Some mage, one of the Highest. Saize."

Elan nodded. "Saize Pallara—the grandson of one of the

four mages who originally crafted the Well. Or . . ." He shook his head. "Or that's what I've always been told. He, well . . . he's remembered for casting the Curse."

"He did this to us," Jae said, one hand clenching a fist. Elthis was cruel, vicious—but Jae doubted even his evil could compare to dreaming up the Curse. "I saw him bind it. The Curse is made of fire and air, the magic bound to a knife. But somehow *that* binding is tied to the binding of the Well."

"The Curse makes the Well's binding weaker," Elan said, reasoning it through out loud. "So to restore the Well, we need to restore its binding."

"Yes," Jae said, but Tal shook his head.

"No. Or, not only that. Jae, tell me if I'm wrong, but . . . even if we restore the binding, the Curse will just eat it away again. Fixing the binding would buy time, but to truly restore the Well—to make sure its magic stays bound forever—we need to break the Curse."

Jae nodded, letting Tal's words resonate in her mind. *Break the Curse.* She'd thought it before, when she'd first discovered her magic, before Elan had stopped her experimenting. That had been the goal: to save Aredann, then to break the Curse and free the Closest for good. It had actually seemed possible, just for a couple of days, before Elan had sought to control her. Before Rannith, before Elthis.

But now here she was. Free. She still didn't know much about magic, but the elemental energies were so much easier to use now that she was unfettered by the Curse. With Tal here, safely away from Elthis and his threats, there was nothing to stop her. She *would* break the Curse. She remembered unraveling the barrier in the desert, and she even knew how.

"I saw its binding—that knife," she said. "If we can find it, destroy it, the Curse will break."

Tal's face lit like the sun. "We can really do it. Save Aredann, save the Well, break the Curse."

"But if you do, there will be war," Elan said. "The Highest will never allow it. They'll fight to the last to stop you."

Just like that, Tal sobered. But Jae's resolve was like a stone inside her, cold and unyielding. "Breaking the Curse saves the Well—and we Closest deserve our freedom. If there is war, so be it. I will fight. And I will win."

"It won't do any good to free the Closest if they all get killed," Tal said softly. "Freedom won't help Gali if she's dead."

Jae started to answer that she'd protect Gali, but stopped, falling silent. Because of course she could. She'd protect Tal, Gali, all the Closest at Aredann. But she wouldn't be able to protect *everyone*, the rest of the Closest across the world. Even with magic, she was still only one person, and the Closest would be untrained against the Highest and the Avowed, with their weapons and guards. There would be war, and even if the Closest won, people would die on both sides.

But maybe it was worth it. Before her magic, if she'd had the choice to risk death for a chance at freedom, she would have taken it. She'd have risked anything for that chance, and as terrifying as it was, she thought Gali would, too. Tal was right, the cost of freedom would be high. But that didn't mean it wasn't worth paying.

Besides, without breaking the Curse, the Well would be lost. Maybe not now—if she could find what remained of the binding, she might be able to restore it—but eventually.

The Curse had ruined the binding once, and the same thing would happen again.

"We'll do what we can to be careful," Jae decided. "But we'll do what we have to."

"Not careful," Tal said. "Merciful."

"The Highest have never shown *us* mercy," Jae said.

"I know," Tal said. "And when we have power—when *you* have power, Jae, you'll need to decide what to do with it. What kind of person you want to be. If you want to be like them."

Jae glanced at Elan, who had gone silent and was staring into the distance, across the Well. Not looking at either one of them as they talked about the fate of the people he'd grown up with, his parents and his sister, his friends. The family he'd loved, who'd lied to him, and now that he was disavowed, who would never forgive him or speak to him again.

She looked back at Tal, who was simply waiting for her answer. She thought about their mother, about Gali and Firran, about the generations before them who'd endured and survived. And Rannith and Shirrad, Elthis's disdain, his cruelty and his lies.

She met Tal's eyes and said, "We'll win our freedom first. Then we'll see."

It was late afternoon by the time Jae had discovered the Curse's binding lurking in the Well, and after fighting the Curse and nearly drowning, she was tired enough that she didn't want to try any more magic without resting. In the morning, she'd try again to find and restore the Well's binding—she'd be prepared to be hit with the Curse this time—but one night of sleep wouldn't be the difference between saving Aredann and dooming it.

They had carried food with them from the orchard on the cliff top, so they decided to camp on the shore rather than climb back up. Not that there was much to their camp—they had no sleeping mats, no tent, almost no supplies. But they had flint, and a handful of branches and sticks had been deposited at the cliff base, stripped clean of bark by the water and rocks. They'd dug a pit in the sand and piled in the wood, but so far, none of them had had any luck getting a spark to grow into anything more. The wood was too damp.

Finally, tired though she was, Jae waved Elan and Tal aside and sat in front of the makeshift fire pit. "Let me," she said, sliding into other-vision. Seeing things that way came to her easily now, and it was getting easier the more often she did it.

But sensing and manipulating fire was not. She struck the flint and forced herself to reach for the spark's energy, but it was blindingly hot—and after a moment, it was gone. She couldn't catch and hold it at all.

She struck the flint again, more cautious and aware of what to expect, already bracing herself for the pain. The energy burned once again, but she'd lived with pain every day of her life. She gritted her teeth, braced her mind against the pain, and held on to the energy, clinging desperately to keep it from fizzling out again. But she couldn't call the energy to her like she could with land, and even holding out against the pain, she couldn't direct it like she had with the wind. The fire's energy didn't just burn; it refused to obey her, and a moment later, despite her effort, it was gone again.

So much for that experiment. At least now she knew that

she couldn't use all four elements, though from what Elan had said, few mages could—and being able to use three was better than most. With the night's chill setting in as the sun sank, not being able to light a fire was more frustrating than not being able to use the fourth element. If only the wood wasn't so damp, they wouldn't need magic to light the fire at all.

When she realized what she'd just thought, she almost laughed. She'd done this before, after all, when she'd first experimented with magic. She studied the wood itself in other-vision, finding the traces of energy in it. Like all things, the wood was a mixture of elements and the strange energy of life, left over from before it had fallen off its tree.

She held her hands out over the tinder and pulled. A moment later, water condensed onto her hands, cool against her palms. She kept tugging until the sticks were drained and brittle, then brought her cupped palms to her mouth to drink. The water tasted brighter, somehow, not quite like what they'd drunk from the Well.

"Did you just pull water out of the air?" Tal and Elan were both staring at her—it was Tal who'd asked the question, his voice awed.

She shook her head and wiped her palms on her thighs. "Not quite. I pulled it out of the tinder. And now . . ." She picked the flint back up and struck it. This time, the spark caught. She leaned down and breathed on it, and a minute later, small flames lapped at the sticks they'd piled up.

"Incredible," Elan murmured.

Jae smiled, her cheeks warming a little.

Tal was the one who attempted cooking over the fire, placing fruit and roots on stones tucked up against the flames.

Cooking brought out the flavors and made the food more tender, so as the sun sank, they were able to have another fully satisfying meal.

They took turns keeping the fire burning through the evening, a ring of rocks in place to keep it from getting out of hand as they settled in for the night. Even during the day, the temperature was cooler by the Well than it had been in the open desert, and at night without any bedding, they definitely needed fire for warmth. As the temperature dropped, Jae leaned against Tal, sharing their body heat, while Elan sat against the cliff's base only a few hand spans away.

The stars came out, twinkling to life above them, beautiful and bright in the endless sky. If she hadn't been terrified for Aredann, the night would have been perfect. She'd been able to eat and drink her fill, without worrying about rations or begging for scraps left after others had eaten. There was no shortage of food or water out here, and she'd had time to rest and recover from the ordeal in the desert. She was truly clean for the first time in years, having scrubbed the sand and sweat from her body and her clothes both. Even her hair, which she'd kept cropped as close to her scalp as possible for years, had started to grow out, and she didn't mind.

And there was no fear. Out here, removed from civilization entirely, no one could try to steal her hard-won freedom, and no one could threaten Tal. He was still cursed, but it barely seemed like it, with no one giving him any orders. There was only the three of them, as if no one else existed.

"I think I could stay out here forever," Jae said.

Tal made a quiet noise of assent, and after a moment, Elan said, "I would stay with you."

Jae blinked, and twisted to stare at him. He wasn't looking at her, and the moonlight was bright against his face but threw the rest of him into shadow.

"Interesting choice," Tal said to him.

Elan shrugged a little. "It's not like I have anything to go back to. No one who knew me will ever speak to me again."

"I'm sorry," Tal said.

"I'm not," Elan said. "Not *too* sorry, anyway. I chose . . . I knew what he'd do if I questioned him. And I did it anyway."

"Why?" Jae asked, letting her genuine curiosity win out over good manners. She only knew what it was like to fight for every scrap she had; she couldn't imagine having so much and walking away from it all.

Elan looked back at her. "I thought that was obvious."

She blinked. That answer wasn't exactly helpful. Next to her, Tal chuckled so softly that Jae felt the movement more than anything else. She elbowed him gently.

"Because I believe in you," Elan said. "And . . . and I wanted to help people. Even back at Danardae, when Lady Palma asked me to speak to my father about her estate . . . I knew something wasn't right, and I wanted to help. I thought my fa—His Highest"—Elan stumbled over the title—"*was* helping. It's his sworn duty. But he wasn't. He's a liar and—everything I believed was a lie, and—once I knew the truth, I couldn't ignore it."

Jae had even less of an idea what to say to that, but Tal mused, "No wonder he disavowed you. But I think you're better off without him."

"So do I," Elan said. "I just wish . . . My sister. I won't miss the rest of them, but if my sister knew the truth, she'd do the right thing, too."

"She might already know," Jae said. "She's the heir."

"She doesn't," Elan said, conviction ringing in his voice. "She'd never stand for the lies."

Jae doubted that, but she'd never met Elan's sister, so she didn't say anything. With everything Elan had lost, if he needed to have faith in his sister, she wouldn't fight him on that. Especially not when Tal rolled over next to her and she thought about losing him. She couldn't imagine coping after that. Losing Tal would be like the brand on Elan's skin. A painful wound that might someday scab over but never fully heal, leaving a scar that would last forever.

Elan had given himself that wound by believing Jae, by following her. He'd done what he thought was right, and had lost everything for it.

Jae rolled away from Tal a little bit, tucked her hands under her head, and went back to watching the stars. She didn't look over at Elan again, but she couldn't forget how near he was, either.

Guilt gnawed at her, a feeling oddly like hunger, but she refused to dwell on it. Sighing, she tried to find a comfortable position on the cold, muddy ground.

Tal nudged her, and when she looked at him, he raised his eyebrows in a silent question.

She frowned, answering with a question of her own.

He nodded toward Elan.

She turned away, not wanting to ask what Tal was thinking. Even out here the Curse would force him to answer honestly, and she didn't think she wanted to hear it.

Chapter 22

ELAN STARED DOWN AT THE WELL. FROM UP HERE ON THE CLIFF top he could see for ages into the distance, but he still couldn't make out the far shore. Even if the Well was going dry the way Jae believed, it was incredible. With rays from the morning sun reflecting and dazzling, it was almost too beautiful to look at.

No wonder people had been willing to fight for the Well, to die to possess it. It was beauty and power both, a hypnotic combination. He'd always lived comfortably at Danardae, knowing he'd never want for water, as his family controlled one of the four enormous linked reservoirs. But they were nothing compared to this. Even if, generations ago, the Highest had somehow rightfully controlled those four reservoirs—a fact he now doubted—he could understand why they hadn't been enough. Nothing would be, compared to this.

He shuddered at the thought. Maybe he could understand the urge to seize all of this, but to actually *do* it—to fight a war that had killed thousands, to enslave generations of people to maintain control—was unforgivable. He hated that he could understand the urge. He hated that understanding made him even a little bit like those liars—those *traitors*—and like his father.

"I think I could watch the water for the rest of my life and never grow tired of it," Tal said.

"I imagine sunset will be a spectacle," Elan agreed. Even dawn, creeping up from the cliffs behind them, had been gorgeous. Watching the sun kiss the water when it dropped below the horizon . . . that would be a kind of magic all its own. Elan had been too exhausted to think to watch last night; he would be sure to tonight.

They'd eaten after dawn, and Jae had decided to try to find the Well's binding again—but from the shore this time. The magic wouldn't be as easy to locate if she wasn't immersed in it, but at least she wouldn't be in danger of drowning. It was Tal who'd suggested that he and Elan hike back to the top of the cliff and explore the orchard while she worked. They could gather more food and see if there was anything else worth finding. If the people Jae called the Wellspring Bloodlines had really stayed up there for so long that they'd grown a whole orchard to feed themselves, they probably hadn't camped the whole time. Maybe there was some kind of shelter left, the remains of a building the three of them could use instead of sleeping under the stars or beneath the branches.

Exploring the orchard required turning away from the stunning sight of the Well. Elan willed himself to do it. Tal joined him, and they made their way from the cliff and into the trees.

"I've never seen anything like this, either," Elan said as they walked. "Even in our finest groves, the trees have to be kept small. But these look like they've been growing since the Well was founded."

Tal reached up to pluck a fruit from one of the trees as they passed, and clawed the rind off. "Well, if Jae's right, they have been," Tal said. "The way she described it, it sounded like they live at least as much on magic as they do on water and sunlight."

"They'd have to. Not much light down here," Elan pointed out. The underbrush was just as enormously overgrown as the trees were. Bushes came up to his waist, and he had to stop and push past them more often than branches from the fruit trees. Most of the trees were so huge that their branches were higher up, the lowest just within reach, and their trunks were so wide that Elan couldn't wrap his arms around them.

"I hope Jae will have a chance to come explore up here," Tal mused. He popped a section of the fruit into his mouth. "She's always been good with plants. She loves the garden at home. I know it doesn't look like much, but it would be nothing at all without her."

Elan nodded a little. He'd grown up with Danardae's splendid gardens, all carefully tended, bright and colorful and controlled. Aredann's had been dismal by comparison. Not just lacking in plant life, but tiny. But after having spent time at Aredann, Elan understood just how hard Jae must have worked to keep the garden alive at all.

"It's good she was placed as the groundskeeper, then," Elan said.

"It was no coincidence," Tal said. "She was good at it—even when she was young. When there was a Twill grounds-keeper, she assisted him. When he left . . . It wasn't long after Lord Savann died in the desert. Lady Shirrad was inconsolable, but she confided in me often enough—it's not as if I could tell anyone her secrets. I managed to convince her that Jae would be best suited to working the grounds."

Elan shook his head in wonder. Shirrad must have been terrified and desperate to confide in one of the Closest at all—to see them as anything more than obedient shadows. Even after his whole world had been upended, Elan still found that strange. The idea of an Avowed guardian conversing with Closest was madness. But Lady Shirrad had, and he could only admire Tal for finding a way to use it to his advantage.

"If you hadn't been born a Closest, I wonder what you'd be," Elan mused. "I think you'd have been *very* successful if you were Avowed. You know, all of this—everything—it would have gone very differently if you'd discovered that magic instead of Jae. I think I'd have had a much easier time reasoning with you."

"Then it's probably for the best it was Jae," Tal said, and though he sounded lighthearted, Elan sensed there was something under that laugh.

"Why's that?" Elan asked. Then, "Sorry, you don't have to—"

But the compulsion had already hit Tal, who gave Elan a dark look as he answered, "It would have been easier for *you* if I'd had Jae's magic. I'd have been reasonable, and I'd have convinced you to be reasonable, too. I would have made sure things were easy for me and Jae and Gali from then on, taken care of them. But I'm not like Jae. I would never have had the courage to kill Rannith—or to attack your father. And we'd never have ended up out here."

"I thought you hated that Jae did all that," Elan said, remembering Tal's comments. He shoved the prickly branches of another bush out of his way. Careful not to ask it as a question, he added, "I thought you wanted her to be merciful."

He held the branches so Tal could follow him. "I do. But you were right—there *will* be war. And I hope she will be merciful, because I think that will make it easier to find a way forward. But I know, I *know*, she will do whatever it takes to free us."

What it might take would be violence. Destruction. Elan shivered in the shade as he edged around one of the enormous trees, only to find that another one had grown so large and so close that there was no room to squeeze between them.

"Then it's lucky she listens to you," Elan said. "If you ask her to have mercy, she will."

"She'll do what she thinks is right," Tal said, but he sounded thoughtful.

Elan kicked his way past a smaller bush, still looking for a gap between the trees. Instead he hit yet another trunk, grown so wide that the two trees were now practically fused into one.

"Odd," Tal said from behind him. "All the trees have been

wide and close, but these are more like a wall than anything else."

"Yeah," Elan said, and then it struck him. "But walls have doors."

"You think . . ." Tal trailed off.

"They were grown by magic. And these are *not* normal trees. They aren't even fruit trees like the others. Look at them," Elan said as he realized it himself. The bark on these trees was smoother, silvery-white instead of brown or red. Their branches were high overhead—much higher than Elan could reach, even by jumping. There were no knots in the trunks, either. Nowhere to grab and climb. A wall of trees like this wouldn't be impenetrable to people with axes, or to fire—but it would be a long, hard job to get through.

The trunk gave way to another, and then another, before he and Tal found it—a gap, not between trunks but carved into one. It was a small arched opening. The shape looked too much like one of the hallway entrances at Aredann or Danardae for it to be natural. Thick, heavy vines grew across and inside it. They seemed to be growing out of the tree trunk itself, like a curtain.

"Looks like you were right," Tal said, and reached for one of the vines. He twisted and tugged, and it broke, but there were dozens left. "This would be faster if we had a knife."

"Or magic," Elan said. If they couldn't get through themselves, they could bring Jae up to try it. But he wasn't ready to give up so quickly. The vines were thick and sturdy, hard to tear but not too hard to move. It took a lot of untangling and pulling, and the vines didn't just block the front of the tree.

They grew all the way through it. He and Tal both worked at yanking and untangling vines until they were sweating, even in the shade of the orchard, until finally they'd pulled open a hole big enough to scurry through, hunched over, with vines still scraping at their faces and limbs.

The sun hit Elan hard the moment he broke through. He tumbled out of the way so Tal could join him, and then looked up. The trees reached like monuments to the sky, but their branches were latticed at the top, forming a patchwork roof that still allowed sunshine through. The space was the size of Lady Shirrad's study at Aredann, and walls had been erected that reached up almost to where the branches began. The walls formed a shape with odd corners, none meeting squarely like a normal room, but they were flat rather than matching the curving of the trees behind them.

And like at any of the mage-built estates, the walls were art.

"Incredible," Tal breathed, walking the perimeter of the room, his fingers brushing the wall. Elan took in the largest of the walls, a long, flat space across from him, and saw that it was a portrait made out of tiny tiles, carefully placed, untouched by dust and unfaded despite the sun. It was a woman, her skin a rich brown, her hair pulled into thick coils and tied into a knot on top of her head. She wore a deep red-and-gold robe and held a knife in one hand and a flower in the other. Her smile was calm and kind—*wise*, Elan thought. The edges of the mural were ringed with familiar vine patterns dotted by bright flowers. Elan traced it with his hand and realized it was the same four circles overlapping at the center that made up the fountain back at Aredann, with the woman placed in the space at the middle.

"It's the same as the fountain," Elan told Tal.

"I don't suppose you recognize that woman," Tal said.

Elan shook his head. "If the Highest didn't craft the Well, then I have no idea who did, but I imagine she was one of them."

Tal nodded thoughtfully, and they both resumed inspecting the beautiful tiled walls. The next largest, across from the woman, was a wall made mostly of tannish-orange tiles, with a handful of bright blue and green circles and a few lines, but again, something familiar tugged at Elan's mind. He studied this picture more carefully, ignored the placement of the green shapes in favor of the blue—

"It's a map!"

Tal stared at him.

"It is," Elan said, calmer this time. He pointed to the familiar cluster of four circles. They were a little messier than the circles of the fountain, but very similar to those and the circles around the woman in the other mosaic. There was a red flower, the only other color on the map, right at the center where the four circles overlapped.

"Those are the reservoirs of the central cities. This one is Danardae," Elan explained. The blue and green splotches ran up against each other, with green almost outlining the four overlapping blue circles. "The blue areas are reservoirs; the green are cities—or at least fields, farmable land."

He knew the shape of the world well enough to recognize other estates, now that he had picked the four central cities and their reservoirs out. He traced a path outward and westward and tapped a finger against another green-blue combination. "This one is Aredann. So this"—he gestured at a much larger blue spot, near the edge of the wall—"must be the Well."

"It's hard to believe we traveled all that way," Tal said, examining the distance. The gap between Aredann and the Well was much wider than between any other blue or green spaces.

Elan traced his route from Danardae out to Aredann, then frowned. He worked his way back and looked at the other cities, found the outlying estates that had been abandoned like Aredann. There were only a few, and they were all also on the outskirts. But there were others, even farther out.

"I've never seen some of these," he said, mentally reciting the names of estates and reservoirs he was sure of, to make certain he was right. But he was. Out beyond even the small, now-abandoned estates, there were others.

"I wonder if this *isn't* the first time estates have been abandoned," Tal said. "There have been droughts before, I think."

It took Elan a moment to realize it was another of his non-questions. "Yes, there've been plenty—but only a few were even close to this bad. The last was four generations ago." He pressed his hand to one of the strange, unknown estates up north. "If the Highest have abandoned estates before, they've made sure they were never mentioned again."

"They'd have had to redraw every map," Tal said. "And forbid people to speak of the lost estates."

Elan could imagine his father doing that. He'd have a lie to explain it—a pretty speech about looking forward instead of back, about leaving the past where it belonged. People would be happy enough to do it, since it would make it easier to forget the Closest who'd been left to die on those abandoned estates.

"They'd have had to destroy every book," Tal added.

"They may have," Elan said. "There's so little writing left from before the War, and what there is, is hard to follow. My sister—that is, Lady Erra—she found some and sent it to Aredann with me, but half of it was indecipherable. I knew the letters, but I swear I've never seen any of those words before."

"Like this, I'd think," Tal said, with a slight lilt in his voice that once again reminded Elan that it was a question. Tal pointed at another wall, one where lines of green text covered yellow tiles. The text wasn't painted on them; it was somehow seared right into the tiles themselves.

Elan had to tilt his head. The text had been written sideways, wrapping from the top to the bottom instead of from side to side, but he could read it well enough. For a moment, he was surprised Tal couldn't—but of course not. Tal was Closest, and none of them knew how to read. Not even all of the Twill did.

Elan cleared his throat and read aloud, *"Here we founded the Well and declared ourselves Wellspring; here our blood was bound together; here we crafted the magic that will protect our descendants. Here our duty to protect our world was sealed with her life. Let us never forget."*

"Well, they've certainly been forgotten," Tal said, wry.

Elan gave a little laugh, even though it wasn't exactly funny.

"There's more," Tal said, and Elan followed him to another wall, but the twisting lines down it were like nothing Elan had ever seen before. He wasn't even sure they were letters. These were white lines against a blue background, still sharp after all these generations, but if they held any secrets, Elan wouldn't be the one to guess them.

"I have no idea," Elan confessed.

"There's more still," Tal said.

This was the last wall he hadn't examined yet. The text here was gold letters over red tiles, and it *did* look like the strange text from the papers and books Elan had examined. He could read most of the individual letters, but they didn't spell out anything at all. It was just nonsense, most of it not even pronounceable. There weren't any vowels, and at the ends of some lines were symbols he'd never seen before. Those looked more like the other wall.

"More history the Highest have stolen from the world," Elan said. He pressed his hand to the wall, as if that would somehow open his mind to its secrets, and the tiles were cool and smooth under his hand.

"Maybe it's magic," Tal said. "Maybe Jae will be able to understand it. This whole place feels important—hidden and protected like this. It must mean something."

"Let's go get Jae," Elan agreed, and he followed as Tal scrambled out. He cast one look back at the vine-covered opening as they left, certain Tal was right. Whatever those other walls said, it was part of the history the Highest had tried so hard to destroy. There had to be a way to figure it out.

❖❖❖

Jae sat alone in front of the Well, legs crossed, back straight. She opened her mind to other-vision and plunged her senses into the Well. She could feel the magic, suspended in the glistening energy of the water, and when the Curse closed in around her, she braced herself and pushed it away.

It was easier from here on the shore, where she could work and breathe at the same time, concentrate on making the energy do what she wanted. But she was also farther removed, which made it harder to find the faint traces of the Bloodlines' magic that were mostly overwhelmed by the Curse.

She sweated in the sunlight as she worked, carefully sifting through the energies. Separating out Curse from water, cringing from the Curse's painful touch, and then finding the tiny glowing pinpricks that remained of the binding crafted by the Wellspring Bloodlines.

She gathered the glowing specks together, reached out with her mind to get a feel for them, and sensed not only the familiar, easy presence of what she knew was magic crafted by her own ancestors—it felt the same as the fountain had—but also, oddly, the steady and solid feeling of earth.

Curious, she tugged a little on the earth energy around her. Yes, the Well's binding definitely called on that, too. Earth and water and magic, all bound together by the Bloodlines—

There was a reason they'd called themselves that. Certainty hit her, but she looked within herself anyway. The mages who'd crafted the Well hadn't just meant that their bloodlines would be their families, their descendants through the generations. They'd meant bloodlines more literally— their *blood*. Which would be passed down from parent to child. Blood wasn't as solid as the rocks that had bound the barrier in the desert, but would do the trick—and as long as the Wellspring mages' descendants lived, the binding would hold, and the magic would continue to work.

But the Curse placed on the mages' descendants had somehow supplanted the binding, weakening the magic. The more Closest who died, the weaker the magic would get, until it was gone entirely, leaving the Well dry and the world in chaos.

Jae reached out for the remnants of the binding, and could sense, very faintly, the presence of the Closest within them. The binding hadn't yet eroded entirely—there was still hope for it. She just had to reenergize it, figure out how it had lost its connection to the thousands of Closest who still lived, and rebuild that connection.

She reached out with her mind, remembering the feeling she'd had when she'd broken the Curse. For a moment, she'd had contact with every Closest in the world. All of the Wellspring Bloodlines, bundled together. She was too far away to reach them now. She could feel herself and Tal, but she had only a vague sense of connection to the others.

That would have to be enough. She touched that connection carefully, not fighting or pulling like when she'd battled the Curse, just bringing the essence of the other Closest toward her. Then she reached for what remained of the Well's binding, pulled that toward herself, too, and tried to mesh the Closest and the binding back together.

For a moment, the lines of energy lit up, tremulous and hesitant. It was working—barely, but the connection was there, joining everything together—

The connection sputtered and faded. Jae grasped desperately for the Closest's essence again, yanking even though the Closest might feel it physically, and pushed them toward the binding again, harder this time. But her effort still wasn't enough. The Well was too vast, needed too much to sustain itself. The Well's magic needed the power of the Bloodlines to keep itself running, but it needed something else, something even more vast, to *build* that binding.

Jae opened her eyes to find sunlight dazzling across the surface of the Well. Everything was calm, unchanged, beautiful, and peaceful. Something faint pulled on her mind, something from the vision she'd had of Janna and her son, but she couldn't figure out what it was. So she sat back and enjoyed the soothing mud on her scabbed feet, the cool breeze against her face.

They'd come this far. She was just missing one last piece. Then she'd be able to restore the Well and save Aredann—and return to the world, and find a way to break the Curse.

Chapter 23

Jae stared in awe at the mosaic portrait of the woman. "That's her. Her name is Janna, and she was the one who first conceived of the Well."

Tal and Elan had been sweaty and tired from hiking back down to the Well, but after a quick lunch had insisted on climbing back to the cliff top to show Jae this strange little room. Its mosaic wall was an incredible likeness of the woman Jae had seen in her vision, Taesann and Aredann's grandmother. In other-vision, the mosaic, the map, and the whole room still had faint traces of magic clinging to them. The room had been built and decorated by mages, and sustained by magic through the years. There must have been a binding somewhere.

Jae didn't think the room had been a shelter. It was too small to have housed the number of mages who had made up the Wellspring Bloodlines. Instead, staring up at the magic-crafted picture of Janna, Jae was sure the room was a memorial.

"We hoped you'd be able to read the inscriptions," Elan said, and pointed at one of the small walls that was covered in spidery, twisting lines.

"I can't read anything," she reminded him, and glanced at Tal.

"We were hoping you could with magic," Tal explained. "Elan read that one." He pointed. "But the other two . . . they aren't the same, are they? I can see that. But I don't know what they say."

She examined the lettered walls in other-vision. Like everything else, they glowed faintly with magic. But that was all; the magic didn't resolve into anything she could understand. Nothing spoke to her, nothing explained itself. She shook her head. "I'd like to know what that one says, though."

Elan read it to her: "*Here we founded the Well and declared ourselves Wellspring; here our blood was bound together; here we crafted the magic that will protect our descendants. Here our duty to protect our world was sealed with her life. Let us never forget.*" Then he raised his eyebrows. "Does that mean anything to you? That is—I'd like to know if that means anything to you."

"Some of it," she murmured, and gazed again at Janna's likeness. "They bound their blood together—that's the binding of the Well, the magic that is supposed to make it work forever. And her life . . ." It tugged on her mind again, the very first magical vision she'd had. Janna had crafted the fountain—so her children and grandchildren would remember her. "I think she must have passed away during the crafting of the Well."

But that wasn't quite right. Janna had built the fountain because she'd *known* she'd need to leave a legacy behind—she'd known she was going to die.

"There's the map, too," Tal said. "Elan and I think maybe the Highest have abandoned other estates before. But that would only make sense if doing it actually helps the droughts—or if they're trying to hide something."

"Maybe both," Jae said, thinking it through. "From what I can tell, the Well will send water to any of the reservoirs where there are enough people—particularly descendants of the Wellspring Bloodlines. So it makes sense that if a reservoir was entirely abandoned, the Well would send its water elsewhere. That would certainly make it *look* like the Highest have control."

"But if they just leave the Closest there, then the Well would keep sending them water," Elan said. "So . . . maybe the Closest still live at those estates."

"Or maybe the Highest have them killed when everyone else leaves," Jae said.

Tal looked stricken, horrified. "We thought we'd be left to die but that we'd have some time. You truly think . . ."

"It would be the only way to ensure those reservoirs go dry," Jae said, grim. It shouldn't have made any difference. The Closest would die either way, whether they were abandoned to sunsickness or killed in cold blood. But somehow this outright killing felt more brutal, even more cruel.

"But Aredann . . . His Highest still ordered it to be abandoned," Tal said. "If he gives that order . . ."

"I warned him," Jae said.

"But he might still . . ." Tal trailed off.

Jae knew he was thinking about Gali and the others. They might restore the Well but get back to Aredann and find it was too late. She bowed her head. "If he has hurt them, I'll make him pay for it. I warned him I would."

She expected Tal to rebuke her, but he stayed silent.

"Besides, if he harmed them, he's sealed his own fate," she continued. "Because each time a section of the Bloodlines has been killed, the Well's binding has weakened. The fewer Closest there are, the less blood there is to bind the magic. Abandoning estates may help the Highest look like they have power over the Well, but sooner or later too many Bloodlines will be lost. The binding will break entirely. There's barely any of it left now—Aredann may well be the last grain of sand on the pile."

"Only if he really . . . really killed them," Elan said. "His Highest knows what you can do—he's not foolish enough to ignore your threat."

"Maybe," Jae agreed. She had no idea if Elthis would harm the Closest at Aredann or not. If he had, it was too late to help them at all, but if he'd simply taken his Avowed and left the Closest at Aredann, then the Closest needed the Well's binding restored immediately. It would give them the water they needed to survive on their own, until Jae could break the Curse and free them.

"For now, let's . . . let's assume they're alive," Tal said. "And help them."

Jae nodded her assent. "I just need to find a way to restore the binding. It must be possible. It *must* be."

Again she looked up at the mosaic of Janna. Janna, who had known she was going to die, who'd crafted the Well and then a fountain to preserve her legacy. Jae reached out, placed her hand against Janna's on the wall, and reached for the magic that had created and preserved this strange little room.

She opened her mind to it, searched for the binding, and found it in the roots of the massive trees themselves. She tugged at it with her mental fingers, pulling and coaxing, until the world went white—

They were gathered near the edge of the cliff, a semicircle of two dozen mages. The air was already thick around them, like inhaling soup, but it still crackled. That was what came of bringing so many mages together, having them all hold their magic carefully, keeping it at the ready. If they'd done everything right, the clouds would burst with torrential rain the moment the binding was sealed, and over the next few weeks, rain would fill the basin below entirely. There was some water in the basin already—they'd built it on top of a natural oasis—but there would be so much more, and the magic would make sure the water would last forever.

Tandan's mother stood nearest to the edge of the cliff, her back to the Well she'd spent so many years preparing and crafting. It was the largest work of magic ever—well, no. Tandan cast a look past his mother and toward what would be the distant shore of the Well. The mountains back there had been the biggest work of magic in history, and the biggest mistake. But the Well his mother had masterminded wouldn't be like that. It would protect and heal, not destroy, and it would keep their land safe forever.

"It's time," she said, taking out her knife. The knife was ceremonial, passed down through the mages in her family since before they had come to this land, imbued with power from everyone who'd used it.

Tandan winced as she drew the blade from her wrist almost up to her elbow. The magic around them soared, sensing the binding she'd already built into her blood. Now she only had to share that blood with the others, to bind all the mages' bloodlines together, and then to bind those joined bloodlines to the Well. It was a complicated plan, with layers upon layers of magic worked in, but in a few minutes, it would all be done.

The mage who stood next to her stepped forward. Janna handed him the knife, and he mimicked her gesture, cutting his arm. Not as deeply, but enough to bleed. They pressed their arms together, blood to blood, and the mage kissed Tandan's mother's cheek and murmured a soft goodbye.

She only smiled at him, serene despite any pain from the cut, and passed the knife to the next mage. They took it one after another, cutting themselves and sharing their blood, linking their families' bloodlines together. Finally she offered the knife to Tandan himself.

She didn't need to. They already carried the same blood, just like his children did, and their children would. But he'd helped craft the Well, too, and contributing to the binding was an honor.

Clouds roiled overhead as he sliced his arm. It did hurt,

but that pain was nothing next to the enormity of what they'd done—and the loss he still wasn't entirely prepared for.

His sorrow must have shown on his face, because his mother said, "No, none of that. No crying."

He wiped at his cheeks. The air was so thick and hot that it was hard to tell water from sweat from tears.

"This is no time to be sad; it's a time to celebrate," she continued, loud enough for all the gathered mages to hear. "Look at what we've built. Our families will live safely forever. That is what we've done here. And I will give myself to the Well gladly to make sure that happens."

Tandan nodded, finally letting her go, and she pressed the knife into his hand. "You should keep this. Pass it down to one of the twins."

"I will," he promised, and slid it into his belt. Then he stepped back, her gaze still on him.

She smiled one last time and said, "I love you." Then she looked up at all of them, casting a last glance at every mage she'd brought together to help her. The Well with its linked reservoirs and aqueducts was too enormous an undertaking for any one or two mages to craft alone, so she'd built this alliance, ignored the mages who'd thought it was foolish or dangerous, and simply done what needed to be done.

As she would now. But this last part she had to do alone.

"Thank you," she said, and raised the hand above her bloody arm in something that was part wave, part salute.

She turned and looked down at where the wind hammered waves up against the cliff. Then she threw herself forward in an inelegant dive. Tandan held his breath, the magic around them surged and crackled, and then—

It started to rain.

The binding was complete. The Well had been sealed, his mother's life providing the energy the binding needed, linking the Well to the Bloodlines forevermore.

Jae startled out of the vision and stumbled back several steps, colliding with Tal. He jumped to catch her, even as she turned to face him.

"I know how they did it," she said, her voice scratchy. "I know how to restore the binding, but . . ."

She shook her head, choked. She would do it. She *had* to do it. She could still save the Closest at Aredann—if they even still lived. She could buy the time they'd need to find and destroy the knife that bound the Curse. Tal wouldn't be able to do that, she doubted any Closest could, but Elan might be able to. She had to hope he could.

She turned to stare at him, and he stepped back, startled. "Jae, I don't understand. What—" He cleared his throat. "I don't understand what just happened, why you look so . . . wild."

"The only way to restore the Well's binding is a sacrifice," she said. "If we're going save Aredann before the Well goes dry, then I . . . I need to give my life to the Well."

❊❊❊

Elan stared at Jae in horror. He barely had time to understand what she said before she was continuing, "It should be easy enough for you to get back to Aredann. When the binding is restored, it will rain. I'm sure of it. You'll be all right in the desert this time. Just walk toward the sunrise each morning."

"Jae—" Tal started, but she ignored him.

"You'll have to find the knife," she said to Elan. "Tal can stay at Aredann—he'll be safe there, once there's water. But the moment he's around other people, it'll be too obvious he's cursed, so you'll have to do that. I don't know where the knife is, but"—she pointed at the mosaic—"it's that one, there. The Highest have it somewhere, and you *must* find it, and destroy it. Break it, melt it down—any way you can—"

"Jae!" Tal shouted.

She finally stopped at stared at him. "It's the only way."

"Are you sure?" Elan asked, then looked away guiltily. Of course it was the only way. She wouldn't be talking like this if it wasn't. She was the one who understood magic, who'd tried to restore the binding already. Whatever she'd discovered in the magic behind the mosaic must have convinced her.

But he wasn't sure he could do what she was asking. He'd try—he'd search for the knife—but he had no idea where to start, or whether he'd even be able to destroy the knife if he *did* find it. It sounded like the knife was magic, too, and he was no mage. Only Jae was. Without her, the idea of breaking the Curse seemed impossible. And Jae giving her life after all this just wasn't *fair*.

But she finally answered him. "Yes. It requires a life."

A life. Hers. Unless . . . He felt like he had when he'd spotted the sandstorm on the horizon. The dread was sudden, the danger definite. But instead of running, he had to face it. "What I mean is, forgive the question, but does it have to be *you*? Your life?"

Jae was quiet for a long moment, and Elan knew the answer before she even spoke. "It doesn't *have* to be, but—"

"Then I'll do it," he said.

Jae and Tal both stared at him, and the words he'd just spoken echoed in his own ears. He'd said it without thinking, but it resonated inside him, felt *right*. He'd lost everything. His status, his position. His family—maybe, *maybe* Erra would help him, but their father would forbid it if he found out. And more than all of that, he'd lost his faith.

Before he'd come to Aredann, his family's history had been as sure as the sun in the sky. He'd believed their every move had been driven by necessity, had been justified because they protected the world from chaos and the desert both. The Highest families had kept the peace, and when they'd been cruel, it had been because they'd had no choice.

But it had all been a lie.

The Closest hadn't started the war. The Well had been theirs, and they had suffered for generations because Elan's ancestors were thieves. That his ancestors had started the war was bad enough, but that they'd forced the world to forget that, to believe they were guiltless protectors, was worse.

Everything Elan knew about the world had changed, and there was nothing left he could trust—nothing except Jae, who had told him the truth, and who had the power to right the Highest's wrongs. The world needed her, but the sun would still rise tomorrow if he died.

"I'll do it," he repeated. "You're the only one who has magic, and we don't really know what it will take to break the Curse. You can't die here, and I can. It's as simple as that."

"No, it's not," she said, but she was still staring at him,

her eyes wide and her voice soft. It wasn't the way she usually looked at him, from behind a blank mask or with a sneer of disdain. But her face hardened, and the moment passed. "The sacrifice needs to be from the Wellspring Bloodlines, to link them back to the Well and restore its binding. If we had someone else here, maybe, but . . . it has to be me."

Elan didn't even have a chance to feel relieved—relieved *or* disappointed—before Tal said, "Or me. We have the same blood."

"No."

"Jae—"

"No," she repeated. "You're the only one I care about saving. If you die, the world can turn to dust for all I care."

"But *I* care." Tal reached out, grabbed her hand. "Elan is right. You have magic. That means you're the most important person in the world. You can change things, change *everything*—"

"But I don't care about that if you're not—"

"Listen to me!" Tal yelled, and Jae yanked her hand back as if she'd been stung. "Back there, in that world, I can't even talk, but here and now, you have to listen to me. This isn't about you, or me, or any one person. This is about all of us. All of Aredann, *all* of the Closest, and—and the Twill and even the Avowed. *Everyone.* If you die here, we can't be sure that Elan will be able to break the Curse—he's not a mage. You are. You're the world's best hope, and if you die here, everyone else might die, too."

"Maybe they deserve to." Jae looked defiant, the way she had when Elan had tried to talk to her after she'd killed Rannith.

"But maybe they don't," Tal countered. "You're not the only one who's been hurt, Jae. But you had your revenge. Rannith is dead. You used your power to kill him, and maybe you were right to do it, but for every Rannith out there, there's ... there's someone like you were, powerless and scared and angry, who deserves better. I'm willing to die to give them a chance, but it's meaningless if you won't help them." Tal stared at her, and she all but squirmed under that fixed, fierce gaze.

Finally she murmured, "It's meaningless if I lose you."

"No," Tal breathed. "It means everything to *me*. To know you'd be free—that Gali could be free, safe, happy—that everyone else could, too. You can protect them. You and I can give them that, together. But not if you throw your life away."

"*You're* willing to—"

"But I'm not. You said it was a sacrifice. Coming from me, it's a gift. From you, it's a death sentence for all of us."

Jae's angry mask was crumbling in front of them, her shoulders shaking as she repeated, "No, no, Tal, *please*," over and over. He held her hand in both of his as she shook.

"There must be another way," Elan said, desperate, even though he knew it was pointless before Jae's head shake confirmed it. If there had been another way, she'd never have planned to sacrifice herself in the first place.

"I don't want to leave you," Tal said, pulling Jae close as her eyes finally went glassy and damp. "I'd do anything to stay with you, but if one of us has to go, let it be me. I trust you to carry on, do things I never could. Please, please let me do this for you."

"But what if—what if— Without you, I can't, I don't

care," she gasped. "Everything I've done has been to protect you, and now—"

"Now I'm protecting you."

"I'd be all alone. I can't do this alone."

"You *won't* be alone," Tal said, and looked up at Elan again. Tal's eyes were damp, too, and his gaze pinned Elan down.

"I'll help you," Elan said. "I'll do anything I can. I'd do . . . I'd do anything for you."

Jae didn't even look at him, just buried her face in Tal's shoulder. "I don't care about anyone else. I don't want to live without you."

"But I want you to," Tal said. "I want you to live, and go on living, and let everyone else live, too. And I want you to finish what we started, and I want you to swear to me that you will."

Jae didn't answer, but Tal wrapped his arms around her and stroked her back. He glanced at Elan, then away, and Elan ached because he couldn't do anything. He couldn't take this burden from them, and he didn't even know how to comfort Jae. Tal was the only one who could do that, and Elan would make a poor substitute at best. But he meant what he said: he'd do anything for her. If the best he could do was give them privacy, then he would.

He turned toward the opening in the tree trunk and mumbled, "I'll find us something to eat," and left them to the pain he'd never really be able to understand.

Chapter 24

THEY BUILT THEIR CAMP UNDER THE TREES AGAIN, THIS TIME closer to where the trees gave way to the cliff and the staircase down to the Well. It required shoving some bushes out of the way, breaking their branches until there was enough room for the three of them to sit and eat.

Jae was numb, and barely even tasted the roots Elan had laid out in a nest of embers to cook. She wasn't hungry, but ate anyway, more from habit than anything else. She'd almost never had enough to eat before in her life; the idea of turning down food was just too foreign. A meal was a meal.

It would be Tal's *last* meal.

She hadn't even had time to accept what rebinding the Well would require when he'd volunteered to sacrifice himself, carving a pit out of her heart. It didn't matter that what he and Elan said made sense. It didn't matter that she'd be better able to protect Aredann, free the Closest, than Elan alone.

"You don't have to . . . Everyone at Aredann might already be dead," she said, her voice rusty.

Tal looked up sharply. "I won't believe that."

"It might be for nothing. You can't—"

"*You* were going to," Tal said. "For that same 'maybe.' And I *don't* think they're dead."

"But—"

"And even if they are," he said, pressing ahead, over her objections, "there are other estates with no water that might be abandoned. If I can't save the Closest at Aredann, I *will* save the others, and give you the time to free them."

Jae looked away from him. She knew she should be ashamed that she was so willing to bargain away other Closests' lives for Tal's, but she'd accepted that awful choice days ago, when she'd been willing to trade him for every other Closest at Aredann.

Tal tossed aside a fruit rind. "I think the fruit out here is better than anything in Aredann's orchards. I visited them once, you know."

"I remember," Jae said.

Tal turned to Elan, somehow managing to smile. Jae knew it was forced, but it seemed to fool Elan. "We were infants when our mother was brought into the household to nurse Lady Shirrad. We came in with her. We were never supposed to leave the grounds, not unless we were ordered to. Which we never were."

"But you found a way," Elan said. To his credit, he didn't ask how.

"Yes. I was . . . twelve, I think. It was before our mother died. Lady Shirrad said she wanted dates. Of course, she probably meant the dried ones they kept in the kitchen, but she didn't specify, so I decided to find some that were fresh. Still on the tree, in fact."

Elan gave a slight, awkward laugh. Tal's smile broadened, and he cast his glance over at Jae. She tried to return the smile that Tal so obviously wanted from her, but couldn't quite manage it.

"Our mother was very, very angry when I told her. She asked where I'd been all day. I could have been caught." He paused significantly, then leaned in a little to add in a conspiratorial whisper, "If any of the Avowed figured out what I was up to, they might have realized *she* got up to it, too. I'd have ruined it for all of us."

"And I suppose all of the Closest did the same," Elan said.

"Only a few," Tal said. "Those of us who were more creative than others at how we carried out orders. And who paid a lot of attention to what the Avowed *really* said instead of what they meant to say. I learned it from her."

Elan cast a questioning look at Jae, who shook her head. "I was never any good at it. But . . ." She cleared her throat. It didn't matter what Tal confirmed now. "But Tal always stole enough for both of us."

"I never stole," Tal said. "The Closest worked the land, grew the crops, tended the beasts—it was as much ours as any Avowed's, when you think about it like that. And it's not *my* fault if no one ever told me not to take things."

"It sounds like you're very lucky no one ever caught on," Elan said. "Though I'm sure you had a story ready in case someone ever did."

"No story," Jae said. "No lies."

"Just a little bit of truth," Tal agreed. Voice going high and tremulous, he said, "It's just, Lady Guardian, I know you always *mean* to care for all of us Closest as part of Aredann. I only didn't want to bother you with it!"

Jae actually *did* laugh at that, despite herself. Tal was mad if he thought Shirrad cared even a little—he had to, if he'd said it—but then again, Shirrad clearly cared for *him*. Maybe that made it easier for him to believe the rest, that all he'd been doing was taking care of the Closest for her.

He'd *always* taken care of them.

Jae's laugh turned into a choked sob, and a second later his arms were around her, holding her close. But only for a moment before he stood up and offered her a hand.

"Come on. It'll be sunset in a minute. Elan said it'll be glorious."

Jae almost felt as if she was compelled by the Curse. She stood, Tal's hand in hers, and followed him through the trees to the bare cliff top. Elan followed behind them, and the three of them stood together and watched the sun as it turned to liquid gold, as the water below dazzled and sparkled and swallowed it, leaving an open, beautiful sky whose stars were reflected on the waves below.

"I'm glad I got to see that," Tal said, and though his smile was genuine, Jae had never seen him look so sad.

*   *   *

Jae hadn't expected to sleep at all, but she found herself waking as a few rays of early sunlight fought their way through the canopy. Elan was already sitting up and rubbing his eyes, and Tal was pacing. So it wasn't a surprise when he turned to her and said, "It's time."

Jae hesitated, staring up at him.

He stopped in front of her and said, "Jae, ask me if I want to do this."

She knew there would be a hundred ways he could answer, none of which actually meant yes, but she asked it anyway: "Do you want to do this?"

"No," he said, but before she could respond, he continued, "But I am *willing* to do it—and I have to. Just . . . promise me . . ."

She watched him, waiting as he chose his words very carefully.

"Promise that you'll remember me. And when you do, you'll remember to be merciful."

Her throat went tight. Of course she'd remember him. She'd remember him with every breath she ever took, every sunset, every drop of water she drank. But mercy . . . She wasn't sure a world without Tal deserved that.

But of course, that was why he'd asked it of her. She knew that, just as surely as she knew his smile. He needed her promise because he wouldn't be there anymore, standing at her side to remind her that even though she was powerful enough to kill, she could also grow flowers.

She caught his gaze and held it, and almost wished she were cursed so he'd know for certain it was the truth when she said, "I promise."

"Then it's time."

When it came down to it, all Jae really knew about magic came from her visions, her instincts, and the scraps of information Elan had found. The web of magic that made up the Well was so far beyond all of that that it was almost impossible to understand, but in her vision inside the mosaic room, she'd seen how the Wellspring mages had bound it all together. So she led Tal out to the edge of the cliff, where Janna had connected the Bloodlines together.

Elan followed them. "I'm here. If you need— If I can— Tell me how to help."

"There's nothing you can do," Jae said, voice hollow.

Elan looked down at the ground, then up one last time. He took Tal's hand and clasped it in both of his, not speaking. Tal smiled wanly, and their eyes met. Then Elan let go and stepped back to sit near the tree line and wait.

Jae and Tal stood there, side by side, staring out at the Well. From up here, it looked endless, and the sky was perfect, cloudless. Even the air was still. The Well's surface was a dark smudge beneath them, brightening slightly as the sun rose, gentle ripples dancing across it. It reminded Jae of Gali's drawings, as though if she stared at it long enough, she might be able to see the picture in it.

But there was no picture, just dawn reflecting back up at them. Falling into the water would be like flying.

"We'll need something sharp enough to break skin," Jae said, looking around. Tal cast around, too, found a jagged stone, and handed it to her. It wasn't exactly Janna's ceremonial knife, but it would do the job.

"Tell me what to do," Tal said.

"Just sit," she said. "For now, just . . . wait. Just . . . be with me."

He nodded, and they both sat cross-legged at the edge of the cliff. When she slid into other-vision, she could feel him. The bright light his energy cast was so close to hers that they were impossible to separate, completely intertwined. The way the two of them had always been.

Reaching out, she felt for the shape of the spell, the ancient framework Janna and her friends had laid out. The Well as a whole was meant to attract and direct water, to seal water to this spot and send it where it was needed. She could feel the Well's purpose, but as the binding had unraveled, so had its power. As much water as there was now, Jae knew there should be much, much more. Eyes shut, she thought about the way water's unique energy felt, and she *pulled*. There was only a trickle in the desert, and she couldn't feel any farther than that.

When she opened her eyes again, three small clouds dotted the sky. In her vision of Janna and the mages, it had been a rainstorm. This would have to be enough.

The other members of the Wellspring Bloodlines were so far away that they were more like an idea than anything she could sense, but she reached inside herself, reached into Tal, and found the connection between all of them. If she pulled on it, all of the Closest—the Wellspring Bloodlines—would feel it. All the descendants of the mages who'd bound themselves together here, and then been bound again by the Curse.

Sure enough, Tal said, "Everything is . . . tingling."

"It's the other Closest," she said. "You can feel them all."

"You know, I like that idea." He let out a breath, and

the glow of his energy expanded as if he were reaching out somehow, even though he wasn't a mage. "That we're all connected."

"That's the connection that will . . . that will save everyone," Jae said.

"I like that even better."

That brought tears back to her eyes, and she forced herself to concentrate on the magic that was around them now. If she didn't make herself look away from him, she'd never be able to go through with this. Even so, she was already blinking back tears as she used the stone to tear at her arm, and the tears had nothing to do with pain.

"And now me, I take it," Tal said.

She nodded. Maybe they didn't have to do this part—they had the same blood, and the Wellspring Bloodlines were already bound together. But even so, she pressed her bleeding arm to his, let the energy that made up the two of them swirl together and merge.

The Well seemed to sing as she did it. The magic in the Well surged, reaching up toward them, as if it was hungry to have the binding restored. The clouds on the horizon grew thicker and darker, the air heavier.

"I can feel it," Tal murmured, taking her hand. "It's . . . it's so big. There's going to be so much water, Jae."

She nodded.

"You'll never be thirsty again."

She made herself nod, but couldn't smile. She'd endured the desert once, and a lifetime of thirst before it. She'd do it all again, resign herself to a lifetime of thirst and sunsickness, if it would keep him at her side.

"And now I . . . ," he prompted, but he was already eyeing the edge of the cliff.

All Jae could do was nod.

"Then it's time," he said yet again.

She could barely hear him over the sudden wind. He was right, it was time, but it would *never* be time. She'd never be ready for this, never be able to let him go.

He tugged his hand away from hers, stood, and held his hand out over the abyss. Their shared blood dripped down, and the magic in the Well flared and roared, roiled. Jae stood to join him, pressed up against him shoulder to shoulder, and could see that the Well's surface had grown choppy beneath them. The sky was suddenly so cloudy and dark that dawn might as well never have happened.

Tal shuffled forward an inch, toes resting at the very edge of the cliff, and took a deep breath. He cast one long look at Jae, smiling with an expression she knew too well hid what he was really feeling. They were so closely linked now that she felt it, too. Despite the brave face, he was terrified, not ready. He'd never be ready, but—

He fell forward, body lurching into motion. Jae screamed, couldn't stop herself from reaching for him. Her hand caught his, the magic surged, and the wind threw the wispy ends of his hair back toward her face. He was moving too fast. She couldn't stop him or let him go.

They both fell. The wind whistled and shrieked around them, the energy they'd built flaring. It reached for them, and Jae grabbed it on blind instinct—

They broke the surface and *stopped*. The water should have killed them both, shattered their bones before it drowned them, releasing their energy into the binding, but instead Jae was dry and terrified and still holding Tal's arm. A bubble glowed around them, sealing them in, even as the magic battered it, desperate to pull the energy it needed from them.

Jae. Tal's mouth didn't move, but she heard him in her mind anyway, felt him clutching at her. *Stop this, let it go, let me go—*

I can't, she told him, clinging now as he tried to pull away. If he pierced the edge of their bubble, that would be the end, he'd be lost.

Let. Me. Go. He stared at her, but she could only make out his eyes. It was nearly pitch black under the surface, the only light the dimly glowing magic around them. Not enough to see by. *You have to. This is my choice. Jae—*

Tal, please—

This sets me free. It's my choice, my free choice. You have to let me do this.

She clutched at his hand, even as he tried to yank it away. But he couldn't. It was too hard to move in this strange, suspended bubble. She pulled him close instead, arms wrapped around him, head on his shoulder.

Please let me go, he said.

Then she felt it. He was scared, yes, but he was determined. He was so sure. He'd always protected her, and the other Closest at Aredann—this was simply more of the same, Tal being Tal. It was his gift, his choice, and even as scared as he was, he wouldn't change his mind.

Goodbye, Tal told her.

She released her grip, let him drift. *Goodbye.*

His last thought was *I love you.*

The bubble burst—shattered, more like, sheets of water cascading in, driving them apart, as the magic pulled at them both. For a moment, she tried to balance the magic, the water, and the binding between herself and Tal. If the magic took half of her, half of him, maybe that would be enough to restore the binding, but she and Tal would be left too weak. Neither of them would be able to swim to safety, and she wouldn't be able to control anything anymore. She'd be alive but useless, ruining Tal's gift.

He believed this was the right thing, and he believed in *her*.

She clawed toward the surface, shoving the magic away from her. It sang in her mind as it found Tal instead, the binding restored and the Well flooding with energy *and* water as the clouds burst. Jae broke through the surface at last.

Rain pelted her as she tried to drag herself toward the nearest shore. The water she'd called was here now, and more was coming. The Well was sealed and bound once again, Tal's gift enough to hold it for now. The binding wouldn't last forever unless the Curse was broken, but Tal had given them enough time to get that done.

When she finally reached the muddy shore, she was barely able to drag herself out as the muck pulled at her, her clothes soaking and dragging her back. She found herself near the staircase and crawled up until she couldn't move any more.

Eventually she'd follow through on her promises, make sure the world was grateful for Tal's sacrifice. But today she couldn't walk any more, couldn't move, couldn't think. She curled up on a wide stair, barely sheltered from the wind and rain. Too exhausted to move farther, she lay there, cold and miserable, her tears mixing with the rain on her face as she mourned.

Chapter 25

THERE WAS SOMETHING STRANGE IN THE AIR. ELAN WAS SITTING A short distance from where Jae and Tal were perched at the edge of the cliff, but he was still close enough to watch. Close enough to *feel*. His skin tingled, hair standing up, as the sky went gray above them. The wind picked up, clouds growing out of nowhere. He shivered, colder than he'd been in years.

So this was what magic felt like. Not quite natural, but not quite *wrong*, just as if there was suddenly *more* in the air around him. He hunched over, trying to catch his breath as the strange energy pushed him down, oppressive and heavy. He didn't know how Jae could stand it, unless it felt different to control it.

In the distance, Jae and Tal both stood. The wind whipped

at them, hard enough that Elan imagined them staggering away from the cliff's edge—but instead Tal leaned over it. Elan held his breath, unwilling to imagine what Tal must have been feeling as he looked down.

Tal fell forward.

Jae followed him.

Elan shouted toward them, knowing it was too late, his voice lost in the howling wind. The clouds burst, and the bizarre feeling around him vanished like a morning haze. The world felt suddenly in focus, the magic back wherever it needed to be. The temperature dropped sharply, lightning laced the sky, and the clouds had grown enormous above him.

Jae was gone.

Elan pushed himself to his feet, rain hammering him, his hair sticking to his face and neck. He shivered uncontrollably but couldn't bring himself to move. Jae was *gone*. After everything, after Tal's decision and her agreement, she'd leapt after him, and now . . .

Her magic had worked. The rain hit the cliff and cascaded over it in growing streams. It would fill the Well, helping it grow back to its intended size. It would rain for days, Elan realized. It would pour out here as magic called water back to the Well, and in the rest of the world, the reservoirs would rise. Maybe the rain would make its way out there, too, ending the drought that had plagued the world for so long, and everyone would celebrate.

No one else in the world would know what had happened, that no one was really saved, that they only had a reprieve. Jae was gone, and with her, their hope.

Elan climbed farther under the trees for shelter, but they

didn't provide much. Wind still battered him, and sheets of rain found their way through the leaves. He curled up in the driest spot he could find and shut his eyes.

He lay there and shivered, unable to bring himself to move, with no idea what to do next. Hours passed, and between the wind and the trees, he couldn't even see the sky to get a sense of how long he'd been in that position. He gave up trying to guess and just lay there, alone.

Finally the rain lessened, though it didn't stop. He was stiff from the cold, desperate to move, and forced himself to straighten out and stretch. After their days in the desert, his body was lean, muscle over bone with almost nothing else to it. He'd gotten used to being sore.

As he stretched out his limbs, he found his resolve. Yes, he was alone, and no, the Well wouldn't last forever, but Jae and Tal had bought it time. Jae had said that the only way to prevent it from drying again was to break the Curse, and she'd told him how.

There was a knife somewhere. He'd have to brave the desert again, but alone this time. He'd have to find his way back to civilization, and find a way to get from Aredann back to his family's land. He'd contact Erra and beg her for help, tell her the truth about what their father knew, what he'd done—what all of the Highest had done. If she helped him, they might be able to find the knife and destroy it. He'd have a better chance with her than he would alone, and then . . .

He would break the Curse, and save them all—unless the Closest then rose up against the Avowed who'd controlled them, rose up and were slaughtered. Without Jae's magic, the Closest might have sheer numbers on their side, but no weapons, organization, or training. There *would* be a war, he was sure of that—and if the Closest lost, if this time the Highest went beyond cursing them and killed them instead . . .

If the Highest slaughtered the Closest, they would seal their own fate. Without the Closest, the Well had no binding. The whole world would turn to dust, including the Highest. They'd bring it on themselves, Jae would have said. But the Avowed would believe they were fighting not just for their lives, but for their birthright. Elan would have to find a way to make them all understand the truth he'd learned about the Well and the Closest and the War. All of it.

He finished stretching and found the waterlogged remains of their camp. Most of their supplies had been lost in the desert, but he still had the satchel and water skin to fill, and a bag large enough to carry food in, plus the flint. It wouldn't be much, but it would have to be enough. Besides, the desert blossomed in the days after a rain. Maybe he could find something out there, once it came to life around him.

There was no point in putting off leaving. Nothing was going to get easier, and no one was going to help him. All he could do was start to gather supplies and force himself to go before he lost his will.

"Elan?"

Elan spun, dropping the bag he'd been holding open, and found Jae standing in the misting rain behind him. He stared, eyes saucer-wide, as she took another few steps toward him.

"You . . . you're alive?" he murmured, almost unable to believe it, as if Jae were an apparition brought to him by magic. He'd seen her fall, he'd felt the magic settle. She'd died. How could she not have died?

"I'm tired," she said.

He tried to answer her but couldn't remember how to speak, and instead stepped forward. She didn't give him her eternally wary look, just stood there, looking lost and alone. He reached for her, pulled her against him, wrapped his arms around her, and breathed her in.

"Tal's dead," she said, and pulled away from him.

He reached for her again, just her hand this time, and tugged her farther under the trees. The rain was light enough now that, aside from when branches grew too heavy and sent showers of drops splattering down, the ground beneath the branches was sheltered. "Sit," he said, and then sat with her. "I'm sorry. I know he was . . . It wasn't easy for you to . . . Jae."

"We can't sit long," she said. "We have to go back. I won't waste his gift."

"Of course," he said. "I was gathering supplies when you appeared."

"Oh." She blinked. "You thought I was dead."

"I did," he said. "But I couldn't just . . . The Curse has to be broken, and I had to try. Even if I was alone."

"Alone," she echoed, and turned away. He reached out, wanting to put an arm around her shoulder, pull her close and comfort her. But she didn't move any closer to him, so he dropped his hand instead.

"But I'm *not* alone," he said. "We don't have to be alone. We have . . ."

She looked over at him, and he couldn't say "each other." He'd sworn to Tal he'd look after her, and he'd keep that vow, hold it more sacred than the vows he'd once said to his father. He'd follow her anywhere, do anything she asked. But as grateful as he was to have her to follow, she didn't feel the same. She'd lost her whole world, and all she had in return was him.

He didn't think he'd ever be enough, but he'd try. So he just sat there next to her, still and quiet in the mist. Alone, together.

❖❖❖

Gathering supplies didn't take them long, and then they set out into the overcast, dreary desert. That felt right somehow. Jae was empty and cold inside, as if Tal had left a tear in her body, one that would never be sewn shut. At least the weather reflected her mood.

Already the desert around them was different from the last time they'd faced it. Even after they were far enough from the Well that the rain no longer reached them, the desert had blossomed. Plants seemed to grow out of nowhere, pale grasses digging their way through muddy sands. Every bush and cactus had blossoms, bright against the dunes, purples and yellows and oranges that looked like jewels. The foliage spread in front of them like an overgrown garden. Wild and unkempt, but beautiful.

Jae felt nothing.

This time, they didn't have to ration water so much, even with only the water skin and satchel between them. There was water to be found in the plants, and even if there wasn't, there was enough water in the air around them for Jae to call.

She could make it rain, if they needed water that badly. So they walked until they were tired, slept and ate and drank, and the next night walked again.

Every step brought them closer to Aredann, but Jae could no longer think of it as home. Home was a cramped, dark room she shared with Tal and Gali. Home was Tal smirking as he handed her a date, smiling as he set a gentle hand on her elbow. Home was her brother, and he was gone.

She almost couldn't do it. The idea of familiar sights turned wrong because he wasn't there left her anxious, stomach clenching despite being full and sated. She didn't know how to face the memories waiting at Aredann, or the years that would follow. It seemed almost easier to turn around, to just wander the desert until she fell.

But she couldn't squander Tal's gift. He'd wanted to protect the other Closest, so she'd protect them in his name. Besides, she had Elan to consider. He followed her without question, and she knew he'd follow her out into the desert, too, stay with her until they were both gone, just as he'd followed her out there in the first place.

He wasn't the same as when she'd first met him. Aredann had sanded off his arrogance and posturing, and the desert had honed him, focused him. He was willing to break the Curse, no longer grudgingly but because it would help everyone. Because it was the right thing to do, even if he had to do it alone. He deserved better than to die because she didn't care enough to live. She hadn't been able to save Tal; she wouldn't fail Elan, too.

It took them longer to reach Aredann than it had to reach

the Well, since they were no longer driven by the threat of sunsickness or starvation. They didn't talk much, just kept moving, falling into step together smoothly.

She felt Aredann the evening before they reached it. Even without other-vision, she could sense life, brighter than the scattered blooms across the desert, and when she really looked, she could see so much more. All of the fields they'd worried about were growing, vital, and plentiful. The reservoir was brimming, and the stream that led directly to the estate house was running high. Yet the town itself seemed empty of people. There were plenty in the fields, but only a few in the estate house and nearly none in the town itself.

When she and Elan arrived at the town's outskirts, the buildings were all dark and no one peered out through the windows. The road was muddy but not trampled, and no one came out to greet them or curse them. Not until they reached the house itself.

The gate was open, and the yard behind it was wild with dark green grass. A lawn at last. Paths had been beaten across it closer to the house, and as Jae and Elan approached, Lady Shirrad ran out, Gali at her heels.

"Jae!" Shirrad threw herself forward, embracing Jae like a long-lost sister. Jae jerked away, then went still for punishment, a habitual gesture. Shirrad didn't notice, but Elan must have, because he somehow pulled Shirrad toward him, let her hug him instead. "Blood and bones, you're *alive*. I knew you would be. When it started raining, I *knew* you were alive out there."

"I don't see Tal," Gali said.

Jae stared at her. She'd spoken—in front of Shirrad, a crime under the Curse. She didn't wince as if she was being punished; she just waited, staring right back at Jae.

Who opened her mouth and said aloud what she told herself a thousand times a day: "Tal is dead."

Shirrad gasped, and Gali's face fell, as if she was going to crumple. Jae wanted to reach for Gali, to comfort her somehow, but how could she? Tal was dead, and nothing would make that easier to face.

"You should come inside," Shirrad finally said, all the enthusiasm gone from her voice. "I think we have a lot to discuss."

Jae let them lead her inside. They went straight to the kitchen, where a few of the Closest were sitting around a stewing pot. They all stared at Jae and Elan, but Shirrad didn't shoo them away or order them to serve anything in the dining hall. She just grabbed and filled a bowl, passed it to Jae, and then gave another to Elan, before getting one for herself. Gali did the same, and they sat down at the kitchen table.

"Where is everyone?" Elan asked Shirrad between bites.

"Gone," Shirrad said. "His Highest"—her voice dripped with disdain—"fled Aredann. He said it was because the second quake meant Aredann was falling down more quickly than he'd anticipated. It wasn't safe to stay and do things in an orderly fashion. Everyone left immediately—except the Closest and me, my punishment for defying him. Disavowed, and left here to die with Aredann."

But Aredann wasn't dying, and Jae's threat must have scared Elthis into leaving the Closest alive. That meant that

Tal's sacrifice *had* saved them all from the drought—and even saved Shirrad, who'd helped get Tal out of Aredann, despite the Curse. Though if he'd stayed, maybe he would be here now, abandoned and alive like the rest of them.

Or maybe they'd all be dead, because without a sacrifice, it wouldn't have rained. The Closest would have died of thirst, even after Elthis had left them alive.

Jae ate a spoonful of stew so she wouldn't have to speak.

"Everything is different now," Gali said. "With only us here . . ." She cast a look at Shirrad, then back at Jae. "We're all the same now. We work together. Shirrad can't give us any orders, so we're free to speak. It's almost as if we aren't cursed at all."

Just like Tal in the desert. With no one around giving orders, what difference did it make if the Closest were cursed to obey? If Gali was sitting and eating with Shirrad, elbow to elbow, then it was her choice. *Both* of their choices.

"It's better this way," Shirrad said. "Now that the reservoir is back, we can stay here forever. There's plenty for everyone, and we don't need to worry about the Danardaes or anyone else. We're safe."

"As safe as we can be," Gali said.

Shirrad nodded. "And now you're with us, home. You saved our lives, and this . . . this is your home as much as it is mine, with everything you've done for us."

"I can't stay," Jae said at last, pushing the bowl away from her. She glanced at Elan, who nodded a little bit.

"Why not? Where will you go?" Shirrad asked.

"To break the Curse," Jae said. She looked at Gali, met

her gaze for the first time since she'd come inside. "This isn't freedom. It's just . . . being left alone. You deserve the real thing. And I promised Tal I would make that happen."

"And you really think you can," Gali breathed.

Jae nodded. The knife was out there somewhere, binding the Curse. They just had to find it.

"I'd love to know if we can help," Shirrad said, twisting her words to avoid a question, just like a Closest would.

Now it was Jae's turn to stare, surprised. Everything really *was* different. Elan had changed so much, Tal was gone, and Shirrad . . . Shirrad was eating with the Closest, speaking like them, and willing to help them. Maybe Tal's sacrifice had given the world that, too.

"No," Jae said. "I have to do it alone—"

"*Not* alone," Elan said.

She looked at him. She'd need his help to find the knife, so he was right. "Not alone. But we need to leave—"

"Soon," he said, interrupting again. "In a day or two, after we've had a chance to rest."

She frowned, wanting to get started as soon as possible. His expression didn't waver under her sharp look, and he was probably right. He was the one who'd made her stop and rest in the desert, who'd forced her to eat and drink when she'd been too haunted to care. So she nodded, letting him make this decision, too.

"Of course," Shirrad said. "You can stay as long as you like. Here, you eat. I'll go draw you both baths—we have plenty of water for it now. There's so much water. You'll feel better when you're clean."

Elan smiled and thanked her, and Jae picked at her food.

Then she followed Gali to Lady Shirrad's bathing chamber, washed the mud and sand off. By the time she'd finished, Elan had trimmed his beard and hair. He looked more like when he'd first come to Aredann, now that he was better groomed, but with the beard he looked older, and he was leaner, sharper, not so careless. When he saw Jae looking at him, he smiled, and it looked more genuine than it ever had in those first few days.

Shirrad offered them a set of rooms that the Avowed had once used, and Jae accepted, because she couldn't stand the thought of her mat in the Closest's quarters without Tal on the next mat over. She dried and dressed but didn't head straight up to sleep.

Instead she wandered down a long, dusty hall and into the garden. Elan followed her a minute later, looking around.

The cactus was in bloom now, and for the first time Jae could remember, lush grass blanketed the whole yard, even where it shouldn't have, growing up between the orange rocks of the path. Bright flowers bloomed around the fountain, and the bushes were deep green and overgrown.

"I like the garden like this," Elan said. "It reminds me of you."

"I didn't do this," Jae said. "I never got the grass to grow."

"Yes, you did," he said. "Look at it, all of this. It's wild, and beautiful, and you're the only one who *could* do this."

She frowned, but maybe he was right. This was her garden, not Shirrad's; it wasn't beautifully trimmed, laid out carefully, well kept so it could compete with what they had in the central cities. Instead it was wild, growing how it wanted to, lush and alive. Hers.

There was only one thing wrong: the fountain. It was still dormant, though that was less obvious now that the plants were growing around it. There was water in the trough, though, deposited there by rain. A good start.

She walked over to it, grass tickling her bare, callused feet, and laid her hands inside, one matching up with where she felt the palm print, though she couldn't see it under the water.

"Maybe . . . ," she murmured, and shut her eyes, used other-vision to examine the fountain. There was plenty of water around the estate now, and no reason it shouldn't have flowed in, but—there it was. An old clog, ancient mud that was more like rock now. All Jae needed was a moment's concentration. She reached out toward the clog, pushed, broke it down until water swept the remnants away and flowed freely.

A minute later, water burbled out of the top of the fountain, then cascaded down. Cool to the touch, beautiful, surrounded by flowers. She cupped her palms under it and drank.

The fountain had been Janna's gift. The water was Tal's. Jae looked back at Elan, caught his eye, and he nodded his approval. They'd been given all this, and with it, a chance.

With Elan's help, Jae was going to break the Curse. That would be *their* gift.

She held out her hand, and Elan took it, held it gently, and led her back inside, the fountain still flowing behind them.

Acknowledgments

The thing about this being my first book is that I'd kind of like to thank everyone I've ever met, but that's probably not practical. So here is an only slightly shortened list of people who deserve enormous thanks.

My fantastic editor, Kate Sullivan, who understood everything I wanted to do with this story and helped me figure out how to get there; and my incredible agent, Hannah Bowman, whose unshakable belief in this book still has me a little bit awed. Thanks also to the full teams at both Delacorte Press and Liza Dawson Associates.

My writing group: Jess, Jen, and Maddy, thank you for all the frozen nights sitting in Panera convincing me that I needed more character motivation and fewer barrels. My other first readers: Margot, Nicole, and Olivia, and Karen, Erin, and Carolyn, who read various in-progress versions.

Plus thanks, of course, to the friends and family who have encouraged and inspired me throughout my life, but especially Rachel (thanks for the Stormy Stories, among many other things), Dad (thanks for promising to always buy me books when I asked, which I know you've since come to regret), and Mom (I miss you every day, but I know how proud and happy you'd be right now).

About the Author

Becky Allen grew up in a tiny town outside of Ithaca, New York, and graduated from Brandeis University with a major in American studies and a minor in journalism. For the last eight years, she has held various positions at TheBody.com, an online HIV resource, and she is currently the website director. Becky loves New York, brunch, and feminism. She cannot function without coffee. Becky lives in New York City with her sister, Rachel, and their cat, Lily. It was a conversation with her sister about irrigation that inspired Becky to wonder about a fantasy world where irrigation was fueled by magic, and what that would mean. Their discussion became *Bound by Blood and Sand*.